GIRLS GONE GROUPIE

First signed copy
is yours!
With Love, from
Barbie, 2017
"BK Stone"

GIRLS GONE GROUPIE

GIRLS OF GLAM ROCK SERIES
BOOK 1

Brenda K. Stone

DANDELION

How I Became a Hair Metal Groupie:
The Step-by-Step Guide to Backstage Action
by Dandelion Dagger, age 16

Copyright 1983

Hollywood, California, nine double oh rock and roll

It happened like this.

The 1980s were just dawning, and an unprecedented event was taking place in L.A.: my daddy, *The* Derek Dagger of Derek Dagger and the Blues Blasters and a hometown hero, was invited to do a year-long residency at Holly Woods, the indoor-outdoor music arena where rock and roll shows became urban legend, not only because of what happened onstage, but what happened backstage. Because we just happened to be at the right place at the right time, Mama and I jumped on board for the ride while Daddy attempted to make L.A. rock history. Don't think for one minute that Mama wasn't going to make some history of her own. I guess you could say that I just got swept away by the wave of self-indulgence and excess that tore through our lives that mad year. Meanwhile, the musical guard was changing on Sunset Boulevard and a new kind of music with a new kind of look was emerging. The apple was ripe for the picking and I reached for it with both hands.

Daddy doesn't like it, didn't like it from the start. But how can Daddy pass judgment when he married the world's most desirable backstage queen and impregnated her with the seed that turned out to be little ole me? I love my daddy. But sometimes I wonder how he can expect any different from me.

"What's happening to my little spring flower?" he'd finally asked me with a shake of his head, when it was becoming apparent that I was turning over an unexpected leaf with an unscrupulous girl I had met at school and brought along to three of his concerts in a row.

"I'm just growing up, Daddy," I'd said without a care or a second thought, that wonderful girl by my side, eager to take me away from him.

He'd turned his back to me and took a secret slug from a guitar-shaped flask in the side pocket of his newly embroidered blazer that he was already referring to as his "favorite." The sting of his rejection was over in seconds.

"What about the little spring flower who gave him that jacket last week?" H.C. had snorted in my ear, reinforcing the hypocrisy of Daddy's words.

I didn't want to be reminded of the petite blonde with giant breasts that had presented Daddy with the stunning handmade jacket before following him to his dressing room so she could "help him try it on." I only wanted to think the best of my handsome and supremely talented daddy, even if I was starting to feel like someone different than the Daddy's little girl that I used to be.

I tried. I tried to stay Daddy's little spring flower for as long as I could, but the pull of the rock and roll world was too much for me. I'd seen the delicate blonde making the rounds backstage for months before I'd met H.C., before H.C. and I watched her offer up the jacket, in awe of her nerve. Daddy's eyes coveted her from every corner of the dressing room. She was only one in an arsenal of crazy young girls following Mama's lead. The power they had over Daddy and his bandmates was a heady discovery for me at the age of fifteen going on twenty-one. A yearning for something I couldn't identify began to tug at my insides. I wanted to be carefree, funny, careless like them, not the dark and brooding teenager I felt like I really was. Mama started to eye me with suspicion when my child's body turned into one of a young and curious adult and Daddy's friends started to whisper and smile amongst themselves when I swayed by in some little halter dress.

"They're looking at her, Derek," I heard Mama yelling at Daddy one night before a concert.

"She's a pretty young thing. They know she's off limits," Daddy brushed her off.

Everything went silent when Daddy's bodyguard appeared with me.

But I heard what I needed to hear.

Things were already falling apart between Mama and I even before I came of age, even before I met H.C., mostly because Daddy wanted me to be a little guitar princess and Mama didn't want me to be anything that would take attention away from her. Well, she didn't have to worry about that. I didn't want to sit still long enough to play guitar. But I had other quests in mind and she must have seen the words written all over my pubescent face.

"You aren't the taste of a rock star. Too skinny and not enough on top," she'd informed me, trying to make it sound not only like a joke, but like she was trying to save me from some horrible rejection.

We'd see about that.

Mama's ways were starting to stick in my craw. I was ready to stick in Mama's craw.

I couldn't explore the idea any further without a vehicle to help me get where I wanted to go, a vehicle that wasn't Mama but could potentially take Mama on. Then, as fate would have it, within the year I would meet the craziest crazy girl of all, a girl so nutty she didn't even have a real name.

H.C.

She was sitting alone in the school cafeteria at lunch time, silently and defiantly daring anyone to get near her. The dangerously beautiful teenager reminded me of a wild animal, like some feral child you read about in the gossip papers that had been chained in someone's shed for the first ten years of her life. I half-expected her to swat at me with a clawed hand when I dared do what she tried to dissuade the whole school from doing with her catty glare: I sat down across from her.

"What's your name?" I was chewing my gum really hard and trying to come off as tough, something pretty hard to do when you go to Hollywood High. I was picturing myself as Rizzo in *Grease*. But this girl in front of me was no Sandra Dee.

"H.C." She pronounced the two letters between clenched teeth and put a pause in between. I had to hand it to her, from the very beginning she was dramatic.

"What's that stand for?" I asked her, trying to guess the first letter: Helen, Hillary, Honey, Heart?

She stuck her face in mine and hissed, "Highway Child." Then, she abruptly swept up the table scraps that passed as "lunch" for her and stomped away, tossing her long curly mane as she tried to leave me behind.

Close at her heels, I spit my gum into the nearest waste-basket.

I was enamored.

H.C. stopped in her tracks and turned back to me as if shocked that I had the gall to follow her.

"What the hell do you want?" she demanded.

"I just thought you might want to see a free concert to-morrow night at Holly Woods. My daddy is Derek Dagger." I don't know where the words came from. All I know is that they came out like words meant to be spoken since the beginning of time.

I saw her face change, soften. Her nose twitched, nostrils flared. Eyebrows lifted slightly, head tipped.

"And my mama is a really famous groupie," I sweetened the pot. Though I didn't really have to, since I had her at the word "free."

H.C. and I were inseparable from that moment forward. At least until she vanished into thin air, just when I needed her the most.

H.C.

Dandelion's Mama Tulip may be our inspiration, but don't think for one minute that Dandelion is the brains behind all these fun and games. I'll give it to her that she invited me to Holly Woods to meet the Daggers. But after that, I have to make the claim of being the true mastermind who propelled us to our lofty and highly lucrative perch. The vision was mine. I built this trio from the ground up. Only, real life turned out to be even better than my day-dream. Not bad for a chick without a name.

Laugh all you want. But Highway Child is the only title I have. No, there's not any hidden normal moniker on some rumpled birth certificate like Lisa or Jane or Kelly, so get over it. I had to. The story I remember being told goes something like this: my loser parents didn't know what to call me when Mommy popped me out in the back seat of their stolen Caddy. So, they said something totally stupid like, "We're just gonna call you the highway child until we think of a name for you." But they were too stoned to come up with a name, so Highway Child just stuck. When I ended up in L.A. when I was fifteen I decided to shorten it to H.C. And there you have it. The End.

Right. Oh, there's plenty more to tell. But it's none of anyone's business, so the whole damn world can go to hell.

Anyway, I was talking about becoming a groupie when I got sidetracked.

Like it or not, this is a business. And as someone who grew up on Eisenhower's Interstates, hustling my little way through mom and pop grocerettes from sea to shining puddle to lift the next meal for the family, I know something about business. I understand something about survival of the fittest, of maneuvering around the competition to nab the biggest prize. And in this business, there's no bigger trophy than a coveted rock star. I liken them to scoring a nice, big steak in the meat section for Mommy and Dadda and me to barbeque in the local campground. Right down the front of the shorts of the innocent little highway waif, the cool beef pressed against my tummy while Mommy bought me a dime candy bar and the dumb cashier smiled sweetly over the wooden check-out counter at me. Sticking my hungry tummy out as far as I could so that clammy meat wouldn't fall down the leg of my filthy shorts and reveal me a thief. I could relate several more comparisons between my young life and my life now, but I couldn't find a better one than the man versus meat analogy.

Whoa, sorry, got a little nostalgic there!

I didn't grow up here in L.A., so to me, Holly Woods was a filthy black hole, not the historic music venue that everyone in the city made it out to be. The Woods was rub up against something and get dirty territory, stick to the cement floor territory. But I was supposed to kneel at the threshold and thank Jesus for allowing me to cross it or something like that, from the way Dandelion bragged about it. To hell with that. You've seen one train wreck, you've seen them all. And Holly Woods was one hell of a train wreck.

My whole attitude changed when we got inside and I saw all the roadies running around loading in the Marshall stacks and gleaming instruments, the talent being doted on and followed around while they acted all self-important, and Dandelion's mama Tulip Dagger looking like the crown princess of slut heaven. Only Tulip had a few problems: that woman had bags under her eyes and crow's feet starting to embed lines in her skin where her upper and lower lashes met. Tulip Dagger was *aging*. I saw my future in the thin layer of cellulite on the backs of her thighs.

I'd never heard the word "groupie" until Dandelion used it to describe her mother in the cafeteria of Hollywood High, but like the static thrown off by a stray bolt of lightning, the sound of it rolling off her tongue made me feel like electricity was coursing through me. I nodded my head like I knew exactly what she was talking about. And in a way, like when destiny hits you, I guess I did.

Dandelion and I had telepathy from the get-go.

"I don't want to be Mama. I want to be better than Mama," she confessed, as her mother flung herself down on her father's lap and struck a starlet pose with legs out and back arched.

Though I could imagine the move went off better at an earlier time in her life, none of the other men in the room failed to take notice.

Tulip Dagger was a legend in her own mind. And if you aren't one there, you aren't going to be one anywhere else either.

"We'll be better than your Mama," I promised Dandelion.

My life suddenly had a direction for the first time ever.

Dandelion's attention had strayed to a sweet-looking blonde with billowing hair who had brushed by us with some elaborately embroidered thing clutched in her graceful hands. She looked a hell of a lot like Elly May Clampett from *The Beverly Hillbillies* and was dressed in what you might expect the ditzy character to wear: a gingham shirt tied below her huge breasts, tight cut-offs with a rope through the belt loops, and macramé sandals. She wasn't any older than us, maybe even younger, and I wondered if she was a student at Hollywood High. Her perfect little feet skittered over to Derek Dagger even as Dandelion's attention-seeking mama continued to put on the pre-concert entertainment. The blond presented the guitar king with her gift like some eager-to-please servant girl then tried to run off, her face pink from being so close to the royalty. But the royalty had other plans. Dandelion Dagger's father pushed her mama off his lap and graciously accepted the girl's handiwork.

"Come to my dressing room and help me try it on, sweet thing," he crooned.

She wrung her hands together, appearing ready to bawl her eyes out, before those willing tootsies followed Derek Dagger's smoking steps to his dressing room.

"Who the hell was that?" I asked Dandelion, as a noticeable, collective snicker went up amongst the band members.

"Some girl from South Carolina that makes jewelry for all the bands that come here," Dandelion explained.

"She just makes jewelry?"

"Well, sometimes clothes, too."

"Just clothes and jewelry?" I pushed.

"And then she goes to their dressing rooms with them." Dandelion reluctantly gave me the information I wanted.

"And your daddy likes her, too."

Dandelion grimaced. "My daddy likes her, too."

"We need her," I decided.

But Elly May wouldn't appear again for months. And by that time, our hunger to see her again had grown to epic proportions.

CAROLINA

"Hey, Carolina, look!"

I'll never forget H.C. saying those words to me.

The day she and Dandelion showed me the framed picture of Elly May Clampett in a gift shop on Hollywood Boulevard was the day that I knew I really did have a sister. Ma and Pa lied to me about so many things, but keeping my sister's identity from me is the worst thing they could've done. I've always had this feeling in me that I'm not whole, that something is missing, and now I know why. I wonder why they sent her away. I wonder how she ended up here in Southern California.

"I have to find her," I cried, to which I received two blank stares.

"Who do you have to find?" Dandelion sneered, looking me up and down like I was acting insane.

"Elly May is my sister! She's a Clampett and so am I!" My hand shook with the picture of my beautiful sibling in it.

Now Dandelion put her hands on her hips and said, "Carolina-"

But H.C. stepped in, taking my side.

"My sources tell me she's in Beverly Hills," H.C. announced.

I grabbed her shoulders half in terror, half in excitement, and almost dropped the picture.

"You know her?"

Dandelion threw her hands in the air.

"Highway Child-"

H.C. wouldn't let her finish a sentence.

"Of course I know her!" H.C. exclaimed, then demanded, "Gimme that," and wrestled my sister's image from me, sticking it, frame and all, down the front of her skirt.

I had a few dollars to pay for the picture. She didn't have to steal it. I'd sold a few bracelets in Venice that I'd created from seashells. But all of that was the last thing on my mind when finally faced with the discovery of the void in my family life.

Out on the sidewalk in front of the shop I suddenly realized the dilemma I faced if I wanted to find Elly May.

"Not Beverly Hills. I'll never find her there with all of those rich, snooty people in my way!" My voice was high-pitched and I sounded really stupid to me, but I couldn't control it. And worse, I was wringing my hands. I hate when I wring my hands. Ma wrung her hands. I don't want to be like Ma.

That's why I ran away from South Carolina at the age of fourteen.

Ma and Pa don't know where I am. But I'll call them someday. Maybe when I'm a famous jewelry-maker to the rock stars who play at Holly Woods.

That's the only reason I started going there. They gave me money for my stuff and then they chased me around their dressing rooms. Don't tell Dandelion, but her daddy Derek Dagger was the worst one. I embroidered him a blazer to get his undivided attention, not an easy task with half-naked L.A. girls running around everywhere. Embroidery isn't my thing, but I put some beads on it, too, which is my thing. He acted all impressed then wanted me to go to his private dressing room to help him try it on. I just figured I should, since I had made the thing and beaded it in red and royal blue because I thought it would look great against his dark hair.

"Well, here we are," he said.

"Yeah, here we are. So, are you gonna try on the blazer, honey? I don't usually bead clothes, but for you I-"

"Comere, little pretty. I want to show you how much I appreciate the gift." He bent his finger at me and lifted his eyebrows, but he didn't put on the jacket I'd worked so hard to make especially for him.

I thought that maybe I should go if he wasn't going to put it on.

Mr. Dagger started to approach me with a look on his face that wasn't exactly saying, "Wow, love the blazer, girl!"

I bolted for the door. But I went back a few more times for the sake of my jewelry dreams, and I thought that maybe now that Mr. Dagger knew me and was still playing at Holly Woods once a week, that maybe before his residency ended, I could get myself a job as jewelry girl or something. I kept bringing the goods not only for Mr. Dagger but for the rest of his band too. But for some crazy reason they just wanted to chase me around backstage and try to lure me into their dressing rooms, sometimes even in front of their wives and children, and it was just too much of a challenge. Gosh, I'm an underage girl! I guess they thought I was like all of those other girls who swarmed the backstage and gave favors to the rude men who set up the equipment so they could get introduced to the musicians. Those men called "roadies." That's what I'd heard them called once when I was back there. But I really wasn't like those other girls.

Well, back then I wasn't.

The worst was when I started to see Mr. Dagger's daughter watching me with curiosity. She was older than me by a year, I think. I'd read about her in some local newspaper article. Dandelion. I never thought at the time that I would become the topic of such interest to the offspring of a world-renowned guitarist and an infamous groupie. When I found out, I was afraid that maybe she and her wild-eyed friend, who started to show up at the concerts with her, wanted to beat me up or something because they thought I was messing with her daddy. So I stopped going.

I let some time go by, getting restocked on beads and sup-plies. Other girls who continued to claw at the back stage doors of Holly Woods told stories about the new music craze heating up in West Hollywood and taking over the Woods. They lived in the same gross building I lived in on Hollywood Boulevard that was run by a lady with a big heart who took in runaways and made sure we didn't end up dead in an alley. These same girls instructed me to start stringing jewelry in black and neon, maybe get some lace chokers in order. And maybe I could somehow get fishnet into the mix too.

"You have to come with us, Carolina. You're missing all the fun," they told me.

I had to get back into the mix. My jewelry-making dream was suffering. I had to prove to Ma and Pa that my jewelry was important. They always told me I was a dumb Southern girl who wouldn't amount to anything. Well, the first part may be true, but I have hopes and dreams even if I'm not all that smart, even if I stutter and sputter because I'm trying not to sound ignorant. I was smart enough to know that when Derek Dagger's shows began to be replaced at Holly Woods with the bands of boys in make-up and lace, it was my cue to go back.

I fell in love with the hair metal scene from that very first concert, not at Holly Woods but at the Troubador on Santa Monica Boulevard. A drinking establishment. And I was only fifteen! Ma and Pa would hate me even more if they knew!

That's when I came face to face with Dandelion and Highway Child. I tried to avoid them but they tracked me down. One morning another girl from the house I live in came running into my room and shook me awake.

"Look out the window!" Bunny Baby, as she was known on the street, all thirteen years of her, said excitedly.

I stumbled out of bed to peer out the dirty pane, terrified that I would see Ma and Pa there. And there they were, looking like Sunset Boulevard's new "it" girls.

Dandelion Dagger and Highway Child. And they wouldn't go away until I appeared.

They wanted me to be part of their groupie trio, out to conquer the hair metal world. I don't know what they saw in me. All I wanted to do was make jewelry. They pulled me in because they were so interested in where I came from and why I was in L.A. making jewelry for rock stars. They were my sisters that day on the sidewalk, before they ever showed me Elly May.

Pretty soon the hair metal boys were buying my jewelry and giving me sexy lace and fishnet clothes because they want me to look like one of their kind. But I didn't wear the leather pants and short camisoles because I like to stick to my Southern roots with my frilly dresses, denim shorts, and heels. So they've started to buy me cute little lace dresses with neon belts and short shorts in crazy colors so that I can be hair metal and Southern Belle at the same time, and that pleases everyone. Still, this groupie thing keeps me awake at night for a very big reason.

Ma and Pa can't ever know I'm a groupie, because then they'll laugh in my face and say, *See? You're a dumb, good for nothin' girl. Just like we always said!*

Oh dear, there I go wringing my hands again, because I know that I've said too much.

Please don't tell them all the bad things that I've just confessed.

Let's keep it our little secret.

TULIP

I noticed when the men started to look at my daughter. She was fifteen with long, dark hair and a darling figure. I warned her father and he blamed it on me.

"She sees you and she wants the same kind of attention you get. Watch what you do around her. I told you this day was gonna come if you weren't careful."

Derek had the roar of the crowd in the background, chanting his name.

Derek Dagger…Derek Dagger…

"They're looking at her, Derek," I pleaded my case against his beloved band mates, a battle I was foolish to start.

"They know she's off limits." With these words, my husband effectively ended the conversation. His beefy bodyguard showed up with Dandelion at precisely that moment, so I couldn't even make an attempt to keep it going. I know she heard some of our heated discussion. But even I didn't know whether I was having it out with Derek because I wanted to protect my child or whether I was trying to protect my reputation as the classic queen of backstage affairs.

Derek Dagger may have married me to make me an honest woman, but good luck taking the groupie out of the girl who's clinging to her hard-earned persona with all she's got. These new girls coming up don't have anything on me.

It's not my fault that rock stars still want me. I became the choice of musicians the world over because I was good to my men. Back then, I was the best and still am on occasion. It's not as if Mr. Dagger is any saint, so why should Mrs. Dagger be? As for Baby Dagger, well, she can blame her problems on me all she wants, and her father can point fingers too, but I know she made her own choices. There is no magic seed that got passed on from me to her. In fact, I warned her that she wasn't cut out to follow in my footsteps. But then she brought that awful street urchin I call Hippy Chick to Holly Woods. I knew from the beginning that she had no decorum. No limits. Derek and I put a stop to that after a few sightings and thought we'd seen the last of her.

I know it sounds ironically funny that a career groupie should be talking about decorum and limits. But I've always had both whether anyone believes it or not. If you don't, you end up being thrown to the roadies. From the beginning I kept myself from suffering that fate and I became a celebrity in my own right. Just look on the arm of practically any rocker from the 60s and 70s and you'll see me. I am a very photographed woman. Hippie Chick won't ever reach such a high post in this world. She's much too depraved, desperate.

A curious choice of friends for my daughter. Which is why even I have to raise an eyebrow.

Speaking of those hallowed men of yesteryear, they were good people under all that hair and bravado. Yes, they liked their women, liked a drug or three here and there, and wanted to have a good time. When you put a musician in a tour bus and send them around the country or around the world they're going to get bored and will need to have some fun. And fun in the 60s and 70s seemed almost innocent compared to what my daughter and her friends have stepped into. Tattoos and make-up? Not on the macho men I knew. I suppose the new boys coming up do have some odd charm and maybe I like the newness of it all. I'm not completely unmoved. But I yearn for the old days.

My life story is the typical hard luck tale of a generation of groupies. I shared a passion for rockers with a big-busted beauty named Miss Moonshine and we joined forces so we wouldn't have to go home. Tulip and Moonshine. Together, we got the boys excited. We were both from broken families and found each other backstage at Holly Woods like so many other lost souls have done. We worked real jobs during the day, painted West Hollywood in rainbow colors by night. As for Dandelion and her cohorts, Hippy Chick and Carolina Clampett may come from nowhere, but Dandelion doesn't come from a broken home and as far as I'm concerned, she doesn't rate as a "lost soul." Her parents are famous and we function as a family unit. Derek yearns to teach his only child how to play like him. She has so many possibilities. I didn't. I had to go out and earn the world on my back. And now my daughter is using my hard-earned notoriety to lasso her own fame.

You have to be more than the usual backstage conven-ience to attract a rock star and well beyond that to marry one. You have to cater to every taste, every whim, and you have to have staying power. I can easily see my daughter burning out very quickly. So maybe I should just mind my business and let her learn her lesson.

As I peer into the looking glass, I'm frightened that I have reached the age that women stop counting the years: thirty-five. Never to be older. But I am a legend, and still beautiful, still coveted. I may have lost my innocent appeal; the baby-silk blond hair, porcelain skin, and willowy smile are all gone. But in their place are experience, reputation, and seniority.

Am I ready to throw in the towel? Hardly. Out of the running just because I'm married? Doubtful. About to be pushed aside by the new breed of underlings? Not on your life. I am still the standard-bearer. Just think of how many times The Rolling Stones have been compared to The Beatles. And how every other band since 1964 have been compared to the four mop tops whom, unfortunately, I was never able to land. Then think of The Beatles in terms of groupies and you have me, Tulip Dagger.

Mind my own business and let my daughter and her friends have all the glory of the 80s? Don't be silly. A new era for Tulip Dagger has just begun.

DANDELION

Dandelion Dagger is the last damn person the bad girls at Hollywood High expected to be sharing a table with the mysterious Highway Child. In spite of my Blues Buster daddy and notorious groupie mama, I was a pretty quiet and inconspicuous girl in my freshman and sophomore years and was, in fact, a straight A- student. But here we are, the Monday after I bring H.C. to Holly Woods for the third time, in the middle of the cafeteria again, together for the world to see, like the day a couple of weeks back when I had dared to sit down with the new nut on campus. This time, she seeks me out. The second half of junior year has suddenly changed course. Good grades and studying music theory at UCLA seem like a long-forgotten fantasy now, even though I just talked to my advisor again about my supposed life goal and Daddy keeps hammering away at me about college.

"You sure are living a dream life, Dandelion Dagger," H.C. says, wagging her finger at me. I can't tell if she's serious or making fun of me. Mama is a bit of an embarrassment even if Daddy makes up for it and allows for a half-impressive family snapshot.

"Dream life?" H.C. can't possibly be talking about me. Daddy had me for lunch and Mama finished me off by having me for dessert yesterday after I dared bring my new sidekick to Daddy's concert again over the weekend, even though they told me after the second time to stop inviting her. Took the air right out of the balloon I've been floating around on.

"The rock and roll life, traveling around the world, rubbing elbows with celebrities…" H.C. prompts.

"A mother who's famous for sleeping with rock musicians…" I add.

H.C. is giddy with the same energy she had on Saturday night until I say this.

"Must be pretty hard having her for a mother." H.C.'s shoulders droop.

"Well, she was okay up until about a year ago and then she started being a shit," I admit.

Mama had started to treat me differently and I had started to feel differently about her around the same time. Funny how our feelings changed simultaneously.

My words effectively put H.C. back on the giddy map.

"Must be the competition factor." She nods knowingly.

"The competition factor?" I look at her questioningly.

"Sure. Women get pissed at their daughters when they start looking better than them. Especially women like your mama who are used to getting all the attention." H.C. chews on the end of a thin straw that's sticking out of her milk.

I have to wonder how H.C. knows all of this stuff. She must've been through it to know so much.

"Is that what happened with you and your mama?" I inquire innocently enough.

Well, I couldn't have said a worst thing. H.C. slams her milk carton down and the white liquid flies up through the spout and all over the table. She fixes me with the evilest glare she can come up with and whooshes away like a freaking hurricane. I follow her, needing to have an answer but not to the question I asked her to set her off. A subject change is welcome anyway. I catch up to her as if we're flouncing off somewhere to raise some hell, which is what I'd rather be doing than chasing her around again.

"Do you think I look better than Mama?" I ask, fascinated that anyone could think that. Mama has such a bloated ego that even I believe her self-promotion.

H.C. is about to answer but we suddenly freeze up when four gangly boys round the corner and come staggering down the hall making a hell of a lot of noise. They're dressed in tight denim with some neon-colored accents added. Their hair looks almost as good as ours. In fact, they probably spend more time in front of the mirror than we do. Their hairdos reach for the ceiling. The four of them are in a band called Hall Pass and they've never paid me a lick of attention. Now is no exception. They act like we aren't even in the hall. Or, let me clarify. They act like *I'm* not even in the hall. One of them feasts his eyes on the twin peaks sticking out of H.C.'s camisole, but doesn't meet her eyes. He whacks one of the other guys on the shoulder, who turns his head to look. H.C. is facing the wrong direction for him to see anything. Other than this, we're invisible, even though our eyes follow them toward the cafeteria.

"You said you wanted to be better than your mama," H.C. suddenly reminds me.

"Fat chance of that when I can't even get Hall Pass to look at me," I moan.

"Maybe we aren't the kind of girls they like quite yet. We can change that." Her words have an air of conspiracy to them.

Mama and Daddy's disapproval of H.C. starts to fade as she grabs my hand and we head back into the cafeteria to see what the Hall Pass boys are up to.

What they're up to are four pouting girls who most of us steer clear of because they're really mean to people not in their circle. They have the attitudes of the girls backstage at Daddy's concerts, but with a twist: this maddening fashion statement called "hair metal." Think neon, fishnet, mesh, leather, animal prints and studs highlighting sky-high hair and heels to match. I'm trying not to like it. It's all so different than the way Daddy's super fans dress. But the look isn't reserved for only fans. It's not even reserved for only females. The new harvest of L.A. bands is dressing the same way. When we drive down Sunset or Hollywood we see them all over the place, day or night. Daddy says they look like girls.

"And they sound like amateurs."

I've never heard Hall Pass play, but rumor has it that they don't play like amateurs. And I have to admit that the girls with the band boys look pretty cutting edge.

"Can you get some money?" H.C. is studying the hair metal girls.

"Yeah, I can ask Daddy for some. You?" I asked.

"Sure. We need some clothes before we do anything else."

"I'll bring some money tomorrow and we can hit Hollywood Boulevard after school." I snap my fingers. "And I'll have Mama's driver pick us up here and bring us over there."

Mama's driver is named Marty and he's this creepy overweight guy in a Dodgers hat and an old yellow cab.

"We'll get some serious attention getting picked up in a limo. Why don't you have your daddy send someone every day? Hall Pass will be in the palm of your hand." H.C shakes her head and rolls her green cat eyes at me like she has the secret to high school popularity all figured out.

Now I have to break the news to her that Mama's driver gets around town in a cab and he is actually a cab driver by trade.

"Your daddy is Derek Dagger and your mama has to get around in a cab?"

I hate explaining to everyone how Daddy enjoys being surrounded by "excess," as he calls it, but doesn't really believe in practicing it for himself. I hate explaining it because I really don't understand it. All I know is that we live in a nice but normal house in Hollywood that has a pool in the back and a security fence around it and Daddy and Mama have nice cars and a boat and Daddy has a tricked-out Harley and an equally badass tour bus. They have parties all the time with lots of weird, stoned friends. But limos and all that are pretty much non-existent, unless Daddy wants to make a grand entrance somewhere. Mama gripes about it a lot. She wants all that stuff, says it's the life she's accustomed to, but Daddy turns a deaf ear and takes a swig from his guitar-shaped flask whenever she applies the heat.

As for H.C., she flipped her lid and slammed her milk all over the table when I tried to ask her about her mama, so why should I have to explain all this to her. Testily I say, "Well, do you want Marty to come and get us or not?"

H.C. penetrates me with a who's-the-boss-here-anyway look. "I'll walk if I have to. It's not that far and I've been thumbing everywhere my whole life."

I shrug flippantly and take note for future reference of the thumbing comment. "Suit yourself," I hiss, and am about to dismiss her when she grabs my arm.

"No, get Marty and we'll go together." I catch a fleeting ripple of the excitement that slips through her body.

Hmph. Guess she knows who the boss is now.

As I get on the bus to go home and H.C. disappears into the crowd of students walking south on Highland Avenue, I wonder where she calls home, wonder who and where her parents are, wonder where she came from. I'll find out someday, but in the meantime, I have no idea that she doesn't have the answers to any of my questions.

As for things at the Dagger household, life is fairly quiet with Daddy doing his contracted residency at Holly Woods on alternating Wednesday and Saturday nights plus one extra concert per month for a total of five. The tour bus is parked in a garage somewhere in West Hollywood, Daddy is in his personal studio in our finished basement practicing several hours a day, and Mama keeps herself busy planning the next party and buying more clothes to keep up with the ragamuffins backstage. I have to use that word to describe them, because compared to those slick hair metal girls they look pretty scrungy with their windblown hair and threads hanging from their cut-off shorts. So 70s. I'm starting to like the idea of having my very own era of fashion and bad boys to immerse myself in.

But first, I need Marty and some money.

One of them is conveniently waiting outside the Dagger residence when the bus drops me off.

Marty isn't quite as weird as Robert De Niro in *Taxi Driver*, but the car he drives looks just like the one in the movie so I have to make the association anyway. I usually try to ignore Marty as much as I can because he makes me kind of uncomfortable, but today I need him so I have to muster up some niceness. I lower my head to look in the passenger side window and say hello.

Marty looks all nervous and sweaty when he sees me and glances toward the house.

"Uh…h-hi, Miss Dandylion," he mumbles, then adds, "Just waitin' for Miss Tulip to come out 'cuz she wants to go shopping," as if I can't figure out for myself that he's waiting for Mama.

"Well, while you're waiting, I was wondering if you might pick me and my girlfriend up from school tomorrow and bring us to Hollywood Boulevard." I add a little grin and hope I look seductive. Marty certainly isn't the boys from Hall Pass, but if he won't succumb to my charms I have no chance with them.

Behind my back I hear the screen door on the side of the house slam. Marty's eyes are bugging out of his fat skull as he looks around me. I turn in time to see, through the black rails of the security fence, that Mama has exited the house with a man who isn't my daddy. They take a few steps down the driveway giggling and cooing at each other, but then the intruder sees me and suddenly takes off at a run in the opposite direction, disappearing behind the house. Mama stutter steps a few times before she turns on the groupie sway that I know only too well and comes out of the locking iron door cut into the fence looking as natural as can be.

"Daddy went to Joshua Tree with his friends for a few days and I'm going out for a little while. Do your homework and I'll bring home some din-din so we don't have to cook."

Ugh. I hate when Daddy goes to Joshua Tree. Because all rock starts go to Joshua Tree to smoke pot and do weird shamanistic rituals amongst the rocks. He always comes home acting like he's been somehow cleansed of his sins even though he's sinning the whole time he's there. Evidently, Mama is doing a bit of her own too, while he's away.

Some dream life I have. H.C. is definitely wacko.

I could say something about the guy who came out of the house with Mama, but now that I know she's my only hope of getting any money for the next day, I decide to let it go and maybe use it against her when Daddy comes home.

"Mama, can I have some money for tomorrow, please? I need it for school," I lie.

"I don't remember you bringing home anything that said you need money for school."

"I need to pay the cafeteria for lunch." I have this response at the ready.

"I'll write you a check later." Mama is sliding into the back of the cab after propping the fence door open for me. "Now, run along and lock yourself in and do your homework."

The discussion ends when she slams the door, but Marty offers me a look of sympathy through the same window I was just talking to him. As I shut the heavy door and walk to the house I see the unidentified man hurling himself over the top of the fence behind the garage. He peers back at me like a scared animal and disappears behind the neighbor's shed. He looks embarrassingly young, like someone maybe I'd chase around.

You bet your behind I lock myself in the house. Glumly I do my homework and try to figure out a way to get cash out of Mama. I even go to her and Daddy's room and look around to see if they left anything worth stealing. I could take the pot roaches in Daddy's ashtray, but I'm not really that interested in selling drugs or even doing them. Just boys for right now. Boys with high hair and tight bright clothes.

H.C. hasn't given me any way to contact her, so if I don't get Mama to give me some cash I can't tell her until the next day at school, a fact that makes me even more intent on cooking up a good lie for Mama.

Mama doesn't come home until after seven, at which point I'm ready to eat trashy leftovers from our refrigerator that have green fur forming on them. The greasy smell of Chinese food that follows her through the door is welcome.

Pretty soon Mama has all the little white paper containers open all over the table and is studying me with an egg roll in one hand and Daddy's checkbook in the other. Leave it to Mama to want to write me a check when I need some good, old-fashion cash-ola.

"Can I have a couple of twenties instead? I'll give one to the lunch lady and I want to buy snacks from the machine with the other one."

Mama narrows her thickly mascara'd eyes at me and me-ows, "How did you run out of lunch money so fast? Have you been feeding that awful girl with Daddy's money?"

There she goes again, griping about H.C. I wonder what beef Mama has with her. I've never seen her act like this before. Then again, I never brought home someone quite like Highway Child.

"No, I just ran out. And Highway Child is not awful, Mama."

She starts using her egg roll as a pointer. I feel like she's wagging a penis at me. Not that I've ever seen a real penis.

"Why don't you tell your mama what you really want money for?"

I must look like a little savage tearing my chicken wing to pieces, but I haven't eaten since H.C. slammed her milk all over the table.

"I want chocolate chip cookies, okay?"

Mama crunches into her egg roll and tucks Daddy's check-book into her bulging bra now. And it fits, too. A business card falls out of mine. Maybe that's why Hall Pass isn't looking at me. Maybe she's right about me not being the taste of rock stars and boys who wish they were rock stars.

"Whatever you're up to you're going to have to wait until your daddy gets home. We have homemade chocolate chip cookies in the cabinet. I'll pack you some tonight and leave them on the table."

Our little twosome is silent after that. Though I think about asking her who the guy was that jumped our fence, I'm dreading too much what H.C. will say the next day to even speak.

I don't see H.C. until lunch. By that time I'm bursting at the seams to level with her, regardless of the consequences. I mean, what is she going to do? Beat me up in front of the whole sophomore class?

"I didn't get any money or Marty's cab."

"Well, that makes two of us," she says, taking a load off my mind.

"Daddy will be back tomorrow to rehearse for his show at Holly Woods. I'll ask him then," I promise.

The same four hair metal girls are enjoying the rapt attention of the Hall Pass boys again. I feel the desire to be them pouring out of H.C. because it's my desire, too. I have to get that money from Daddy.

"Look." H.C. produces a neon yellow and black flier. The combination of colors makes my eyes do funny dances, but the message is clear: Hall Pass is playing at a house party in less than two weeks and the whole damn school is invited. *Dress to impress, the higher the hair the better we like you*, the flier says. A cheap picture of the boys dressed in really weird clothes is copied onto the paper. Striped pants that make them look like they're a circus act and vests with nothing underneath, sequins belts, feathers, chokers. Daddy would flip. H.C. and I are flipping for other reasons. I don't care what Daddy says. He's just mad maybe because he's old news and they're the latest and coolest thing going.

"I'm going to that party," I proclaim.

"When's your daddy gonna be home?" When H.C. asks this I feel like the whole scheme is riding on Daddy's money, both for her and for me. Because I don't know the first thing about her, I don't even know if she has parents or anyone to ask for money, or if she has any other way to get it. H.C. definitely has the air of being a shyster, but it's one of the things that draws me to her too.

"Tomorrow. But maybe I can figure something out today," I answer with determination.

Later, when I get home from school, the house is empty and Mama has left me a note about being out "shopping" again and how she'll be home with dinner "so we don't have to cook." Which really means so she doesn't have to cook, because I certainly don't know how to. Mama only makes quick meals. The best meals come from somewhere else. But that's not what's on my mind right now. What's on my mind is that I have time to dig around for spare money. Daddy is pretty careless with cash, so it wouldn't be so strange to find a few stray twenties lying around. I never cared about it until now, but I just have this feeling that Mama is going to put a bug in his ear about me asking for money and lying about what I needed it for. After a quick sweep of the house to be sure that Mama isn't hiding out somewhere to try and trick me into thinking she's gone, I abandon my school books in my room and head to their bedroom.

My parents' bedroom is about as close to rock star excess that Daddy will allow, and it's such a weird place that I always hope that I wasn't conceived there. I'm afraid to ask, because I think that maybe I'm better off not knowing.

The bed is the biggest problem for me. It's this giant waterbed with a high, cushioned black leather head and deep red fur top that holds the water in. The entire base of the bed is also black leather. Black velvet pillow cases on four large pillows round out the look. A polished black Lucite table sits at the foot. A large silver thing that resembles a genie lamp dominates the table today, though right now two empty beer steins are there too. One of them has Mama's favorite color of fuchsia lipstick smeared around the edge. I don't even want to think who was drinking out of the other one. I can't help but lift the top off of the genie lamp that's usually stashed away. Daddy would scold Mama for being careless; it's filled with their sweet-smelling pot. I decide that I'll have to make off with it if I really get desperate Something tells me that H.C. would be able to hustle the pot in a few hours and make at least a couple hundred bucks.

The bedroom has white floor-to-ceiling curtains behind the bed to add some light to a very dark place, but I still have to turn on one of the guitar-shaped lamps with musical notes cut into the shades to see what I'm doing. I've liked the lamps since I was young, because the notes are projected all over the walls when the bulbs are lit.

Daddy's safe is in the closet. I don't know the combination. But I do know from seeing it unlocked that he hardly ever opens it because he has all kinds of stuff packed tightly into it like jewelry and a couple of antique guns. Keeping money in there is too inconvenient because the other things start falling out when the door is ajar. What I'm looking for is a polished redwood box made by a fan which has "Derek Dagger and the Blues Blasters" carved expertly on the cover. Like the jacket that the missing blonde created for him, the box is special to him. The heartwarming thought that my daddy thinks so highly of his fans momentarily stops me in my pursuit of the box.

I am his little spring flower.

No, I used to be his little spring flower.

I start pushing hanger loads of clothing and boxes of expensive shoes aside, looking for the case. Everything is in such a haphazard way that they won't ever know I've been in here. But I am making a lot of racket, so much that I wouldn't even know if Mama arrived home. I pause in my pursuit of the all-important box and let the silence of the house settle in around me. Good. Still safe. Now, back to work.

Mama's shoe collection is over the top. Every color, every texture, every thickness of heel over three inches. In fact, I unearth a pair of neon pink pumps that look hair-metal ready and discover that Mama just bought them the day before when she left me to go shopping in Marty's cab. The sales slip from a place called Another Man's Treasure is still in the box and unless I'm mistaken, she tried to hide it from prying eyes, also known as Daddy's eyes. As I finger the eye-popping shoes, I have two thoughts and neither of them are good. One, something tells me that Mama is getting her own idea about the new boys on the rock scene. Two, something else tells me that the shoes will look much better on me. Therefore, they now belong to me. Slipping the cover underneath the box, I place them just outside the door so I can sneak them easily into my room when I'm done.

Just a little more digging brings me to the coveted redwood box, which has a lock on it. I know where the key is because I've seen Daddy retrieve it before. It's in the pocket of a motorcycle jacket that he was wearing when he slid twenty feet on pavement after dumping his Harley. The jacket is scarred and he doesn't wear it but refuses to throw it out because he thinks it has some special powers that saved his life. The key is in the zippered breast pocket closest to the wall. I can't see the pocket but manage to slither my hand in between other clothes without pulling the jacket out of the melee.

Ziiiip. The key is now in my possession. I stare at it for a minute and smile to myself before I bend at the waist to unlock the small gold padlock on the side of the box. Opening the cover is like opening a buried treasure. A massive wad of bills makes my eyes widen. My hands are shaking when I pick it up. I can hardly breathe when I thumb through it and discover that the whole thing is made up of one hundred dollar bills. Ben Franklin's chubby face and half-bald head repeat themselves as I ruffle the valuable paper like an expert card dealer. Knowing my daddy and the way he takes care of his money, I figure he isn't ever going to miss two of them. Two hundred smackers are plenty to dress both H.C. and me for Hall Pass's party in ten days. I peel two off and slip them in my bra.

A feeling of exhilaration and fear passes through me as I

go through the motions to close the box and return it to its place amongst the shoe collection. As I rustle cardboard boxes and clothes around again, reality streams through my teenage mind: I am stealing money from my daddy. I have infiltrated his secret hiding place. I can't turn back now and be his little spring flower after this. I don't want to be. I want to be a hair metal groupie.

The key falls back into the pocket of the leather jacket and I pull my hand out.

That hair-standing-on-end feeling creeps up the back of my neck.

Someone is right behind me.

Oh my-

"Any good thief would zip that pocket back up," Daddy's voice says suddenly from behind me.

I do a dramatic half-spin to find him sitting casually on the edge of that obnoxious black leather bed.

"Daddy, I-"

Daddy shakes his head at me and motions toward my chest, indicating that I need to hand his money over.

"My little girl, robbing me blind," he tsks.

When did he get home from Joshua Tree? Where was he hiding when I arrived home from school? I can only imagine that he was down in his studio. A prevailing smell of hard alcohol tells me that he was likely passed out cold down there, as I've seen him before.

"Mama wouldn't give me any money." I start to sob, as if my actions are perfectly justified because of Mama's denial.

"So, why didn't you just ask me instead of stealing it, sweetheart? Now the answer is definitely no." He rips the two crispy bills out of my fingers. "Does this have something to do with that girl you've been bringing to the concerts? Did she put you up to this?"

"Mama said you wouldn't be home until tomorrow and I needed some money today," I bawl.

"You didn't answer my question about that girl. Mama is pretty sure she's going to be a bad influence on you and maybe Mama is right."

I can't help but think that Daddy is so handsome with his side-parted brown hair that reaches his shoulders, his full lips that are pouting slightly as he awaits my answer, his facial hair that he manages to keep looking like it's always growing in but isn't quite a full moustache and beard. He's well aware of the fact that it's a very attractive look for him. I'm well aware of the fact that I look a lot more like him than I do Mama. Minus the facial hair, of course.

"Daddy-" I throw myself at him. He accepts my arms around him but his response is cold. He is just barely patting my back with one of his long, thin hands.

"Your mama and I are going to put a stop to this before things get any worse. You're grounded for at least a week, maybe longer. We'll talk about it more when she gets home."

The only way I know what "grounded" means is because I've heard other kids at school use the term. But I've never done anything until now to earn the terrible punishment. My shoulders droop and I drag toward the door.

"Are those your shoes in the hall?" Daddy asks before I leave, making me turn toward him again.

The shoes. The neon pink hair metal shoes that I've left

by the door. I scoop up the box, putting the cover on now. "Yes, Daddy. They're mine."

"Did that Highway Child girl give those to you?" Annoyance wrinkles the skin around his eyes.

"Yes, Daddy."

"You have to give them back to her. Tomorrow. Bring them to school and give them back to her. No daughter of mine is going to be seen in those shoes. What do you want with that trash anyway?"

I shake my head at him now, and say, "I don't know, Daddy. I guess there's a little bit of Mama in me."

Wow, am I ever getting brave.

The punishment is just about unbearable. First, I have to sit at the kitchen table when Mama gets home from spending Daddy's money, which is exactly what I want to be doing, and listen to the rock star and the professional groupie while they give me a lesson on picking friends.

"Rule number one: all friends must possess a real name," Mama scolds.

Daddy has to hold back his laughter even as she gives him a hard look.

To add irony to the stupidity, Mama has her shopping bags on the counter, since Daddy roped her into this "family meeting" before she could even get to their bedroom, and it's no mystery to me that they're stuffed with black lace and neon. I don't know how Daddy doesn't notice that she's getting stocked up on the fashions of the moment even as they try to tell me that I can't jump on the bandwagon of my own generation.

"Rule number two: you won't see this Highway Child in or out of school again." That's Daddy's rule. And it leads to the second level of discipline that makes our "family meeting" look tame.

The following morning Mama and Daddy roll out of bed before noontime for the first time this decade. They look like shit at seven in the morning, but I guess they think they really have to stick it to me so they suck it up just this once. Daddy backs his 1963 black Lincoln Continental out of the garage and they demand I get into the back seat. I feel like I'm either riding around the south side of Chicago with Bad, Bad Leroy Brown or am about to be assassinated by Lee Harvey Oswald. The car is so embarrassing. At least the top isn't down. I may be able to save face by darting out the driver's side when Daddy pulls up in front of Hollywood High. Mama is berating me from the passenger side. My only saving grace is that I'm clutching my book bag with a special delivery in the bottom: her neon pink shoes from Another Man's Treasure. She hasn't discovered them missing yet, and once I'm standing in front of my locker and slamming the door closed with the shoes inside, I'm home free. But first, I have several other blush-worthy moments yet to endure.

Just my luck, half the school is outside when we pull into the parking lot. Half the school includes Hall Pass and the four girls they seem to prefer over the rest. About the only good thing that I can hang my hat on is that H.C. isn't anywhere to be seen. Daddy's car draws a lot of guffawing from my peers, and the fact that he basically leaves it in the middle of the lot and alights with Mama on his arm like they're the King and Queen of who knows what doesn't make things any better. They're so busy looking like rock royalty I could almost escape if they didn't turn around and give me a "where's the court jester?" glare.

"We need to see the principal immediately," Mama demands when we get into the office, even though the overworked secretaries are speaking with other parents and students.

"We'll be with you shortly, ma'am," a dumpy woman with terrible hair tells her.

"Never mind *shortly*. We need to see the principal *now*." Evidently, Mama thinks she wields the same power in the school front office that she does backstage at a rock concert.

Evidently, she's right. The lady who so desperately needs a makeover picks up a phone, says a few words, and like magic, Principal Paulson appears looking not unlike Ben Franklin on those bills that I still want to be feeling in my bra.

I hate Paulson like most students do. We're pretty sure he likes young girls. His once-overs are barely hidden by his professionally necessary demeanor. He takes in an eyeful of Mama, which isn't that tough, since her ample bosom is popping out of a black camisole that crisscrosses in the back and doesn't allow for any kind of bra but for a strapless, which Mama sans.

"May I help you, ma'am?" he asks, regaining his composure after the scan.

"Yes, my husband and I need to talk to you about our daughter Dandelion." Mama tosses her chin at me.

"Dandelion, yes. She's a lovely young lady, has never been in my office for anything." Paulson smiles kindly at me, but I see the creep behind the polyester suit.

"Well, we're here to be sure that it stays that way," Daddy adds.

"Of course. Right this way." Paulson offers a sweep of his hand that sure does look like he thinks they're some kind of royalty, too.

We turn quite a few heads as we are ushered into Paulson's office. The staff people are hitting each other on the shoulder to get each other's attention so nobody misses the show.

No, I'll never live this down.

Inside Paulson's cave, which looks like the Santa Ana winds just hit it leaving papers scattered everywhere and stacks of books ready to teeter over if anyone dares breathe too hard, I go from the "lovely young lady" of a few moments ago to the new disease to keep from spreading. A whole lot of butt-kissing is going on:

"Of course, Mrs. Dagger, I completely understand."

"Mr. Dagger, we wouldn't have it any other way at Hollywood High."

"Dandelion, you know how strict we are about student conduct around here."

After Paulson puts on the Ritz, he calls my homeroom teacher and asks her to send H.C. in to see him.

"She hasn't come in yet today," I hear Ms. Kravitz crow through the receiver in a voice that sounds distinctly like she's telling Paulson where to go.

"Well, if she shows up in the next few minutes please send her to me." Paulson hangs up before Kravitz can belittle him anymore.

"All of this will be taken care of immediately. And if you would like to come back in when the other young lady shows her face that can be easily arranged." Paulson's attempt at a helpful smile looks beyond fake. I see his eyes slip down to Mama's cleavage when she and Daddy look at each other to decide if they're done with me. Paulson wiggles around in his swivel chair uncomfortably while they agree to his terms. I know they must be wondering how they could possibly show up at seven in the morning again. Their exit matches their entrance in grandeur.

Glory hallelujah! I'm set free! I hightail it to my locker, throwing a few cautionary looks over my shoulder to be sure Mama and Daddy aren't following me. I'm anxious to deposit the shoes in my little hiding place and hope that H.C. really is somewhere in the building. Maybe she saw Mama and Daddy and was smart enough to hide. H.C. may be a little rough around the edges, but she's definitely wise. I'm dying for her to see my little treasures.

The hall is pretty much empty now with everyone checking into homeroom before first class so they don't get marked absent. I know I have to do the same. But not before I stare at my gleaming shoes, the first concrete sign that my new goal in life has started to formulate in reality.

I guess you could say that I became a hair metal groupie from the ground up.

So now, we wait. And wait and wait. "We" meaning me and the shoes. And who we wait for is H.C. Little do I know that I'll be spending days and weeks of my life waiting for H.C. now and forever. Being a "lovely young lady" is pretty easy without her. But I'm ready to explode, wanting so badly to see her.

Meanwhile, the Hall Pass Honeys, as they have come to call themselves, make it a point to walk by me an awful lot and giggle, or maybe they just shoot me looks then turn the other way if I happen to catch them. Their behavior prompts me to abandon the idea of going to the Hall Pass party unless H.C. appears again. I'm afraid they want to start trouble with me and I don't want to give them any reason to gang up on me.

I'm such a wuss. I'm never going to make it as a hair metal groupie this way.

H.C.'s absence grows and grows, extending past the Hall Pass bash. I can't sleep that Saturday night, wanting to be at that party with hair to the sky and my shoes propelling me there. Because Mama and Daddy are throwing one of their usual shindigs, sneaking out would be easy. They wouldn't even miss me. I consider it, but remember those Hall Pass Honeys. And let's face it, above the shoes, which I left in school anyway, I'm severely lacking in fashion.

Dandelion Dagger, I decide, will do nothing half-assed.

Monday at school, the halls are abuzz with news of the party.

"Oh my god, Mikey Morris is the most gorgeous guy ever!" a senior girl is squealing to her two friends about one of the band guys. I've gathered from other comments that he's the blond lead singer.

"We'd better be careful or Cherry Red is gonna scratch our eyes out!" another in the trio warns.

"Did you see how amazing she looked at the party? No wonder she can get a rocker guy!"

"Shhh, here she comes!" The three girls titter as they

look down the hall over their shoulders and rapidly disappear from sight.

Cherry Red is, of course, one of the Hall Pass Honeys and she's strutting down the hall in full hair metal glory: black fishnets, snug black mini skirt, black patent spikes with ankle straps, cherry red leather bomber jacket studded with rhinestones. Her name is Sherri but her nickname is appropriate because she has long, curly red hair. Her skin is perfect porcelain white and she has a beautiful face with her make-up always done like a professional. Today, her lips match her jacket and her eye make-up is black like the rest of her clothes.

I just want to stare at her and take notes. Opening my locker door, I try to hide myself behind it so I can watch her as she passes by. Right now, I can only dream about looking that good. I make like I'm taking things out of my locker just to catch another glimpse of Cherry Red as she sways by. But she doesn't sway by. Suddenly, her black shoes are right next to me and I'm staring right into her pore-free face. Uh-oh. I'm going down now.

"Sweetheart, you can't possibly be hiding those deadly shoes in your locker and not wearing them!" Cherry Red looks down at Mama's shoes that I've taken out of the locker and put on the floor in front of me in my attempt to look "busy."

"I-I don't have anything to wear them with." Wow, could I have said anything worse? I'm ready to hand the damn things over to her to save my own life.

I'm stiff with fear and the feeling only deepens as I see one of the other Honeys making her way over to me. The other two have to be ready to climb out of the woodwork and crush me like a hapless bug under their coolness.

What did I do to deserve this? In high school, you don't have to do anything to end up on someone's hate list. Sometimes, you just have to *be*.

"C'mon, sweetie, with that Daddy of yours playing Holly Woods for the next century and your Mama making the Friday night boys spaz out when she shows up in her black leather, you don't have anything to wear with these?"

Like when Daddy caught me with the money in my bra, the hairs on the back of my neck are standing tall. Friday night boys spazzing out over Mama in black leather? What could Cherry Red possibly mean?

My thoughts are interrupted as Tinkerbell, the other Honey, grabs Cherry Red and, shaking her by the shoulders, bubbles, "Ohmigod, I can't believe you're talking to her!" She's vibrating all over as she gazes at me with awe. I'm trying to clear my head, but soon realize with a great deal of confusion that if I'm fascinated with them, they are equally as fascinated with me if not more so. I guess they weren't staring at me because they wanted to chop my head off.

"Your Mama is so smooth with the rock stars. How does she do it? You must know all of her secrets," Cherry Red swoons, leaning in closer like I'm about to share the key to life.

I can't believe I'm standing here with one half of the Hall Pass Honeys and that they actually like me and have been trying to figure out a way to approach me. I really need to see H.C. now. My good fortune has transcended a fabulous pair of shoes. In fact, those shoes have built a bridge between me and the coolest girls in Hollywood High.

"So that's really your Mama backstage at Holly Woods making it with the hair boys?" Tinkerbell asks, wide-eyed and leaning into me on my other side, making me a human sandwich between two Honeys. After a moment she sighs and leans her head against the locker next to mine, her eyes closed.

Something clicks into place for me. For the past couple of Friday evenings Mama has been telling Daddy she's going "out with the girls." Which really isn't completely surprising, since she has two friends her own age that haven't grown out of being groupies and they're always going out on the town like teenagers. Only she doesn't usually leave the house with a bag stuffed full of clothing and accessories that she's obviously going to change into when she gets out of the house. When Daddy asked her what was in the bag the first time, she said she had "presents" for her friends. There in the hallway, I put two and two together. I've seen the marquee at Holly Woods for the past two Fridays. Hair metal extravaganzas both nights. Glamour boys in lipstick and spandex.

Damn her.

"That's my Mama," I say with an unfortunate nod, because it has to be true. Then, I speak in a more intimate tone to my new friends. "I sure would like to give her some competition, but Mama and Daddy won't give me any money to buy the clothes I need. All I have is these great shoes and nothing to go with them." I shake my head in a full-blown attempt at sympathy, which I get without hesitation.

"Clothes, honey? You get us backstage with the hair boys at Holly Woods and we have all the clothes in the world for you," Cherry Red assures me.

"Well, there's a problem. Mama and Daddy have to trust you in order to let me out of the house with you," I conspire.

Tinkerbell and Cherry Red meet eyes and giggle. I envy the connection I see them make. They seem to know what the other is thinking. I want that same kind of communication with someone.

"Sweetheart, we know how to make lasting good impressions on mamas and daddies," Cherry Red speaks for both of them. "When should we meet the folks?"

I scratch my chin. Being that I'm still "grounded" I know I have to play the caution card. Mama and Daddy did say last night that I've been so good that maybe they'll let me out of punishment as long as I promise not to join forces with H.C.

"H.C. isn't even in school. She's gone," I'd moaned.

But then they'd dipped into the silver genie lamp that they'd moved from their bedroom onto the coffee table in the living room and pretty soon they were droopy-eyed and drooling with silly marijuana laughter.

"We'll talk tomorrow," Daddy had mumbled, when I'd inquired further if I was off being grounded.

"I'll let you know in a day or two," I promise the Honeys.

"Only four more days to the next great show at Holly Woods," Tinkerbell is quick to remind me.

I missed the Hall Pass fun. I can't miss the Friday show at Holly Woods.

I'm on perfect behavior when I get home, other than a little sulking. I dutifully do my homework while Mama repairs some of her clothes at the kitchen table, her sewing kit strewn all over the place and a pile of decidedly groupie fashions draped over one of the chairs. Daddy is down in his blues cave with band members. I can tell they're working on new songs by the frequent stops and starts and repetition of song fragments. These noises might make other people crazy, but they always remind me that I'm not from a normal family and I don't have a normal life. No matter how bad things are with Mama and Daddy and being grounded, I wouldn't trade my life to have my parents coming home from offices and complaining about their boring existences. What needs to change is that Mama and Daddy need to let me start growing up and making my own kind of fun. I'm ready to do that whether they let me or not.

Rather than do my work in my room I choose the roll-top desk in the corner of the kitchen, because I have to somehow tell Mama that I have new friends that I want her and Daddy to meet, friends they'll surely approve of. But I'm patient and wait for her to open up conversation.

Mama hums for a while, looking self-satisfied. She doesn't look like a woman with a secret, just a woman that is getting exactly what she wants out of life. Mama is getting what I want out of life too. Something is terribly wrong with this.

When she starts talking I jump a little because she's been ignoring me for almost a half hour.

"Daddy and I think you've learned your lesson about that H.C. girl," she says in a little sing-songey gush that she uses on Daddy a lot when she wants something, like money.

"Mama, H.C. is gone. I think she moved away or something." The truth of my words doesn't want to leave my tongue, because then I might have to accept it.

"Well, you're better off without her around. You can find nicer friends than her. A few bad choices in life and you'll end up like…" Mama's voice trails off and a fleeting shadow passes over her lovely face that once was lovelier, though she is still a beautiful woman by any standards. I wonder if she wants to say "like me" but is too afraid to admit that maybe she isn't the finest role model I could have. Sometimes it seems to me that Mama doesn't know whether she's happy with the way she built her notoriety or not. Other times it seems like the room isn't big enough for her ego. But that's not my main concern right now.

"I already have, Mama. I've been talking to two real nice girls in school."

Her sewing needle stops looping in and out of a button. "Oh?" She tries to be nonchalant, but I know she's intrigued. "Nice girls?" she repeats.

Time to lay it on good and thick the way Cherry Red and Tinkerbell told me to.

"They go to church on Sundays and don't smoke or drink. They don't even go to concerts."

The last part is what really gets her to put her sewing aside.

"They told you that?"

"No, that's the rumor around school. I figured that I'm in enough trouble, so I'd better start making some good choices, like you said. I don't want to spend my whole life grounded. Sherri and Tina are the nicest girls I could find to make friends with." I have to be careful not to lay it on too heavy, but I can tell by Mama's compelled expression that I'm doing just fine.

"Well, I'll call your principal and have him confirm that," Mama throws an unexpected right hook that I have to recover from quickly. She's watching me closely to see if she can put a chink in my armor.

I shrug nonchalantly. "He'll tell you the same thing. Everyone knows them and they get picked on sometimes because they're so boring." I have a picture of Cherry Red and Tinkerbell in my mind. Tink is a cute but average looking dirty blond so probably won't have much problem appearing godly when dressed down. But I don't know how Cherry Red is going to hide her inner slut. She's such a knockout.

"I'll call him anyway." She continues to study me. Then, her eyebrows shoot up. "Or, maybe you could bring them to the concert on Saturday night. I know they don't go to concerts," her tone is mocking, as if she doesn't believe me, "but it wouldn't hurt them to meet your Mama and Daddy in their natural environment. I've seen girls as saintly as Mother Teresa turn into strippers when they get backstage at a rock concert."

Panic is setting in now. Saturday is a day too late. I'll miss the hair metal show on Friday night. But I know I have plenty of Mama in me and I reach down into my inner brat to get her and allow her to put words into my mouth.

"Maybe they could come to the Wednesday show instead." By my calculations, if they came on Wednesday, Mama and Daddy could approve them as friends and we would still have time to doll me up for the Friday night concert. What a perfect week to have Daddy's extra show on a week night!

Mama gives my comment consideration. "Well, I guess we could meet them on Wednesday, but it's a school night, so I propose Saturday. Besides, Saturday is when all the fun happens so they'll really be put to the test."

I know what Mama is getting at. Daddy's Wednesday night shows at Holly Woods attract an older, quieter crowd, whereas Saturdays draw the party crowd replete with L.A.'s best groupies, celebrities, and the "lunatic fringe" as Daddy calls the druggies, dealers, and super fans who follow him around the globe. It's not hard to figure out that Mama doesn't completely believe my description of my new friends and she wants to see them in the midst of the real action. But I play dumb even as I remember how H.C. had talked about the "competition factor" she suggested that Mama is worried about.

"Mama, what do you mean they'll really be put to the test?"

"If your friends are as innocent as you say, they won't be at all interested in the backstage scene. I don't want you to end up a groupie, Dandelion. And something tells me that you're going to go any means necessary to be one." Mama's chest starts to heave up and down and she's blinking back tears from glassy eyes. I can't let her know that I see she's fighting hard to contain her emotions, but I have to wonder why she's trying not to cry. Either she's really mad at me because she doesn't want me to be better than her, like H.C. said, or she wants better for me. Either way, I'm not buying it. I just want to be who I want to be. The world needs to see a new Dandelion. Kind of like that song "Georgie Girl."

"No I'm not, Mama. I'm going to UCLA music school like Daddy wants me to."

Sure I am. More likely I'm going to study the anatomy of boys with hair as long as mine.

"That's what I like to hear." Daddy appears from his basement studio and heads right to the refrigerator for a full six-pack of beer. "Sounds like my little spring flower is back?" He comes around to the desk and leans down to kiss my cheek. Gosh, I love my daddy. It's a lot harder to lie to him than to my mama.

"Daddy, I'm trying," I tell him, wrapping my arms around his warm and stubbly neck. His long hair brushes against my shoulders and I wish it was the mane of one of the boys from Hall Pass.

Mama looks at me suspiciously and gives her version of the new leaf I'm "supposedly" turning over.

"Church girls, Derek. Can you imagine?" She tells him about how she has invited them to Holly Woods on Saturday night to see if I'm lying.

Daddy cracks open a brew and takes a swig that empties a third of the bottle. "Tulip, why can't we just believe her? She's learned her lesson. Let her have her new friends. We can invite them to dinner on Thursday or Friday and that will do."

Dinner on Friday? No!

Mama actually looks panicked too. Friday is her new fun night!

"I'll cook dinner. But I still insist on seeing their behavior at a concert," she decides stubbornly.

"We'll talk later," Daddy growls at her before kissing my

head and telling me to invite my new friends to dinner on Thursday.

Cherry Red, Tinkerbell, and a third Hall Pass Honey, Dove, join me for breakfast the following morning. I do my regular sweep of the cafeteria for H.C. before they sit down but come up empty. Cherry Red and Tink introduce me to Dove whose real name is actually Dove. She's tall with stick-straight jet black hair and long, skinny legs. If she doesn't have modeling in her future she's barking up the wrong tree. She's equally as fashionable as her friends. Because I seem to be the new flavor, Dove accepts me immediately even though I need some sprucing up.

"You sure are pretty, precious. You're the perfect new Honey," Dove's smooth voice informs me.

The fourth Honey doesn't seem to be around, so I wonder what Dove means.

"So what did your mama and daddy say?" Cherry Red croons.

I sigh deeply at Cherry Red's question. "They want you to come to dinner on Thursday and then to Daddy's concert on Saturday night. Mama wants to put you to the test to see whether you're going to turn me into a groupie or not."

"Can all three of us come?" Tink asks.

"I only told them about you and Cherry Red, but I can get Dove invited, too."

"That's perfect, sweetheart. We'll be the nicest church girls they could ever ask for," Cherry Red assures me with a confident nod.

"But I won't be able to come to the concert on Friday," I say mournfully.

Cherry Red gives me an apologetic look over her orange juice bottle.

"Me and the girls talked about your makeover and we decided we need ample time to get your look in order. So relax, doll face. Rome wasn't built in a day. You'll be glad we took the time to make you the model of hair metal groupie-ness." Cherry Red winks and the other two girls titter with excitement.

The enthusiasm grows when a pair of hands touch my shoulders. I look around hoping and half-expecting to see H.C. there, but instead it's one of the Hall Pass boys, a cutie with poofy dark hair and a silly grin. He's rocker lean and has a look of love on his face. The other three boys are making room for themselves at the table between us and I'm making even more new friends.

"This is Dandelion. Isn't she perfect?" Dove beats Cherry Red to the introduction. The guys all greet me. The one with his hands on my shoulders is Ricky Rude and he says he's the drummer. Mikey Morris, the blond singer, has Cherry Red on his lap already. But where's the fourth Honey? I have to ask because curiosity is killing the new metal cat.

Tinkerbell looks downcast as she runs her finger over her throat as if to draw blood. "She got put in private school starting today because her parents found out about us."

I blink. That's the last thing I want happening to me because of my new crew, especially after Mama and Daddy flipped their lids over H.C.

"Bye, bye Easy Ellie, hello Dandelion Dagger." Ricky laughs, bringing me back to reality.

Ricky squeezes in next to me and makes a point of leaning his arm against mine. I'll bet he thinks that I'm a fast girl because Daddy is a rocker and Mama is a groupie. But I'm about as slow as they come. I've kissed a few boys and maybe my bra started to come off once, but that's about it. I have a lot to learn if I'm going to be a world-class backstage fixture.

Because so much has happened since Cherry Red talked about my groupie "make-over," I have to bring the subject back to the forefront.

"How long do you think it'll take?" I ask giddily.

"We'll have you ready for the next Hall Pass party in a couple of weeks," Cherry Red promises.

"We're having a big metal fest up in the desert with five other bands," Ricky explains, his face inches from mine, watching my expression intently.

I get a whiff of his breath. I'd like to say I'm pleased with the aroma, but I'm not. It's the morning-after-not-brushing-your-teeth smell, which kind of reminds me of sausages. But then I remember that this is Hall Pass and I'm surrounded by the most desirable students in Hollywood High, so a little bit of bad breath doesn't matter.

"Mama and Daddy will never let me go to that if they find out about it," I moan. And if they knew I was sitting so close to a hair metal boy it would be even worse.

"Who's gonna tell them? You'll be having a pajama party at my house with three other nice girls that night. We'll watch a movie and drink soda pop and go to bed at ten o'clock," Cherry Red explains, then smiles sweetly.

Wow, do these girls know how to spin yarns. All I can do is smile back, because frankly, I'm out of my league. But ready to play ball.

"Hey cutie, think I can get your phone number?" Ricky follows me down the hall after we all have lunch together later that school day. I can remember a day not very long ago when this same boy didn't even know I was alive, but now I'm enamored with Ricky and he can't stay away from me.

Ricky is chewing gum so it helps to disguise his breath odor from breakfast.

"I don't think it would be a good idea to call me at home. But we can definitely talk here." I'm not ready to tell him that I have my own private number in my bedroom. At least I did until Mama and Daddy unplugged the phone from the wall and stuck it in their closet with all the clothes and money.

"Hey, cool," he agrees easily. "See you at the end of the day?"

"Yeah, at the end of the day." I sound confident, but I'm totally overwhelmed by how quickly my life is moving all the sudden.

Ricky walks ahead of me but keeps looking over his shoulder at me. I feel like I should be doing something besides smiling back and waving. I'm nervous because I don't usually feel this way about boys who actually pay attention to me. It's more likely that I'll like someone who doesn't want anything to do with me. I haven't gotten it quite right until now.

That's when a gorgeous blond girl intercepts Ricky, taking him by surprise. Her thin arms slide easily around his hips and she coos, "Ricky, I heard Ellie is gone. Does that mean I have a chance now?" Not that Ricky minds. He hardly looks uncomfortable with the sexy blonde in his face. She's wearing a big lips-and-teeth grin.

I feel my feet start to move slower and an unpleasant heat rises through my body when I see this girl's arms around Ricky.

"Hey, Jacqueline-" Ricky is drawling as I approach their twosome.

I don't let Ricky finish his sentence. Instead, I pierce "Jacqueline" with an evil glare and hiss, "Hands off my man. And don't mess with him again, got it?"

Ricky's eyes go from being full of mirth to what I presume are "bedroom eyes," or maybe "eyes only for me." Jacqueline, on the other hand, looks fearfully at me before hurrying away without a word.

"Did you still want that phone number?" I ask Ricky teasingly.

"More than ever, baby," he says softly, one side of his mouth rising in a cute smirk.

I take out a random piece of paper and scribble the number.

"I'll tell you when it's okay to call," I say before I leave him intrigued, staring.

Now I'm getting the hang of things.

For the next couple of days Ricky is desperate to talk to me out of school, but Mama won't let Daddy plug my phone back in.

"Let's meet these new friend of hers before we cave in so easily, Daddy," she tells him when I keep begging for the phone back.

"But Mama, I want to talk to my new friends so we can make plans for Thursday!"

Mama's making dinner for all of us, including Dove, on Thursday, with the all-important concert on Saturday.

"You can talk to them at school and make plans," she counters.

Mama won't budge, so all I can do is follow her instructions and keep holding Ricky off.

"You can't come over either? My mom and dad are at work when we get out of school," Ricky keeps reminding me whenever we have a few minutes at school when no one is listening to our conversations.

We've managed a few of those moments and they're great, because we've started to cuddle and kiss and it's so warm and new and exciting for me to have his hands and lips on me. I know he wants more and maybe I do too. He tries for more when no one is looking, but I have to be careful. You never can tell who's a spy for Principal Paulson. A locker door or the bleachers during gym don't offer much of a shield to our new-found interest. If Mama and Daddy find out before they meet the girls, I'll never be trusted again.

"I'm still grounded, but once Mama and Daddy meet the Honeys, I'll be able to come over," I whisper. Then I add, "Like, maybe next week."

"I can't wait," Ricky assures me with a passion that turns my arms to goosebumps.

And the Honeys can't wait to meet Mama and Daddy.

But there's a problem.

"You can't come to my house like that!" I howl on Thursday morning when I see that Cherry Red, Tink, and Dove are dressed in their bad girl clothes.

"Don't you worry about a thing, doll face. We have it all under control," Cherry Red purrs, patting my hand on the breakfast table.

They've agreed to come for four o'clock, which gives them very little time to transform themselves after school. When I voice continued concern, Cherry Red nods across the table to Dove.

"Look, sweetheart," Dove alerts me, pulling her long hair away from her face and donning a pair of glasses with thick black frames. "We have it down pat."

My eyebrows shoot up. She looks totally different just taking those two easy steps.

"Trust us, girlfriend," Tink says, as if the conversation is over.

And it is. Because what choice do I have but to let the con artists do their conning.

I'm right behind Daddy when he opens the door to my three co-conspirators. I've never seen so much plaid and innocence. I hardly recognize them. Pleated skirts to mid-calf, dark stockings, saddle shoes, sweaters with collared blouses on underneath. And those damn big glasses. Cherry Red has her unruly hair in a messy braid. Tink and Dove have pigtails. Their faces are void of make-up. Even knowing them I'd never guess what lies beneath all this goodness.

"Hello, Mr. Dagger. We're Dandelion's friends from school." Even in school girl fakery, Cherry Red is still the spokesperson, her pale hands folded in front of her. She wrings them nervously for good measure.

Dove takes her index finger and pushes her glasses further up her nose when they slip down right on cue. "Wow, Mr. Dagger, I've never met a famous guitar player," she gushes.

A winning grin spreads across Daddy's pleased face.

"Well, aren't you the nicest girls," he decides, and invites them in with a flourish of his long arm.

Tink winks at me when he turns his back and I have to be careful not to laugh.

"Mr. Dagger, we can't stay too long because we still have to do homework tonight. We have a homework club and we want Dandelion to join," Tink warbles.

"Isn't that great. You girls can come do your homework here with Dandelion whenever you want. Mama, look at these terrific girls who are Dandelion's new friends."

We enter the kitchen. Mama is standing by the stove watching the doorway like a hawk. She's trying to look cool and casual but I see her straighten up when my new friends enter her field of vision. Immediately her face softens. Mama is pleasantly surprised. The plan is going like clockwork.

I can tell that my friends are more impressed with her than they are with Daddy. You might say that Mama is the gold standard as far as groupies are concerned. The worshipping gazes on their faces as Mama comes over to us may not be as much of an act as the rest of the façade. But the girls are walking a fine line. If Mama even starts to think they know anything about her and her claim to fame, she's going to smell a rat. And Mama is looking for a rat. Her face takes on a business-like hardness now. The business? Protecting her backstage turf.

Mama strikes the perfect mother stance even as she flips her long blond hair behind her back. I have to admire her for being able to emulate both a mother and a sex symbol at the same time.

"Hello, girls. I'm Tulip Dagger. And who's who?"

The girls chime in with their real names, which I've provided my parents with.

"You're so beautiful, you must be an actress," Dove breathes, a pretty good actress herself.

Mama smiles coldly at her and shoots me a sidelong glance. "Dandelion didn't already tell you I'm a model?" she asks. Modeling is her go-to occupation when people don't know her and is supposed to be what I tell everyone. How could I forget to tell them to mention it?

"Of course, Mrs. Dagger. And Dandelion told us how beautiful and nice you are, too," Cherry Red pipes up. I can count on her every time to smooth over the rough edges.

Mama has already heard the word "beautiful" twice in the past minute, so life must be going pretty good for her. She lets the girls off the hook momentarily and invites them to sit down. Daddy has already taken his seat at the head of the oval table that our weekly maid put another leaf in to accommodate three more chairs. He's ready to open his mouth to talk, but Mama starts in again.

"You've never seen me in magazines?" she pries.

"Mama, what's cooking?" Daddy asks, trying to get her off her crusade.

"Homemade chicken soup, and I'm baking some of that bread we love, too," Mama says flippantly, like this isn't a big moment in her culinary output, when I know it really is. She's rolling out all the punches to have the chance to interrogate Sherri, Tina, and Dove. She asks the magazine question again.

"Mommy and Daddy really don't want me to look at magazines, so I don't know anything about fashion," Tinkerbell answers.

"What about other kinds of magazines?" Mama persists as the chicken stew steams and bubbles behind her.

"Tulip-" Daddy is ready to blow his stack. All three girls jump when he raises his voice and he has to smile kindly and apologize.

"Mrs. Dagger, we don't really have permission to look at any kind of magazines. Our priest says they're corrupting to youth like us," Cherry Red explains.

Mama doesn't seem to care for any of these answers, even though they're going her way.

"So, what do you girls do for fun?" Daddy asks quickly, and with put-on cheerfulness, before Mama can pounce again.

"I like to read books a lot," Dove answers. "I'm reading *War and Peace* right now."

"And I'm reading the Holy Bible cover to cover," Tinkerbell says, competing for the biggest lie.

Daddy is nodding his head with a sparkling grin on his face.

"I think you girls are perfect for Dandelion."

"She's an awful nice girl, Mr. Dagger. And a fourth girl for the homework club sure would be great."

I shiver at Cherry Red's words, because I know what she really means is that I'll soon be christened the new Hall Pass Honey in place of Easy Ellie, who was packed off to private boarding school in the High Sierras. All I need is permission to be friends with these girls.

"I can't see any reason why she can't join the homework club right away," Daddy decides.

"Hooray!" Tinkerbell celebrates.

Splat!

Mama slams a large potholder into the middle of the table. "Time for chicken soup!" she barks, giving Daddy a hard look.

Mama reels around to get the pot and I swear she's going to intentionally scar us for life by dumping it all over us. But it somehow lands on the potholder anyway.

"Dig in, girls!" Daddy claps his hands together.

"Mr. Dagger, do you ever play church music at your concerts? Mommy and Daddy want to know, because they're a little worried about me going to Holly Woods on Saturday night." Cherry Red is ladling chicken soup into a deep bowl.

I've asked her to try and get us all out of the concert, so we can have our first "homework club" meeting while Daddy is performing at the Woods.

"Tell your Mommy and Daddy that Mr. Dagger plays beautiful music at his concerts and they have nothing to worry about at all. We'll take very good care of you," Mama assures her.

"I'm so scared to go to that big place!" Dove is wide-eyed.

God, I love these girls.

"Don't worry, girls. Not everyone gets a backstage pass to see Derek Dagger. You might want one someday, so you should take it while you can get it. You'll see people you watch on TV and hear on the radio. It'll be fun for you." That is Daddy talking.

"But Derek, they probably don't watch TV or listen to the radio if they don't look at magazines. I'm sure the priest says no to all of those evil influences." Mama is mocking my friends. Testing, testing. But the girls hold their ground.

"Well, we cheat once in a while," Dove says, putting her hand over her mouth like she's getting away with something big. Her cornflower blue eyes are sparkling with mischief.

"See, Derek? They aren't perfect after all. I wonder what else you're cheating on? Yes, you really have to come to Holly Woods and see Mr. Dagger's show." Mama isn't budging on this one, even if Daddy might.

Daddy narrows his eyes at Mama and I know there's going to be a big fight once my friends leave. Then Daddy will get drunk and play music all night and maybe Mama will get dressed up and go out with her friends. Maybe I can make some points with Daddy once she's gone and try to get my phone plugged in again.

The most hair-raising moment of the dinner is when Cherry Red's thick glasses get fogged up by Mama's soup to the point where her vision gets clouded. Mama, who is sitting closest to her, takes the liberty to reach over and remove the offending glasses.

"You certainly are a pretty girl without those things on. Do you really need them?" Mama asks coyly.

Cherry Red squints and reaches out for her spectacles as if she's useless without them.

"Mrs. Dagger, thank you, but could I please put them back on? I can't see what I'm eating."

Mama is taken aback by Cherry Red's apparent need for those glasses.

Another killer look comes from Daddy as Mama hands the specs over.

Mama is stumped. She's met her sixteen-year-old match.

Cherry Red, Dove, and Tink leave at seven in a car driven by Mikey Morris, whom Tink says is her "older brother." It's a showy gold Trans Am with a black eagle on the hood and t-tops. Even Mikey is dressed down in case Mama and Daddy come outside, which they don't. Only I walk to the car with the three Honeys.

"One more night of convincing and we'll be home free, honey bun," Cherry Red promises as we all hug.

"Hey, Ricky said hi. He wants to call you tonight," Mikey addresses me through the open passenger side window.

"Tell him not tonight, but I'm working on it," I warn.

He holds out a folded note to me. "He sent this."

I snatch it from his fingers. A love note! My first really meaningful love note!

"Thank you," I gush, gratefully.

As Mikey rumbles away the white lettered tires on his sexy car hypnotize me. I wish I was riding with them and going to see Ricky in that muscle car. But for now, his note will have to do.

It's on plain white lined paper and when I open it up I see that Ricky has scrawled "This is what I want to do to you, gorgeous," in a childish hand. Beneath his message is a pretty good drawing of the male anatomy sliding into the female anatomy. I gulp and feel a shot of desire between my thighs. Mama and Daddy can't see this or it's really all over!

The only place I have to put it is in my underwear, as I'm wearing a sun dress with a halter top. I can't exactly put my hand down my panties in front of our house even with that big fence there, so I have to wait until I get back up to the front door and then, quick as a wink, I lift up my dress and stick the note in the back of my undies. I can feel and hear it crunching around in there while I'm walking through the house back to my bedroom, but it hardly matters. As expected, Mama and Daddy are having a battle royale in their black bedroom. What isn't expected is that Daddy leaves on his loud Harley and Mama goes to sleep.

Guess I'm not getting my phone back tonight.

Ricky's note keeps me up all night. I can't decide if I like it or if I think it's gross. Maybe he doesn't want to fall in love like I do. I don't know how I'm going to act when I see him again. After a lot of worrying for nothing, Ricky and the other boys from Hall Pass aren't even in school on Friday. The girls are tweeting happily about their performance the evening before, but they're also impressed with both Mama and Daddy.

"Your mama sure did things right, baby. Got wild with all those yummy in my tummy rocker boys from the 60s and 70s then found one to marry. Just what I want to do after I have a whole bunch of fun," Cherry Red purrs, while Tink and Dove nod their agreement.

Which raises a question about something that I don't quite understand.

"But Cherry Red, don't you have Mikey Morris?" I ask, my eyebrows drawn together in confusion.

"Oh sure, honey. But Hall Pass is small time. We want to make it with the big boys," she explains. Then she looks at me pointedly, and adds, "And remember, what they don't know won't hurt them."

That's where I come in. I can use my name to get us backstage at Holly Woods. Just like I'm concerned that Ricky only wants me for what those little drawings on the paper are doing, I'm worried that my new girlfriends are only looking to trade their Hall Passes for backstage passes. But I remind myself that without H.C., I need a catalyst, or two or three, to help carry out my own plans.

"Remember, honey, by Sunday we'll be dolling you up for the big time, too," Cherry Red sings, pulling me from my deep thoughts.

"So, make sure you save all of your homework until then," Dove reminds me.

Yes, the homework club. My ticket to becoming the hair metal queen I'm meant to be. Wow, life sure works in mysterious ways.

Daddy may know how to work a crowd at Holly Woods, but Cherry Red, Tink, and Dove are the real showstoppers on Saturday night.

Oddly, Daddy hires a limo for the event and we all slide into the back and leave the Dagger residence for the music venue.

"Wow, Mr. Dagger, this is just the coolest thing! I've never been in a limo before now!" Dove marvels.

"You'll have to thank Mrs. Dagger for that. It was her idea. We really wanted to show Dandelion's new friends a great time." Daddy beams as he looks from one girl to the next. I'm the last one and he saves his brightest smile for me. A pang of guilt for lying to him stabs me in the gut. But, the show must go on.

The girls are dressed similarly to the way they were on Thursday night. Mama is in sequins, feathers, and heels, looking every bit like the rock muse that she is. Her skin is gleaming right along with her diamond jewelry from Daddy. And Daddy can't be without his embroidered jacket from that girl from South Carolina who is nowhere to be found. Not that it matters to me anyway, what with my ticket to ride the hair metal express just about secured. Maybe it's even okay that H.C. is gone.

Tink chimes in with a thank you to Mama that we all echo. Mama responds by coolly lighting a cigarette in a long black holder and with her first long pull from the plastic tip, successfully seals the deal that she remains the ultimate force of the backstage scene.

Cherry Red, Tink, and Dove take control in another way. Creamy hands folded in their laps, cross necklaces around their necks falling over their schoolmarm blouses, they sit innocently in the rear of the limo and stare out the window like they've never even ridden in a car before.

Like when they first met my parents, their awe at the Holly Woods scene is part real but mostly exaggerated. They have to keep up the façade, because Mama's scrutiny is ongoing, even when she appears to be busy with something else.

Daddy's bandmates are hardly put off by the nervousness of my girlfriends or the less-than-reveling and downright ugly frocks they're wearing.

"I love innocent school girls," his bass player Leon says within my ear shot.

"I'll bet that little red head has something nice to offer under that long skirt," answers his drummer Pete.

"A nice little red and pink-" Leon notices me listening and doesn't finish his sentence. But I know what part of Cherry Red he's talking about. Pete and Leon distance themselves from me but keep on talking as they eye my friends.

The three girls continue the fish-out-of-water act, asking Mama ten thousand questions and acting frightened by the whole scene. We follow Mama around everywhere to the point that we're obviously cramping her style. As soon as Daddy goes onstage a young local blues guitarist starts giving her the eye and she tries to shake us.

"Dandelion, take your friends over to the side of the stage and let them watch the band from there!" she barks.

"Mrs. Dagger, I don't like it here! All of these people make me nervous! I think I'm gonna have an anxiety attack!"

Cherry Red exclaims, sitting down hard on a strong equipment box that is conveniently behind her. She starts holding her chest and gasping for breath. Tink and Dove hold their hands over their cheeks and "oh no" as they try to comfort Cherry Red.

Mama sighs out loud, exasperated. I have this feeling that this is the last straw in convincing her that the girls are perfect companions for me. I know I'm spot on when she leans into me and hisses, "What catechism class did you pull these girls out of? I'm telling the driver to take them home. I've had enough now. Why don't you ask one of them to take you in for the night? And stop at home and get your homework." Mama clicks away on her silver heels, leaving me staring. My early admission into the homework club has even taken me by storm.

Cherry Red begs Mama to bring her to a phone before we go out to the limo. Mama, impatient to be off with the beautiful and brooding guitarist who looks like a better fit for me than for her, only complies because it means getting rid of us. Cherry Red says she has to call her parents for permission to bring me home. But something tells me that she isn't talking to her mother as I watch her pressing the phone intently to her ear and speaking into the receiver in a secretive way as she peers around at us. She hardly has to hide anything. Mama is too busy passing desirous glances at the guitarist. After the phone call she rushes us down a hall toward the back door of Holly Woods. Following a short conversation with the chauffeur that includes some motioning toward us,

Mama unceremoniously disappears back into the building and slams the door shut. I hear the dead bolt lock. It should be the sound of being locked out. Instead, it's the sound of freedom.

The chauffeur has the door open for us. Dove pulls her glasses off and tugs a tie out of her hair that's holding it back from her face. It fans out gloriously around her shoulders. Then she unbuttons her Peter Pan collared blouse a few buttons until the lace of a sexy bra is showing.

"Aren't you cute, baby! But we already have a ride home." She giggles, eyeing our driver seductively.

"Young lady, I have orders to bring the four of you back to Miss Dagger's house for homework then continue to the home of a young lady named Sherri," the stiff but handsome guy says robotically. But I see that his eyes can't stop from slipping down to Dove's chest, which is ample even though she's model-thin.

"No really, baby. We'd love to join you, but we have other plans," Dove murmurs, as she drops her hand down to his crotch and starts to expertly work on his zipper. I turn away, shocked by her behavior, even as Cherry Red and Tink snicker. My heart is smashing again the inner walls of my chest as Dove jumps in the back of the car with the chauffeur and the door lazily shuts.

"Make it snappy, honey. Mikey is waiting," Cherry Red calls in a casual voice, as if this is all perfectly normal.

Wait, is this perfectly normal? Is this how Mama operates behind closed doors and away from my daughterly eyes?

Cherry Red produces a pack of cigarettes from her matronly purse and after tapping the bottom, pulls one out with her teeth. Tink takes one when offered but I shake my head. If I end up with a butt habit Mama and Daddy will nab me right away, since they don't smoke anymore. It's one of the few bad habits they've given up. And I don't want to give them any clue as to what I'm really up to with my "good girl" friends.

I'm getting antsy behind Holly Woods, while Dove does naughty things with the chauffeur who's supposed to be bringing us to Sherri's house to do innocent things. Because what if Mama decides to come out the door with her youthful conquest? Dove works fast in the back of the limo and both she and the driver come out looking very satisfied.

"All set, girls. Let's go find Mikey," Dove announces, sweeping her hands together to indicate that her job is done and done well. As we walk down the dark alley out to the street the limo comes up behind us to light our way before disappearing into the night.

The streets around Holly Woods are bursting with action and the sound of Daddy and his band rocking the house echoes into the night sky from the open-air arena.

"I told Mikey to meet us in front of lot 3A," Cherry Red tells us as she leads the way across a busy street while men in their cars at the red light lean out of windows and call us "baby." The girls are still in their dull clothes, though Tink lifts her long skirt and flashes some cheek. I'm imagining what will transpire when we're all in our hair metal regalia. I shiver at the thought and look over my shoulder once at the Woods. After that, there's no looking back.

Lot 3A is one of the nearest lots to the Woods. Mikey is parked on the side street in front of it, revving up his Trans

Am. Three other heads with high hair are in the shadows of the rumbling car. I make one out to be Ricky and I remember the note with the male and female anatomy. My throat suddenly feels parched. He's in the back seat with Johnny Buzz, the lead guitarist, who is Dove's man. Nate Money, Tink's guy, is in the passenger seat. Something tells me it's initiation time for me. Something else tells me that if I really want to be a groupie like Mama I'm going to have to lose my pesky virginity sooner than later. Like, maybe on the way to wherever we're going.

And where are we going anyway?

"Don't you worry, sweets. My mommy and daddy said you can come over anytime. They have a big party going on tonight and will be up all night, so we'll have plenty of time to start getting you ready for the big event in a couple of weeks," Cherry Red says confidently.

Ricky's grin is twelve miles wide when Johnny Buzz pulls the passenger seat back to let Dove and me into the rear of the car. Ricky immediately tugs me onto his lap. I feel his hardness against the back of my left thigh and those hands of his that were so warm and cautious at school are curious and furious. He sticks his tongue down my throat without hesitation.

My three new friends go from church girls to depraved whores in two point five seconds. Dove, whom a few minutes ago showed the chauffeur what she's made of is now straddling Johnny and bouncing up and down with her long skirt hiding most of what they're doing. Tink has the same thing going on in the front with Nate and, proving herself a contortionist to be reckoned with, Cherry Red somehow has her face buried in Mikey's lap and he's swerving all over the road. Looking over his shoulder I can see he's doing more than sixty miles an hour.

If only Mama could see me now.

"Did you like my note?" Ricky's breath is hot on my shoulder and his voice is a low moan as he reaches around me to slide his hand under the front of my sundress, not a hard transaction considering how short and flimsy it is. His spindly fingers work my thighs apart as my body tenses up. I close my eyes as his mouth continues to ravish mine like he'll have me for late night snack.

"Mmmhmm," I murmur as I prepare for his trespass into my panties.

Ricky doesn't waste any time in finding his desired destination. Both of his hands are around me now, one to pull my panties back and the other to take the plunge inside. His probing for my hot spot, which is lukewarm at best, is frustratingly unromantic and before I can even decipher the fact that I'm being touched so intimately by a boy, he's demanding that I straddle him because he's "ready." *Someday, I tell myself, you're going to be good at this and things will be different. Right now, you have a lot to learn. Be a willing student.*

Ricky's hands are moving at warp speed to unzip his pants and pull out his stiff throbbing member that has to be the ugliest damn thing I've ever seen. Like a sloppily made eggroll with a life all its own, it looks only a little more inviting when he produces a condom and rolls it onto the tip. I pull off my panties and let them fall to the floor of the car before I follow his lead. Ricky is desperate to separate my moistening folds and watch that god awful thing as he pushes into me. And it *hurts*. Ricky holds my waist and guides my body down onto him and I swear I'm going to tear and bleed. But Ricky suddenly grunts and holds me so hard I can't move. He's groaning into my chest, his teeth grazing my skin. The next thing I'm aware of is raucous laughter all around us.

"Two second Ricky strikes again!" Mikey crows from the driver's seat as he screeches to a halt for a red light.

"Poor Dandelion! Bet she's never had such a quick lay in her life!" Dove, still bouncing and obviously enjoying herself a lot more than I am, shrieks gleefully, her head thrown backward and her silky hair fluttering in the wind coming in from the open windows.

Little do my friends know, Dandelion has never had any lay in her life. So a quick lay is better than no lay, especially when you aspire to be a groupie better than your coveted Mama.

Ricky is taking the ribbing well, but even as our friends continue to make a lot of noise, he promises me privately, "Next time will be better." He pulls the condom off and flicks it out the driver's side window.

Such is the mad life of the rock and roll girl.

I'm a sucker for the excitement.

Mikey burns down the Sunset Strip into West Hollywood. Once the sex is over it's time for the pot. A fat joint starts going around the car and I decide that since I'm not going home tonight, I may as well try it. Maybe it'll take my mind off the chaffed feeling I have between my legs. Like with the loss of my virginity, I have to play the experience card and act like smoking "dope" is second nature to me. I've seen Mama and Daddy do it enough. It's one of their only vices that they've actually done in front of me, so I should know how it's done.

Seeing and doing are two different things, but I manage to hold the smoke in my lungs for several seconds without choking every time the joint comes my way. By the time we pull up in front of Sherri's house, located just above the Strip, we're giggling and flopping all over each other.

Cherry Red's parents own a house that's way nicer than the one I live in and I know they aren't rock stars. In my heightened state of first-time highness, the multi-level Mediterranean-style white stucco pad reminds me of something out of a Dr. Seuss book with its jutting façade and odd third-story lookout that Cherry Red is quick to say affords the best view of L.A. on the Strip. Drippy palm trees and lush gardens surround the home that's lit up like a Roman candle and is surrounded by cars. Party voices, a sound so familiar to me because of my parents' knack for having a good time, drift into the driveway that Mikey pulls into like he's the guest of honor. He speeds right up to the three-car garage before he screeches to a stop and kills the motor.

"Great place," I gurgle as I tumble out.

At my heels, Ricky squeezes my rear end with both of his hands. My eyes roll around in my head and I fall back against him so that he has to hold me up. I'm going to be easy prey tonight.

"Daddy is one of the biggest real estate agents in town, so that's why we have such a rad house. When we get sick of one we just sell it for a big profit and move to another one," Cherry Red explains offhandedly, sounding very, very spoiled and without a care in the world. She leads the way to a set of glass double doors on the side of the house.

We enter into a scene in the large living room that I've seen a thousand times before, only this time I'm a welcome guest. Usually I have to hide in my room or am expected to socialize with the children of the other rockers at Mama and Daddy's parties. No such expectations will be placed on me here.

I immediately know who Cherry Red's mother is, because she's the older version of her daughter. A flame-haired, catty, stunning woman in a black spandex body suit and leopard-print boots with long fringe, her eyes are drooping and she looks wretchedly amazing even if she can hardly stand up on her high boots. I recognize Cherry Red's father, Stash Carter, from hundreds of "For Sale" signs in front of properties around L.A. He's even on billboards. The man is flashy and handsome but clean cut enough to sell real estate when he's not throwing a really big party for the movers and shakers of L.A.

"My baby!" he declares when he sees his daughter.

"Daddy, we had so much fun tonight!" Cherry Red throws herself into his arms and receives his overdone affection; he's kissing her face all over. I would never let my father do that to me. It comes off as more than a little disturbing.

"Well, it looks like you won the fight. But you always do! Is this the famous Dandelion?" He lifts his eyebrows to me, and not in a fatherly way. I get the distinct impression that if he's going to kiss me it's going to be in a much different fashion than most fathers would kiss their daughter's new comrade, especially considering the way he just handled his own daughter.

"This is her. Ain't she great, Daddy? Mommy?"

The smashed but fashionable mother strokes my cheek with a long black nail. "You have a lot to work with. Great hair and a face like your father's. Very nice." I expect her to start purring and maybe even to draw blood. But she quickly loses interest in me as Ricky rescues me from her clutches by encircling my shoulders with his arms from behind.

"Let's find a room," he groans in my ear.

I'm game for his suggestion but want to check out the who's who of guests before anything else happens.

Unlike Mama and Daddy's parties, hair metal is well-represented here. I see a few faces that look familiar from the covers of the rock and roll rags on the news stands. Not high school band boys like Ricky and the other boys we're here with, but the real pioneers of the new look and sound who are way too cool to even look in our direction. One particular group consists of two high-energy blonds with crazy hair and a tall looker with hair too black to be from anywhere but a bottle. The most beautiful blond woman I have ever seen is with them. I've seen her on the covers of high-fashion magazines before. They look completely unapproachable.

"C'mon, we'll go hang out in my rooms," Cherry Red beckons. "It's about time to get out of these get-ups."

I notice how she uses the plural of "room" and can't figure out why my daddy is a household name and I only have a normal-sized bedroom in a normal-sized house. Meanwhile, Cherry Red's father sells houses and is well-known around the city but likely isn't known outside of Southern California, and she has "rooms."

Before we can get away, the real estate expert himself says with pride, "The church girl act fools them every time, doesn't it? That's my girl."

Wow, it sure must be cool to have parents who know that you're a trickster and are proud of you for it. I'd be so grounded for the next three lifetimes if Mama and Daddy even imagined what I've been doing for the past hour since leaving Holly Woods.

It really has only been an hour since we left Holly Woods and already I've ceased to be a virgin and I'm about to find my wings as a hair metal harlot.

We're barely out of the living room and away from the guests before Cherry Red, Tink, and Dove start stripping and throwing their schoolmarm clothes at the Hall Pass boys. Cherry Red is butt naked as she turns a key in a door and lets us into a splendid suite of rooms with a walk-in closet at one end. She isn't two steps through the door before her and Mikey are on the floor rolling around and his clothes are coming off.

"I call the bed!" Ricky grabs my hand and pulls me with him to a downy canopy bed draped in filmy red chiffon to match the silky bed clothes. If we can't have better sex the second time around in this bed I don't know that we have a chance in hell to do it right.

"Maybe you'll make it for ten seconds this time, Ricky!" one of the other boys says, but I don't know who it is because Ricky is already on top of me and is working me over with his drummer's hands. Priming me with a driving hard rock rhythm, he tears my panties off and dives in with his spindly fingers, wanting to get me ready quickly.

Maybe it's time for me to start taking some control over the situation.

"Slow down," I whisper, taking his wrist and willing him to drum a calmer, smoother beat that I like better. I feel like I've done this before. It must be the Mama in me. I instinctively know what I want and Ricky is begging me to "show him how it's done." All these new friends in my life seem to think I'm an expert at these things. Why lead them to think any differently?

The room is suddenly empty of the others and Ricky is pulling off his clothes before working on mine. Before now, when I imagined being with a boy, I wondered how I would feel about not having a stitch on in front of him. I thought I might be bashful, but I'm not the least bit shy. I feel extremely sexy and desirable and I love Ricky's long, scrawny body. He looks like a rock star even if he's not. He has a small tattoo of a pentagram on his chest. I lick it and he moans. He wants to do it all to me and I want to let him. I'm not prepared when he abruptly announces that he's about to "go down on me." The most incredible feeling in the universe grips me a hot minute later and now I know Mama's secret. The secret of groupies and rock stars. The secret of the world. The secret of the ages.

Two second Ricky is left in the back of the Trans Am. And nice little Dandelion Dagger? I wonder how she ever saw the light of day for so damn long as Ricky turns me into the fourth Hall Pass Honey and the rock and roll party girl I was born to be.

Like in the car, sex is followed by pot, only now we all lounge around in the buff on pillows and beanbags and no one is blushing, though the boys seem a little concerned about their deflated love toys dangling around looking very small indeed. Mikey Morris can't leave his alone and finally covers it with a pillow when he has no luck hiding it behind his hand.

"Are you ready to be a new woman?" Dove asks me with a stoned smile.

"I already feel like a new woman," I admit, on my back and staring at the ceiling while Ricky lies with his lean leg thrown over me, stroking my hair.

"Well honey, look at all those clothes in there. All the metal finery you could want." Cherry Red nods lazily toward her massive closet.

"You sure are gonna look hot at the party in a coupla weeks," Ricky mumbles, sounding like he's about to nod off.

"And at Holly-"

"Come in here, sweets," Cherry Red has picked her magnificent body off the carpet and sharply interrupts my musing about my desire to be at Holly Woods on a Friday night in black leather and Mama's neon shoes.

My body feels warm, relaxed, and satisfied and I hardly want to move. Won't there be plenty of time to talk about clothes now that I have permission to be a part of the "homework club?"

I get up anyway, because the hostess seems intent on showing me her collection. Just inside the door of the closet, she whispers to me, "Remember how I told you that we can't let the boys know about going to Holly Woods? They'll get real jealous and will want to tag along and meet the bands. Then we'll never get to rock with the big boys...if you know what I mean." Cherry Red is firm, her face almost touching mine until the end of her warning. Then, she winks twice at me like we have a special secret between us and giggles to relieve some of the tension her tone has implied.

Now that she has given me my second warning, I recall the first one about keeping our ultimate goal a secret. So now I not only have to keep our ploy from the ears and eyes of Mama and Daddy, but from Ricky, too.

That's when it hits me that the plan won't even work for me in the long run.

"Cherry Red, Mama and I are gonna be competing for the same boys at Holly Woods. As soon as she sees me, I'm grounded and all your hard work is for nothing." How could I be so stupid as to not realize this until now? I've been blinded by my visions of grandeur and not even paying attention to basic logistics.

Cherry Red shines one of her confident looks on me and rubs my shoulder.

"How old are you, baby?" she croons.

"Sixteen," I squeak, feeling like a child with an adult craving in my loins.

"And how long are you gonna let your mama and daddy tell you what to do?"

I shrug nervously, getting her point but not fully comprehending my own rebellion, which has only just begun. "Not much longer, I guess," is the most assertive answer I can muster.

"Right. And if they don't like the new Dandelion, you can come and stay here with me. Mommy and Daddy take strays in all the time. They love having my friends around."

I think of the smile Stash Carter gave me and I'm sure that Cherry Red is speaking the whole truth, even if the word "stray" makes me feel like a lost puppy more than anything else.

"Thanks," is all I can say, thinking that maybe I am a lost puppy.

"So are you ready to get busy with the transformation, honey?" Dove has stumbled over to join us.

I turn in a circle to look at the neat rows of hanging pants, skirts, blouses, purses, and accessories against the cream-colored walls and the organized cubby holes of shoes, shoes, shoes. I get dizzy both from the amount of pot I've inhaled and because I'm overwhelmed by the possibilities of becoming the groupie I've set out to be. It's all right here waiting for me. Yet, as much as you want something it's still mind-boggling to actually have it staring you in the face.

A shot of nostalgia grips me for a moment as I think of H.C. and wish she were here with us. Something about that confusing girl has a hold on me, even as I'm surrounded by new comrades who have spun my life around one hundred eight degrees at one hundred and eighty-five miles an hour.

But I answer, "As ready as I'll ever be."

Let the transformation begin.

Downstairs, Cherry Red's parents are partying all night with their fancy rich and super-hip friends. Upstairs, we four girls are having our own little shindig even as the boys snore in Cherry Red's bedroom.

"They do lots of drugs, so they're always sleeping," Tink explains, throwing a ripped-up neon pink rhinestone-spangled camisole over my head to try on with the outfit the girls have been attempting to figure out for an hour now. The top barely covers my breasts. It's made of spandex and I love the feel of it against my nipples.

Dove adds another torn piece in black nylon that looks like a pair of stockings with holes in them but that goes over my arms and shoulders and the top of my chest. Skinny black leather jeans are wading around my hips, encircled by a heavy silver chain belt with "Rock and Roll" across the front in hammered letters, and an additional black belt with silver studs. They won't let me in front of a mirror until they're satisfied that I'll to be floored by their make-over, but I'm forming a picture of me in my mind.

"Step into these and then you're done." Cherry Red places black patent leather spikes embellished with silver sequins in front of me and I put them on, even though I know that my look won't be complete until I put Mama's shoes on.

"Ready?" Cherry Red is pushing an oval mirror in a hardwood frame into the middle of the room. It's on wheels and Cherry Red proclaims it her favorite mirror, better than the ones placed on the walls between the conglomerations of hanging clothes.

I'm only five foot three, but the leather pants and spikes make me look six feet tall because I'm so thin. I gape at my refection in the mirror. The girls have hot-ironed my tailbone-length chocolate hair arrow straight and given me a side part where I usually wear a middle one with slightly wavy beach-girl hair. Tink has done my make-up but said I didn't need too much because I'm so pretty. What she has done with a little bit of foundation and powder and a helping of eyeliner and lipstick is liberating. And still only four hours have gone by since Mama demanded that we leave Holly Woods because we were cramping her style.

Clearly, Mama doesn't know how much we can really cramp her style, but she'll find out.

"I want to look just like this for the party," I whisper, enthralled with everything about me.

"But with those amazing pink shoes from your locker," Cherry Red reminds me.

"And you don't even need a groupie name because Dandelion Dagger is already the perfect backstage pass," Tink says with a high-schooler giggle.

Who knew that I had so much already at my disposal? But now that my girlfriends have enlightened me, I'll use my natural resources to my best advantage.

Going home the following evening, homework complete, is a terrible come down. The Carter family's maid has washed my sundress from the night before and I'm reduced to the Dandelion Dagger that Mama and Daddy are trying to keep me as. Cherry Red and her mother drive me home. It turns out that Black Cherry, as her mother calls herself, is the original charlatan of the Carter clan. She has the Christian bible thumper right down to the Oldsmobile station wagon, which she drops me off in even as she tells me that her usual car is a Ferrari Testarossa. Gone are any traces of the party queen from the night before. Both she and her daughter are dressed in their church clothes.

Mama is waiting for me inside our gate, as I've called her to let her know that I'm on my way home. She has never waited for me before and I wonder if she's still looking for something to incriminate me with. That time, of course, will come. And when it does, I'll be so far into the thick of things that there won't be any turning back.

Black Cherry and her carbon-copy daughter wave at Mama from the Oldsmobile. Mama looks stumped as she waves back.

"Looks like you had a wonderful time," she snorts. "Could you have picked more boring people to hang around with?"

I squeeze my pelvic muscles together, excited by the illusion that it's up to me to keep creating.

"Well, I'm just trying to please you and Daddy," I murmur, though the thoughts of what Ricky was doing to me for most of the day and the night before have me ready to scream out in desire.

How am I ever going to live this double life in secret?

"You're really overdoing it, aren't you?" Mama asks from point-blank range, as if she's concerned that someone is going to hear us. Only, no one else is around, though Daddy could be lurking somewhere. "You can't possibly be replacing that awful Hippy Chick girl with Miss Bible and her drippy mother."

I know it's a trap, and I respond appropriately.

"Mama, I've already told you that H.C. stands for Highway Child, not Hippy Chick. And she's been gone for weeks now and I don't think she's ever coming back." My final words stick in my throat as thick as honey. Honey makes me ill.

"I'll know it if and when she shows up again. And you'd better not invite her to that house you were at this weekend just to see her."

So that's what Mama thinks! And that's exactly what I'll let Mama think: that seeing H.C. at Cherry Red's house is the worst case scenario.

"Sherri's parents would never let that happen. H.C. wouldn't exactly fit in with Bible study every other night and homework club too."

A moment of silence falls between us and I realize that I have rendered my mother speechless. I've finally beat her at one of her games. The first victory of many, with any luck.

"You'd better get ready for school tomorrow. Leftovers are in the fridge," she dismisses me.

I can feel her eyes on me as I sweep into the house. I immediately hear Daddy practicing down in his studio. Everything is normal. I have work to do to keep it that way.

"Why don't you invite your friends over to do your home-work here?" Daddy asks me one evening at the dinner table during spring break, a night when Mama actually cooks chicken soup that tastes pretty good.

"It's okay, Daddy. We don't have any homework over spring break. And Sherri's parents don't mind us being there all the time, plus they have a lot more room than we do."

After a week and a half of being at the fantastic Carter house that's a lot fitter for a rock star than the house we live in, I'd like to ask Daddy why we live in such a regular house in a regular neighborhood but I hold my tongue. The homework club, which is basically Cherry Red's really smart younger brother giving us the answers to everything while we listen to hair metal and prance around in trendy clothes, is going really well and I don't want to arouse suspicion. I don't dare tell Mama and Daddy who Cherry Red's father is, because then they'll start making phone calls. Already they're asking to meet her parents but I keep holding them off.

"But we want your friends to come over. We're so proud of you for getting back on track when it looked like you were going in the wrong direction there for a little while. How about Saturday night? You can host a pajama party and Mama will buy some fun food and drinks for you." This speech gets Daddy a hard look from Mama.

As for me, I have to keep myself from jumping out of my chair. Saturday night is the Hall Pass party in the desert! The night I've been waiting for! My big debut as hair metal starlet! Pajamas and my parents nosing into my business are not part of the plan! In fact, I don't plan on finishing the evening wearing anything at all, even if I start the night in the get-up the girls put together for me. Black Cherry has a rich friend up in the desert and the woman is putting us all up, Hall Pass boys too, for the evening.

"Daddy, we already have plans at Cherry-" I'm so distraught I almost forget that my parents don't know that Sherri is better known as Cherry Red. "At Sherri's house.

Her parents are letting us have a pajama party just like you talked about." This is the lamest thing I've said yet, but I needed a quick explanation.

"Why don't I call her parents and change the location? They must already be getting tired of having all four of you girls there all the time. I feel a little guilty about not doing my part. Parents do need a break sometime."

Wow, Daddy sure picks the wrong time to have a conscience!

Mama looks amused at my discomfort and gazes expectantly at me, awaiting my next rebuttal. I'm tongue-tied.

My phone suddenly starts ringing in my room. They allowed me to plug it back in the previous weekend and Ricky has been calling me when I give him a specific time that I know Mama will be out and Daddy will be jamming. I pray that it's not him.

"Why don't you let that ring and we'll continue this conversation," Mama suggests.

"Tulip, it's a damn teenager calling. Do you think they're just gonna hang up after five rings?" Daddy is looking for a squabble. I'm just looking for a way out of this hole I'm digging. Daddy nods and motions toward my room.

I drop my soup spoon and dash off.

It's not Ricky on the phone. It's Cherry Red. I close the door and before she can tell me why she's calling I blurt, "Can you have your mama call my daddy and tell him that we already have a pajama party planned on Saturday night? He wants us all to come here to give your parents a break."

I'm frantic. Cherry Red, however, is as cool as a red-headed cucumber.

"Oh sure, doll. No problem." She yells to her mother to call Daddy, then comes back on the line and tells me, "I'm taking the day off from the Honeys tomorrow so I'm just calling to tell you the plan for Saturday. Daddy is driving us all up to Palmdale in his van. Mommy and me will pick you up at three in the wagon and we'll come here first and load up. Sound good, baby?"

"That sounds great." I already feel calmer.

"So I'll see you then?"

"I'm gonna miss talking to you!" I exclaim.

Cherry Red is hands-down my favorite Hall Pass Honey. She runs the group like a business, keeping everyone in line. She even insists that I can't start wearing hair metal gear to school until after the party, "Just in case we don't have your look quite right yet."

"I'll miss my girlies terribly, but Mommy and me are going shopping all day. Sometimes we do that on Fridays."

Wow, all day shopping. As rock star daughter, I should be doing that too.

My throat gets that full-of-honey feeling again as Cherry Red and I wrap up our conversation until we meet again on Saturday.

By the time I get back to the dinner table Daddy is talking to Black Cherry on the kitchen phone. His face is glowing and he's smiling a lot while Mama glares at him, her soup barely touched. Daddy is hardly saying anything other than, "Yes, Mrs. Carter," and "I understand." Black Cherry must really be smoothing him over. Her daughter didn't fall far from that tree.

Daddy looks beyond satisfied when he hangs up the phone.

"Well?" Mama demands.

"Mrs. Carter said they don't mind the girls over there at all, but she'll let us know if they need a break. She thought it would be nice if you sent some cookies for the pajama party on Saturday night."

"Thanks for volunteering my services," Mama says frostily before she pushes away from the table and disappears.

Daddy beams at me over the pot of Mama's chicken soup, which is steadily growing cold between us.

"That Mrs. Carter sure seems like a nice lady. I'm so proud of my little spring flower." He winks at me.

And I wink right back.

The Saturday plan is executed right down to the tiniest detail. The two Cherries know that Stash Carter can't pick me up in his custom-designed van with the three girls and the four rocker-wild Hall Pass boys filling up the back. So they roll up in the Olds, also known as the "Wimp Wagon" because it's used so often to make a lasting impression of a dull, staid existence. Mama and Daddy come to the car with me, which my friends already planned on. Mama continues her suspicious looks, but Daddy is won over by Black Cherry's number one mother façade. Daddy's a pretty smart guy and he's just about done and seen it all, but we're dealing with some real experts here.

"Wow, your daddy is hot stuff, kiddo!" Black Cherry meows as we pull away from the curb, leaving Daddy with the same mellow smile he had on his face after they talked on the phone. I can see Mama out of the passenger side rear view mirror as she whispers in his ear, staring intently at the Wimp Wagon.

"Well, what do you expect with this cute daughter of his, huh?" Cherry Red teases, poking me in the side.

I giggle comfortably and snuggle in between the two gorgeous redheads, feeling loved and wanted.

The van is loaded up and ready to go when we arrive at the Carter residence. Ricky bends me backwards in a romantic smooch before we pile into the vehicle, which is outfitted with plush blood red cushions and velvet curtains on the windows. A kicking stereo is built into the floor and is soon blaring a cassette of a new band called Mötley Crüe. They look amazing on the album cover, which Mikey has brought to show us. Ricky sings a song called "Piece of Your Action" into my ear as Cherry Red and her mother, the last ones in the van after changing out of their good-girl clothes, jump in. Stash Carter peels out of the driveway and we all howl joyfully as he takes us on a wild ride down the curving road that leads onto Sunset Boulevard.

Stash doesn't do any less than ninety all the way up to Palmdale and he and Black Cherry are smoking dope. Cherry Red opens a large duffel bag stuffed with our clothes for the night and shows us that she has our four outfits in their very own neat piles in the sack. I'm woozy when I see mine, but I don't see Mama's neon pink shoes, which I brought to Cherry Red's house the previous week from my locker at school. I only see four pairs of black pumps.

"You didn't forget my shoes, did you?" I ask anxiously.

The first side of the cassette ends so the stereo goes silent. Everyone in the back of the van gets quiet too and Cherry Red's hand goes up to her mouth.

"Oh Dandelion, I'm so sorry honey! I don't know how I could have ever forgotten…"

I don't hear how she finishes the sentence because the sinking feeling in my chest is so intense. *It's not a big deal. Just wear the black ones*, I try to tell myself, even though Mama's shoes are symbolic of the new life I'm living behind her back.

My friends all look around at each other as Nate Money leans over Tink to flip the cassette over. Ricky kisses my arm because he knows that I'm crestfallen.

The music starts screaming again and everyone starts laughing as Cherry Red pulls the shoes out of the bag and yells, "Surprise, baby! Just up to my old tricks again!" And I'm too happy and relieved to feel embarrassed or to be upset that the trick is on me this time.

I guess that every once in a while the trick will have to be on me. I'll need to have my turn just like everyone else. Because I certainly am pulling the wool over an awful lot of eyes these days.

The house that we're staying at in Palmdale is a sprawling Spanish style manse, slightly crumbling but still the biggest private residence I've seen since we started rolling through the desert town. It's at the end of a road that doesn't have much else to offer but for tumbleweeds and other desert scrub.

"Kinda weird, don't you think?" Cherry Red asks me as I stare at the place out of the window before we stop.

"Kind of," I agree.

Any trip that I make into the desert for the foreseeable future will have the same air of oddness.

Lulu, the mistress of the house, quickly proves herself a loo-loo indeed. She resembles a neurotic fortune teller with her standing-on-end kinky ink black hair, several scarves wrapped around her from head to toe, and giant gold loop earrings. She wards off Stash and Black Cherry's attempts at affection with a "Not today. The planets aren't aligned right." It doesn't take long before I find out that the fortune teller look is on purpose as she throws her hands into the air and proclaims, "Free readings for everyone!" As she brings us up a marble staircase that was likely grand at one time but has seen better days like the outside of the house and like the governess herself, I marvel at the dragons and coats of armor and hanging crystals that surround us. Peering down on the wide open but shadowy living room which has furniture that looks like it belongs in a dungeon, I see a massive crystal ball in the center of the room that reminds me of the one in *The Wizard of Oz*.

Lulu throws open a door that leads to a suite of rooms that's as dark and eerie as the rest of the house. Flicking a light switch doesn't even take the weird out completely. Some contraption that resembles an ancient torture device is in a corner of the front room. I don't ask about it because I really don't want to know what it is. Some things are better off not knowing. The great thing about the room we're in is that it's tiled in mirrors which provide lots of fragmented but compelling images from every angle possible.

"Is this the perfect room for my young friends?" Lulu shrieks dramatically, tossing her arms out.

I get the feeling that every time she speaks it has to be a real production.

"Oh, Lulu honey, it's the greatest!" Cherry Red sighs and drops the bag of clothes that she wouldn't let anyone else carry up the stairs.

"And four beds in the back!" Lulu adds.

We all peek into the back rooms. Two large beds each are in the two rooms. An antiquated bathroom with a toilet with a pull string and a bathtub with feet is also at our disposal. Everything here is old and has the smell of another time. I hope I don't smell like the house at my big "coming out," as my friends are calling it.

"Thank you so much for putting us all up, Lulu," Dove gushes, making the same mistake as Cherry Red's parents did of offering affection to the hostess and getting the same result: "The planets still aren't aligned right."

"Well, you kids have yourselves a good time and if you get hungry or need me to look into your future, just come down and let me know." Lulu spins around and heads for the door.

I'm the one closest to her exit and before she leaves Lulu stops in front of me and peers at me. She's so near that I have to pull back because her face is kind of disturbing in a soft and doughy way. She has on a thick mask of make-up too, especially around her eyes. Lulu's older than I first thought, perhaps in her 50s.

The strange woman reaches for my hand. Hers is cold and stiff and I'm inclined to pull mine out of her grasp. But I don't. And she squints her bright blue orbs at me and whispers, "You will have a life that others envy."

I blink and whisper back, "Thank you."

"Starting tonight. But many changes have to be made before you really hit your stride." After Lulu says this she bows her head away from me and hustles out the door looking like a hunchback, leaving me staring after her.

A life that others envy. I like that part. *But many changes have to be made.* That sounds an awful lot like work.

"Come on, Dandelion! We're gonna smoke a big one before we start getting ready!" Tink chimes from one of the bedrooms, sticking her head through the doorway.

I'm in the mirrored room alone. No one has seen Lulu talking to me and I'm so mesmerized that I didn't see my friends leave me with her.

"Coming," I say, regaining my composure.

Cherry Red and Mikey are already in bed in one of the bedrooms and everyone else is in the other with a joint burning.

"Know what I want tonight?" Ricky murmurs as I lie down in front of him on the bed he's stretched out on.

"What?" I take a long drag of the joint.

"I want you to take care of me with your mouth."

"Not in front of everyone." We've been talking about this for a week now. It's another thing I won't admit that I've never done.

"Let's go in the bathroom after we're done smoking." He rubs up against me to signal me that he's ready to go. At seventeen, Ricky is always ready to go.

So now I have another move to perfect if I expect to be a world-class groupie. Isn't it too bad that with all Mama knows about the subject that she can't be my teacher? Who could I possibly learn more from?

If the walls of the public bathrooms around Los Angeles could talk, they would tell quite a story about the city's groupies. It's time to start writing my own chapter. Because a paragraph isn't going to be enough for me. Maybe I'll even need my very own book.

Lulu has an ultraviolet light in an ornate lamp in the mirrored room. We put it on as we dress in our black spandex and neon and watch our bright parts glow in the myriad mirrored tiles covering the walls. Mama's shoes look crazy good under the purple light. The Hall Pass boys put on a cassette they made one afternoon at a recording studio in Hollywood and it's actually pretty good.

"When we get a recording contract you'll be my main squeeze," Ricky tells me.

I blink and draw my brows together. "Main squeeze? I won't be your only squeeze?"

"No way, baby. I'm gonna bang every stripper and starlet from here to Bangkok!" Ricky laughs and pokes me, so I don't know if he's serious. But he has to be. His plan makes me think twice about getting too close to him, or getting too cozy with the rest of my new troupe. A cool breeze from the window that makes my skin stand up in small bumps sends me the message that this intimacy is all very temporary.

I'll have the life that others envy, but I have to make a lot of changes before I get there.

The transformation from high school girls to hair metal

queens is complete as the sun is setting below the desert horizon. We look amazing. Stash takes pictures of us in Lulu's dark living room with a very expensive camera. Then, Lulu brings us out the back door where we feast our eyes on the Mystical Express, an old school bus that Lulu has painted in psychedelic colors. The windows are darkly tinted so no one can see in.

"We're going to the party in that?" I ask Cherry Red.

"Sure, honey. Lulu does readings in the bus. She's gonna set up at the party and make herself lots of money," Cherry Red explains.

The inside of the bus looks a lot like the inside of Lulu's house and a lot like the woman herself: scarves of all sizes are hanging everywhere along with candles, moons, stars, crystals, and velvet tapestries with celestial scenes printed on them. A circular couch covered with pillows surrounds a round table with two chairs that are bolted to the floor on opposite sides. Lulu is starting to make sense to me now. In fact, she's starting to seem a little bit like a genius. What a life she must lead, riding around in her funky bus and telling people about their futures.

Lulu takes the wheel while the rest of us, including Stash Carter, flop out on the couch. Black Cherry sits up front with Lulu. The bus bounces out of the parking lot of the falling-down estate that doesn't have a single light on and is nothing but an eerie black shape against the blackening sky. Stash takes more pictures of us and seems to take a particular interest in me, posing me on the couch in suggestive positions.

"I'll develop them when we get home and send them to school for you with Sherri," he promises me.

"Daddy has a dark room at home," Cherry Red says, nodding proudly at her daddy.

I continue to be a little weirded out by Stash's attention and am pleased when Lulu's bus lumbers into a wide-open parking lot that's strewn with cars and people. We all observe the scene from our side of the tinted windows as we pass a small sign that says "Vasquez Rocks Parking." Even though the party has already started, dozens of guests have begun their own smaller celebrations in the lot. I recall Daddy saying he's been to parties here with his band, so it must be a rocking place to let it all hang out.

The sound of Lulu turning the bus engine off is yet another sign of my old life ending. I was born ready for the moment that she opens the creaking school bus door.

"Let's party!" Cherry Red says it like it's an order to her underlings. I may be wearing her clothes, but I'm no underling. Especially if I'm the ticket backstage at Holly Woods. Especially if I'm going to have a life that others envy.

Heads turn to look at us as we make our grand exit from the bus. And then eyes go past three of us and focus on one Honey in particular, and it's not Cherry Red. It's me. I'm an instant hit. Ricky picks up on the attention I'm getting and links arms with me. I pick up on my early fame and get my strut on. His acquaintances come to greet him but their interest is in me. The natural groupie in me is screaming out. I've found my niche. And Mama's shoes are my magic carpet ride into rock and roll excess.

I feel like a haughty queen leading my court into Vasquez Rocks, a popular tourist destination by day, something totally different tonight. Streams of humanity fall into step behind us, ready to rock. A crude stage is set up in front of a giant shelf of striated rocks and an infernal bonfire is reaching thirty feet into the sky. A four-piece band is pounding out hairspray metal while they prance around the stage in leather, chains, and lipstick. Trailers are open for business selling junk food and alcohol. The prices are dirt cheap and the lines are long.

"Free beer and snacks for us!" Ricky says proudly. "You're with the band." He licks my neck.

I know what it's like to be with the band. I've been with the band my whole damn life.

After Ricky's spiel about strippers and Bangkok, I'm not so impressed with him. My impression slips even further when we all meet up with Hall Pass's "manager" Fred Grossman and Ricky introduces me as his "friend."

"Hey, you must be the Dagger girl," is all he says to me, nodding his head in my direction.

"And I'm the boy with the golden dagger," Ricky guffaws before I have the chance to brag about my daddy.

Fred and the other boys appreciate the stupid comment. I think it's rather ridiculous, but the adolescent laughter soon fades as Fred delivers some pressing information.

"Hey, some reps from Double Take Records are here tonight to look at the bands, so play like your life depends on it and you'll walk out of here with a recording contract. Rumor has it that they're really here to see you guys," he says.

A collective "Aaah" goes through my circle of friends. Cherry Red's eyebrows shoot up and her face takes on a look of intense interest that I've never seen her display for the Hall Pass boys until now.

She flings herself at Mikey. "Oh baby, that's so exciting!" she squeals.

Double Take is not only the most lucrative label in Hollywood, it's also the label with the hardest and most popular rockers on it. So lucrative and so hard rocking, in fact, that they turned down Daddy three years ago when he was looking for a new label, saying that he's a "has-been." Hearing the company name leaves a bad taste in my mouth for that very reason, even though it sure would be something if Hall Pass could land a contract with them.

"Don't you worry, Freddie. We're gonna knock 'em dead!" Ricky promises.

"Oh my god, can you believe it? A recording contract with Double Take Records!" Dove exclaims as she embraces me after hugging Johnny Buzz.

The girls are acting like it's a done deal and as if we're somehow part of the contract. But their reverie is interrupted by a scene straight out of Hair Metal Babylon.

Fred, who seems to start every sentence with "hey," catches sight of several young women heading with determination in our direction and announces, "Hey, these girls want to meet you boys really badly. Why don't you just say hello?"

The band boys are then surrounded by the group of beautiful blondes in bikinis who are already drunk and have slathered their bodies with some kind of neon paint, which they announce is "edible."

How nice. And they could care less that we girls are with our men.

My three girlfriends act like they don't care and step aside. I can't deal so well with the reality of seeing the boy I'm learning how to give oral sex to accepting the over-the-top affection of three of these girls, one whom is pouring beer foam all over her voluminous chest. Ricky smiles at me over her shoulder and gives me a little wave before he dives in to lick the foam off. I see his hand slip into her bikini bottom. It's like he's doing it to see my reaction, to see if I can handle it. I can't. But I have some changes to make anyway. What those changes might be are already becoming evident.

"It's okay, honey. It just goes with the territory. They'll be back. And I'm not gonna let some little whores bother me when our boyfriends are gonna have a recording contact pretty soon. Are you?" Tink soothes me.

Heartbreak must be written all over my face in red permanent marker. But it has to be better than believing something monumental is going to happen when getting signed to the hottest label in music is such a long shot.

I learn a lot that night at Vasquez Rocks.

I learn that I can drop Daddy's name to open doors. I learn that Ricky Rude is hardly the only boy available to me and he isn't even the best looking or the most rock and roll boy available to me. I also learn that the Hall Pass boys think they can do whatever they want with whatever girl they want, but we girls have to be waiting for them when they're through with their hijinks. Their egos soar even higher with the news of the record company having people there to see them. What's worse, I learn that my other girlfriends find this behavior perfectly acceptable and, even though they led me to believe something completely different, they aren't finding their own fun at the party. Instead, they're waiting around for the Hall Pass boys to pay them attention again after they hear about those reps from Double Take Records that will probably never even materialize.

I'm very disappointed by their behavior. Evidently, their bad girl act has a limit.

But mine doesn't. That's one change I don't have to make.

The Monday after the party is my big debut in school as a Hall Pass Honey. My coming out is rather bittersweet, considering that the other three Honeys chose the pesky "waiting girlfriend" act all night at the massive hoopla in the desert that lasted until late Sunday afternoon. I expected something a lot different from them. It's the first of many chinks in their hair metal armor that I'll see over the next several weeks. And for all their faithful girlfriend poses, no reps from Double Take Records seemed to be chasing around our boys.

But the news is different when we meet in the cafeteria at lunch time and the boys walk in after being absent from breakfast.

"Girls, you're looking at the next big thing. Double Take called Freddie about us and we're going into the studio tomorrow after school to record a few more tracks for our demo!" Mikey Morris announces, and I can see his head blowing up so big that it's ready to explode.

Cherry Red, Tink, and Dove are beyond themselves. I reluctantly accept Ricky's affection and can almost smell the blond from Saturday night on his breath, on his hand. Not only that, but there's something about this whole scenario that doesn't quite ring true. I feel like I'm being taken for a fool even if the other girls don't.

As the band prepares their demo for the record company the homework club façade continues and so does the full schedule of parties featuring Hall Pass and other amateur bands. All we ever talk about now is how Double Take Records is going to take Hall Pass to the top and we're going to be celebrity lovers, the girls who the boys go home to even if they're enjoying all the other flavors of ice cream backstage. As a result, if we even talk to another boy at a party our boyfriends get testy, which is a real cramp in the style I'm trying to develop as smart, funny, entertaining Dandelion Dagger. Life of the party, Dandelion Dagger. Second generation groupie starlet Dandelion Dagger, thank you very much.

Nevertheless, I perfect oral and coital sex with Ricky Rude and find my love of spandex over leather thanks to Cherry Red's expansive clothing collection. She even hands over a couple of great brand new outfits that she doesn't like. Now, I could almost do this on my own.

But I don't want to do it on my own. I want my friends to keep their promise and let me lead them into temptation backstage at Holly Woods. The way the chips are falling, we have more chances than ever to make a name for ourselves with the bad boys of the new metal scene.

Daddy suddenly has his twice-monthly Wednesday nights at the Woods taken away from him because his audience is starting to dwindle with hair metal gaining momentum. Now, hairspray and lipstick bands are in flashing lights all week but for the Saturday night slot every other week that Daddy is still hanging on to.

"I can't believe those little punks are making it," Daddy whines the first Wednesday night we have dinner together following his ouster. He's pushing pieces of steak around in homemade gravy that Mama has put in the center of the table.

"Derek, the world still loves you. We've seen a lot of trends come and go and still you've survived. This one will pass like the rest of them," Mama says softly, even though I know she continues to make her own contribution to the rise of the new look and sound, taking off in Marty's cab every Friday night with the excuse of "shopping with the girls."

I know just what she's shopping for.

Daddy looks pointedly at me and shakes his head. "I'm so glad that my girls aren't involved in that scene."

I manage a fake smile but stay silent. Mama may lie to Daddy's face, but I'm not going to kick the man while he's down. The truth of my secret maneuverings will reveal themselves in due time.

I don't get much sleep that night. Holly Woods is calling my name. I can almost hear the Sunset Strip sound raising the roof off the old stomping ground and curling like a fragrant smoke through the air and into my bedroom window, enveloping me in its beautiful newness.

The next morning I'm hanging around with the other Honeys at breakfast and can hardly sit still.

"Let's go to Holly Woods! What are we waiting for?" I shriek, a desirous shiver overcoming me. We've been avoiding the subject of our original plan for weeks and weeks now. I have to take over. Now is the time, as it's one of the few moments that our boyfriends aren't with us.

I remember the days earlier in the school year when it looked like being with the Hall Pass boys was the best thing that could ever happen to me socially and being a Honey was the greatest accomplishment available to me. I know plenty of Hollywood High girls who would gladly step into my neon shoes. The word is out that Hall Pass is getting signed to a dream label. But I also know that I can go further without my so-called friends.

I get a cold look from Cherry Red. Tink and Dove lower their eyes to their corn flakes and milk.

"We'll be at Holly Woods with our guys soon enough. I'll wait it out. Won't you, Dandelion?"

Cherry Red's tone makes me feel like the sole option I have is to agree with her, especially since the only time she calls me by my name instead of "honey" or "baby" is when she's annoyed with me.

"What happened to 'what they don't know won't hurt them?'" I want to say, to remind all of the girls how Cherry Red called Hall Pass "small time" and how she said she wanted to "make it with the big boys." But I'm not very popular right now and I've been banking on these girls, assuming that bigger and better things were coming without Hall Pass involved.

"Sure, I'll wait it out." I say instead.

"Ricky said he wants you as his main squeeze when they make it big, baby face. You wouldn't want to miss that, would you?" Dove asks.

"That would really put your mama in her place," Cherry Red adds with a sneer.

Again, I don't upset the apple cart. "Of course not. I wouldn't miss it for the world."

"Then I guess Holly Woods will have to wait for us, won't it?" Cherry Red makes it clear that this is a subject she wants closed.

"I guess so," I agree.

But I know the rock and roll world better than any of them, because I've seen the machine chew Daddy up and spit him out many times. The machine doesn't wait for anyone, especially four high school boys with stars in their eyes who are still playing non-paying gigs at house parties.

The Hall Pass boys can lie to these fame-hungry girls all they want. Somehow, I need to blaze my very own trail to Holly Woods.

The Dagger residence is a cold, dark place even as spring arrives in Southern California. Happiness doesn't blossom even if every flower in L.A. County does.

"I know they're gonna cut me out of Saturday nights to make room for all those talent-less hoodlums roaming Sunset Boulevard," Daddy boo-hoos at dinner one night.

Everything seems to come out a dinner. But Daddy isn't lying. The young girls that normally crowd backstage at his concert are starting to dissipate. His sell-out crowds are starting to sell out other nights of the week at the Woods. Daddy's herd is thinning. But at least his hair isn't. He's wretchedly handsome drowning in his own worry and misery.

I'd like to share my pain with Daddy but can only listen to his. I'd like to tell him that my friends, the same ones that worked so hard to get me out of the house by acting like nice girls, are not only letting me down, they're believing the unbelievable: that Hall Pass is going to hit the big time. So he's not the only one with problems that he can't see a solution to.

Mama offers this diamond in the rough: "Derek, you know that when the chips are down, something always happens to turn you in a new and better direction. How many times has it gone that way for us? Let's have faith that it will happen again."

Mama and Daddy have been as thick as thieves since Daddy's residency at Holly Woods started falling apart.

Daddy nods and bows his head. "I don't want to lose this gig. I love being home in L.A. with my girls. But you're right, Tulip. Something better has to be waiting for us all." He beams one of his ten thousand megawatt star blues guitarist smiles at me. "You're included in this, too, my little spring flower. Something better is waiting right around the corner."

"I hope so, Daddy," I moan. Because I've gotten myself into a real bind with these girls who think they own me now. They think I'm playing a waiting game with them to follow Hall Pass into superstardom that isn't ever going to come.

"One day soon, honey. One day soon," Daddy concludes with a wink.

Between Daddy's prophesy and Lulu's prediction for my future, I'm mad to find out what's in the cards for me. My mind takes off on a flight of fancy. For days, I'm looking over my shoulder, trying to spot the rainbow that will lead me to my pot of gold. Maybe it's a new boy who will sweep me off my feet. Or a new group of hair metal girls to join. I'm pulling my hair out when nothing happens, no matter how I try to manifest my own destiny. Wouldn't it figure that the moment I throw my hands in the air in defeat, divine providence intervenes.

That corner Daddy promised me turns out not to be a proverbial corner, but a real one at Hollywood High. A corner that I turn every day, to nothing new but the three Honeys waiting for me at the same table in the cafeteria wearing hot trends meant to impress the Hall Pass boys. A corner I've learned that I have to take just a little slower than I used to now that I'm clicking on Mama's high heels donned in the girls room just off the school bus along with my spandex and neon. A meaningless corner on any other day. But not meaningless on this day.

On this day, with the merry, merry month of May just beginning, someone enters my line of vision. Someone beautiful, pissed off, and making a cutting-edge fashion statement that screams to be backstage at Holly Woods.

Someone I've been waiting to see again for a hell of a long time. Someone I never thought I'd lay eyes on again. Daddy's nightmare, my fantasy. The one person who will change the face of our family forever.

H.C.

Our eyes lock.

"Where the hell have you been?" I demand like I just saw her yesterday.

"Never mind. I'm here now, right?" she shoots back.

I don't need a mirror to see my own image of the here and now and the great beyond looking back at me.

HIGHWAY CHILD

Usually, I'm running away from something or someone. This time, Hollywood High pulls me back into its clutches. Not because I want to further my formal education, but because of that girl who rolled out the red carpet at Holly Woods for me and showed me a world that I want so badly to be a part of, the only world I've ever craved. Dandelion Dagger, the rock star's kid. I've hardly stopped thinking about her since I last saw her face months ago. This isn't like me at all, so the whole thing must mean something. The thought of her has kept me going through some weird shit. But damned if I'll tell her that. I'm running this show, not her.

I often wonder if I have a sister, if Mommy and Dadda knocked out another kid or two in the back seat of some stolen station wagon with wheels that never stopped turning. When I see Dandelion round that cafeteria corner at Hollywood High in those ridiculously perfect shoes the wondering is over and I know. Proof is further cemented when she gives me the *Where the hell have you been?* line with an attitude that could almost rival mine. Almost, but not quite.

"So your daddy finally gave you some money." I motion to her hot spandex get-up that consists of skinny black pants that go all the way down to her shoes and make her look more like a human toothpick than she already is, and a tight black and white mitered striped camisole that I'd be pouring out of if I wore it.

"No, I figured things out for myself. I run with the Honeys now and the Hall Pass boys."

Dandelion glances briefly at the three tricked-out girls at a table across the cafeteria who're glaring at me like I'm a tumor or something before she looks back at me with a roll of her eyes.

"Nice work." I roll my eyes back at her, not for any other reason but that I'm jealous she wasn't mourning me the whole time I was gone the way I mourned her. A lump of rejection sits in my throat and I swallow it the way I've had to gulp so many other things in the past sixteen years.

"And what about you? Where did you get the money from?" Dandelion is nodding at my black leather motorcycle jacket and matching bustier dress that I made sure I was pouring out of before I left the motel this morning.

I shrug. "Long story. Let's just say I got it. We need to talk." I'm abrupt and bossy.

I motion toward a round table with no one at it and expect her to follow me. Great organizer and business person that I am, I have The Way Thing Are Going To Be all settled in my head and am ready to fill her in and let her decide whether she's in or out, though I'm really not going to give her a choice. With her rise in status, we're already several steps ahead of the plan.

But she doesn't move. Instead, she drops the unexpected on me.

"I want to know where you were and where the money came from. I missed you."

No one ever misses the girl with no name, until now. The jealousy of a moment ago was for nothing.

After momentarily savoring her words I take a deep breath and promise to tell her everything when time permits.

"You may as well come over and meet the other Honeys now," she decides, turning her back to me so I have to follow her.

And I do. What the hell am I doing?

The Honeys look at me with more and more contempt the closer I get to them. Not part of The Way Things Are Going To Be. Now the whole damn plan is going haywire. I'm supposed to make my escape before anyone knows I'm here and Dandelion is supposed to be a sweet school girl yearning for adventure when I appear again like a leather-clad tooth fairy.

The last time I crossed the threshold of Hollywood High Dandelion was a pretty and innocent teenager in soft sundresses and flat sandals in spite of her rock and roll roots. Now, she flings herself down at the table with the girls and motions to me in an offhand way, mumbling my name under her breath.

"Who's this little cutie, honey?" The striking redhead of the bunch is filing her long black nails and attempting nonchalance. But I see a monster behind her darting eyes. "Did you just say Highway Child?" Her eyes fill with mirth now and she looks around the table at the other two girls who perk right up with giggles as if she has granted them permission to laugh.

I've been nice for five whole minutes now, a new world record, and it hasn't been easy. Time to add some shock value to the situation.

I slam my leather purse down on the table and every damn one of them, Dandelion included, jumps and blinks.

"Yeah, she just said Highway Child. You have a problem with that?"

Now Dandelion Dagger is looking at me with love in her eyes.

That's more like it.

The redhead, introduced to me as "Cherry Red," settles back in after my little tantrum and yawns. The table is uncomfortably silent for a few minutes. When Cherry Dead, as I resolve to call her, because that's what she's going to be if I decide to kill her with the buck knife that has become my constant companion, starts to talk it's like I'm not even there. I can't blame any of it on Dandelion, though. She would clearly rather be talking to me, but these girls have some kind of hold on her. When the four boys from the school band Hall Pass come bounding over to the table and surround us I figure out the picture a little better. Four bad boys for four bad girls. Ricky Rude, who wanted to take me into the broom closet and do something nasty to my chest one day at lunch, gives Dandelion a wet kiss. All the boys are sneaking looks at me and my assets and Cherry Dead is looking mighty concerned.

I'm the odd girl out, but what's new? I'll get Dandelion away from them. We were made for bigger things than some high school pretenders.

"So, how's the recording coming along, honey? Did you sign the contract with Double Take yet?" Cherry Dead glances at me, obviously wanting me to be listening to what she's saying to her boyfriend, a pretty blonde in eyeliner and black mesh.

"Nah, baby, but we're still working on it," he answers casually, like she asked him how he'd slept last night.

Dandelion holds my gaze over Ricky's shoulder. I know she's trying to tell me something, but I'll have to wait until we're alone before I find out.

I have to sit through a whole bunch of private jokes and other bull before the bell rings for the first class. My window of opportunity is about to slam shut, because I can't possibly be considered part of the student body anymore after my extended absence and I'm not about to sign myself back in.

Dandelion hesitates to join the others in streaming out of the cafeteria.

"C'mon, baby. What are you waiting for?" Ricky coaxes, obviously used to getting his way with her.

"I just want to talk to H.C. for a minute. I'll see you at lunch," Dandelion explains sweetly.

"Whatever you want, babe." He gives her an annoyed wave.

Cherry Dead glares. I glare back.

"What the hell?" I whisper for Dandelion's ears only.

"Listen, I thought they were cool at first but they aren't. And Hall Pass isn't getting any recording contract with Double Take." She's as frank as Sinatra and now I know what the long look meant.

"So?" I ask expectantly.

She glances carefully in the direction they're exiting. Ricky is still looking back. But as soon as they turn a corner she grabs my arm and says, "Let's get out of here."

Now she's talking my language.

We walk through a few alleys and end up on the seedy end of Sunset Boulevard.

"Where should we go?" Dandelion asks as we stand on the sidewalk looking west, which is exactly where I aspire to be.

"Let's go to West Hollywood."

"Well, I can't walk that far in these heels," she decides, folding her arms.

"Let's just go as far as we can and then I'll get a cab. I have money." I'm fairly busting with pride that I can tell her that I actually have cash in the same purse I have my knife in, the one that I slammed on the table and scared the piss out of her lame friends with.

She presses a questioning look on me. "So, are you gonna tell me now about how you got enough money to look that good?"

"Let's walk."

Strutting down Sunset at eight in the morning looking hair metal fresh isn't exactly easy. For one thing, the derelicts are asking for change, oral sex, or both, men are pulling over to the side of the road and offering us rides to wherever we want to go, and pretty much everyone else looks like we would look if we dressed to kill the night before and haven't been home since. The trend setters don't look quite as impressive twelve hours and several beers later. In fact, I feel like we've stepped into a low budget horror flick.

"Well?" Dandelion sure is anxious to hear my story.

"Do you ever look at *L.A. Tonight*?"

L.A. Tonight is this sleaze ball weekly newspaper that gives me ideas. Lots of ideas.

"Why are you asking me that?" Dandelion explodes.

She must think I'm stalling, but I tell her, "It's part of the story."

"Yeah, I've seen it." She's a little calmer.

"I looked at the ads in the back and found this club looking for dance hostesses in downtown L.A. and I wanted to see what it was all about."

Dandelion is speechless, but her raised eyebrows convey her interest.

"So, I got myself a job there and make a couple of hundred dollars a night dancing with creeps. They rub up against you and put their hands on your ass and try to put their hands down your bra. If you let them feel your nipples it's a few extra dollars. And if you let them put their hands down your panties it's-"

Her hand goes up and she bellows, "You quit that job right away, Highway Child! It sounds terrible!"

I wave my hand at her dismissively. "Aww, they're just a bunch of lonely guys who don't have anyone to be with, so I give them someone. And they give me money and I get what I want with it. I even have my own room now at a motel." Maybe I shouldn't have told her about my room. Now she's going to want to visit me, and then what.

"Why didn't you just become a waitress or something?" She's shaking her head at me and putting distance between us.

"Not enough money, not fast enough. I wanted to have this look, like, yesterday. And by the way, aren't you the one who wants to be a better groupie than your mama?" I get defensive because I really thought she would understand my mission to make money any way I can for our common cause.

Miss My Daddy is a Rock Star and My Mama is a Groupie stops those neon shoes from hitting the pavement.

"What the frig does that have to do with making money letting guys touch your boobs?" she yowls.

"I'll touch your boobs for free!" some drunk splayed out on the sidewalk gurgles.

I want to kick him in the shin but I have to explain my reasoning to my new sister.

"What do you think rock stars are gonna be doing to us if we become groupies?"

I can see by the look on Dandelion's face that I've stumped her momentarily. But she recovers like a pro and shoots back, "You can't tell me these guys at that club are rock star material!"

My shoulders slump. She's got me now and I love her even more. "Well, no. They're thugs and drug dealers and-"

Dandelion's eyes widen so much I swear they're going to pop out and I think it's because she's so shocked that I'm rubbing bellies with criminals. But she takes me by the arm again and starts trying to drag me down the concrete, both of us on heels as skinny as ice picks.

"Oh shit! It's Marty! We have to hide!"

"Wait! Who the hell is-" I'm about to fall flat on the sidewalk like the drunk who wanted a free feel as a rickety yellow cab pulls up to the curb and a big guy in a Dodgers cap turned backward peers out the passenger side window.

I vaguely remember the name Marty. It soon comes back to me that he's the "chauffeur" of Dandelion's mama. A chauffeur in a cab. Some big deal she is.

"Miss Dandylion, what are yous girls doin' out on the street lookin' like that when yous are supposed ta be in school? Your mama and daddy aren't gonna be happy," he mumbles, trying to sound tough.

"Marty, we-" Dandelion starts, and I just know she's going to make up some stupid reason that we're walking down Sunset looking like tonight's hot stuff. So, I step in. After all, I've got the funds.

"Hey, big guy! You know, Miss Dandylion and me were just looking for a cab to West Hollywood and, boom! Here you are!" Marty is suddenly the missing transportation link that I was looking for in The Way Things Are Going to Be. After all that thought about how we're going to get around the city on our groupie business, the problem is solved that quickly.

Marty looks from Dandelion to me and seems torn between two courses of action.

"Uh, Miss-Miss-" Marty searches my face for a name.

"Just call me H.C., big guy." I wink and shove a boob through the window.

"Uh, Miss H.C., I don't know if I can do that. Miss Dandylion is supposed to be in school and-"

Now I have both boobs in the window and a twenty in my hand.

"Come on, big guy."

Sweat droplets pop out on his forehead. "Well-"

"Well," I cut him off again. "Isn't Miss Dandylion better off in the back of your cab than out on this hot, dirty street?" I say "hot" and "dirty" like I'm in a porn video.

Marty is heaving to add to the sweating. He fans himself with the Dodgers cap which is glistening with his perspiration.

"Yeah, I guess so. Yous girls better get in. But I just know that Miss Tulip is gonna fire me for this."

"Don't you worry about Miss Tulip, doll. You have some new customers now."

I jump into the back of the cab even as Dandelion, silenced, stands reluctantly on the sidewalk.

"Marty, if you blab anything to Mama I'll tell her you tried to have sex with me in the back of this heap of junk!" she threatens.

"Uh boy, yous girls are really puttin' the screws to me now, just like Miss Tulip does when I bring her someplace that your daddy doesn't know about."

"He may not know about it Marty, but I know exactly where she's going."

When I poke Dandelion, she quietly informs me that her mama is enjoying all the young hair metal boys around town even while she presumes her daughter and husband don't know her secret. She's wrong about at least one of them.

As Marty barrels down Sunset Boulevard toward the Groupie Promised Land, I broach another subject that's part of The Way. Knowing that Tulip Dagger is crossing generational boundaries makes me even more anxious to fit all the pieces together that I've shaped in my mind.

"Have you seen the blonde?" I ask.

"What blonde?" Dandelion looks at me with confusion.

"The one from South Carolina that beads and embroiders," I say impatiently, because there's only one blond as far as I'm concerned, and she's the one we need.

"Oh, *that* blonde." Dandelion frowns and shakes her head. "No, she disappeared just like you. And anyway, I don't even go to Daddy's concerts anymore most of the time because I'm with the Honeys."

"Oh? Which reminds me... I told you where I got my style, now you tell where you got yours."

Dandelion's eyes burn holes in the back of Marty's head for a minute, then she shrugs and says, "Oh, what the hell."

She starts talking about going to some house off Sunset that belongs to the real estate agent Stash Carter, who is the father of Cherry Dead and has his face on more billboards than John Travolta, and how her three girlfriends put on a big act for her parents to convince them that they were church girls and not the mad metal mavens that they are. Her mama and daddy think she's going to a "homework club" but she's really going to big parties all over the city and having mad sex with Ricky Rude.

Marty is pretending not to listen, but I know megaphone ears when I see them.

"So, what's the problem?" The whole situation sounds perfect to me.

"The problem is that they don't want to go to Holly Woods cuz they think that Hall Pass is getting that recording contract and they want to follow them to the top."

Now I understand.

"Well, you got some great clothes out of it anyway. And some relevant experience."

I crack myself up.

"Yeah, I know." Dandelion isn't as entertained by me as I am.

"I'm ready for Holly Woods whenever you are," I tell her, in case she has any doubt in her mind.

"Ms. Dandylion, it's gonna be real hard for me to keep everything I'm hearing a secret," Marty warns from the driver's seat, thus interrupting the flow of a very crucial conversation.

"Sex with a minor isn't gonna look really good on your resume, Marty. Or your police record for that matter." Dandelion leans forward to remind him.

Marty clams up but he's sizing me up in the rear view mirror every time I look through the front window to see if we've reached the Groupie Promised Land yet. The boarded up Whisky a Go-Go looms up on the right side. Right next to it, the Roxy. Made it!

"I've been trying to get into the Roxy on my nights off but they haven't let me in yet." I squint my eyes to make out the Roxy's marquee that reads "Fri and Sat Scarlett Rouge." Then, I tell Marty to pull over and let us out.

We two girls bail out and I hand Marty the twenty

through the window. "Can you come back and get us so that Dandelion can get on the bus at the end of the school day?"

Dandelion hits me on the shoulder and annoyed, tells me to forget that scheme. "I'll just tell Mama and Daddy that I went home with Cherry Red. I do it all the time anyway."

As for Marty, he pulls away from my money like it's poison. "I don't want no money from yous girls. Yous just call dispatch when yous want to get picked up and I'll be here." After a pause he narrows his eyes at me, throws his pudgy index finger in my direction, and in his best private investigator tone says, "Now I know who yous are. H.C. stands for Highway Child. Yous the girl who Miss Tulip doesn't want Miss Dandylion around. Yup, it's gonna be mighty hard to keep a secret."

"I have total faith in you, Marty." Dandelion ends the discussion with a slam of the back door.

As we watch him pull away, Dandelion stares after him mournfully.

"You don't look as happy as I do to be standing in front of the Whisky a Go-Go," I hint, wanting her to cheer up. "Even if it's closed now," I add when she doesn't speak.

"Well, I want to be as happy as you, but there's a big problem that keeps coming up in my mind," she finally says.

"Spit it out!" I demand, tapping my foot impatiently on the hallowed ground in front of the Whisky. And who knows who's touched this pavement before now. Jim Morrison? Those naughty Led Zeppelin boys? Or more recently, the New York Dolls?

She turns and faces me. "The minute I start showing up at these places and at Holly Woods, Mama is gonna snitch to Daddy and the whole plan is gonna go in the toilet. Dandelion goes back to her no excitement life. That's about the only reason I can think of to keep hanging around with the Honeys and going to lame high school parties that Hall Pass will be playing at for the rest of their natural lives."

Toward the end of her spiel I can tell she's trying to hide tears from me. She turns her back and her hand goes up to her face. I walk up behind her and put my chin on her shoulder. Of course I already covered this base when she told me about her mama's secret.

"You're forgetting something, Baby Dagger." I heard her mama call her this in a condescending manner the night I met her at Holly Woods. Only I make it sound like an important moniker, not an annoying nickname.

"No I'm not. I've thought about it inside and out I'm just gonna have to go head to head with her and hope she doesn't open her mouth. And hope that Marty doesn't open his mouth either," she wails.

"Listen." I take her shoulders and, in spite of her reluctance, spin her around to face me. She hangs her head until I tell her the solution I've already found. "How can your mama tell on you when she's guilty of the same thing? If she sees you it means that she's where she's not supposed to be, right? So my guess is that she's gonna keep her mouth shut because she doesn't want to reveal her sins either."

A moment of enlightenment takes place and she lifts her head to me. Her whole spirit seems to come alive again.

"Why didn't I think of that?" she whispers.

"Because I think of everything, that's why. Come on. Let's go have breakfast at the Rainbow and make some plans." I feel like a damn genius as I clomp further west down Sunset. But like in the cafeteria, Dandelion doesn't follow.

Looking around, I see she hasn't moved from in front of the Whisky. I put my hands out as if to say, *What are you waiting for?*

She folds her arms smugly on her chest and starts the foot tapping like I did a few minutes before.

"If you think of everything, how come you don't know that the Rainbow doesn't even open until eleven?"

Wow, every time I try to declare my superiority she gets me on something. And I kind of like it. I've met my match.

"That's three freaking hours from now. What do we do until then?"

That's when Dandelion tips her head to the side to look around me and a look of disbelief crosses her face. "We'll figure something out. Let's go." She's in a hurry to split now.

I look behind me to see why she's in such a twist.

As if on cue two guys are stumbling down Hilldale Avenue, the first cross street west of the Whisky, which runs up a hill before the Roxy Theatre. They look stinky and hungry and drunk. I think I'm in love.

"Hey girls, wassup?" one of them stutters, waving his hand to flag us down.

They're trying to hold each other up and it's not working very well.

All I can think of while I watch them is: *rock and roll*.

Dandelion is shaking her head at me now and waving her hands like a referee calling a play dead.

"You guys live around here? We're looking for some fun until the Rainbow opens," I tell them.

"Nah, we hail from Van Nuys. But we've got some friends up the hill," the second one says. "You girls got a car? We can go back to Smut Central and get bombed."

"Nope, no car. Nice to meet you guys. See you later," Dandelion says hastily, and pulls her token move of taking my arm and trying to drag me away.

"Well then we can go back up the hill and get bombed." The first one is talking again, calling to us as we hurry away, but he's moving his head back and forth like he doesn't know what direction he came from or where he wants to go next.

"Come on, let's go get bombed," I beg, trying to pull free of Dandelion's clutches.

"They're already bombed. Don't you get it? And furthermore, they're gross."

I look behind us and decide that she's right. One of them has long, stringy blond hair and a chipped tooth, though his face is handsome. The other is basically unreadable because his hair is covering his face and he's drooling.

"We know the doorman at the Roxy," Chewbacca mumbles.

Four high-heeled feet stop on cue. But then Dandelion shakes her head and hisses, "It's a pick-up line."

"It's working," I hiss back. "Let's go."

Our two new friends practically have to crawl up steep Hilldale to a small two-story house that has several cars in the driveway and even more on the street. As we near the front door the prevailing smell of vomit wafts out but is soon replaced by the aroma of pot, which I've smelled a lot because my parents smoked it all the time.

The house isn't bad looking but is so quiet that it brings back an unfortunate memory. Now my feet are hesitating and I hold my breath.

"Mommy and Dadda ripped off a house once that was a fresh crime scene. The cops weren't even there yet," I reveal to Dandelion.

She glares at me and between her teeth growls, "Just what I want to hear right now. Anything else?"

"Yeah, when we went in two people were dead on the living room floor. The guy had killed his wife and then blown his own head to pieces. Blood was everywhere, even on the TV set, but we put it in the back seat anyway and took the stereo too."

"Good-bye. Have a nice life."

She's ready to turn and leave when a somewhat normal looking woman opens the door, smiles, and says, "Welcome back, boys. Oh good, more new friends to join in the fun."

I hit Dandelion with a look of superiority as the woman, who identifies herself as "Mother Sandy," holds the screen door ajar and we trudge over the worn welcome mat.

It occurs to me that we don't even know these guys that we're entering a strange house with. I ask Mother Sandy, a dead giveaway that we can easily be murdered and buried in the back yard without anyone discovering our decaying bodies for years. But what the hell. It would be nice to know what to call our new friends, even though they're already about half asleep on beanbag furniture that's strewn all over the living room.

"Oh, that's Diesel with the blond hair and the other one is Bullshit. Did you girls eat breakfast?"

As we follow her into the kitchen some guy walks through rubbing his head, naked as Adam. And what do you know, his name just happens to be Adam.

"Is he your son?" Dandelion asks the most ridiculous question possible after he locks himself in the bathroom off the kitchen. We can hear him peeing into the toilet through the thin door.

"Sure, sweetheart. I have a lot of children. You're my children now, too. How do you like your eggs?"

While Sandy is cooking Dandelion and I spend a lot of time looking at each other, silently communicating. The other part of the time we're looking around the house which isn't at all dirty or disturbing in spite of the vomit smell outside. The place is filled with cheap travel mementos and equally cheap furnishings.

"I've been a roadie for four different rock bands. When I'm not on the road with anyone I take in all the rockers from the clubs on Sunset if they need a place to stay," Sandy explains. "And I work backstage whenever I can."

Sandy doesn't seem like she's lying. She actually seems normal and nice, if a little rough and masculine. She's got on a Harley t-shirt and a red kerchief wrapped around her head.

Well, this news is all too wonderful to ignore.

"We'd love to go to the Roxy," I gush.

"You look like you're ready to go right now. Where are you girls supposed to be? School?" Sandy asks without turning from the stove.

"No, Mother Sandy. We're supposed to be right here at your table," Dandelion answers.

Damn, I admire her smoothness.

Mother Sandy has a big grin on her face when she turns with the steaming frying pan. She's missing a tooth on the far right and it gives her a tough but kind of cute look.

"Something about you looks familiar," she says to Dandelion as she serves us.

"My daddy is Derek Dagger."

"And her mama is a really famous groupie," I add.

"Oh yes, Tulip. You look like a cross between your mama and daddy. Half and half. Tulip has been around the clubs a lot lately. That woman can change like the seasons! And she looks good no matter what crowd she's dressing for!"

Dandelion's brows rise in interest.

"Is that so, Mother Sandy? My mama in the clubs?"

I know she's searching for information.

Sandy suddenly clams up. "I get the feeling that I'm snitching on her."

Before the conversation can go any further, a tremendous racket tears through the house, originating in the living room. A screaming guitar, a booming bass, sticks smashing drums.

"What the-" I jump up from my chair and run to the doorway that separates the living room and kitchen. Dandelion is at my heels.

"Whoa-" she echoes my very thoughts.

The two losers we followed up Hilldale have transformed themselves into a three-piece band in a matter of minutes. Diesel is shredding the guitar on a sagging couch, Bullshit is thrumming the bass while flat on his back on the floor, and some other creep who wouldn't look good doing anything but mangling the drums is doing just that. And they sound amazing.

Love rushes in again.

"They started a band a couple of weeks ago and call themselves Smut. They can't practice at their house so I let them do it here," Sandy explains, a big, proud grin on her face and her pretty blue eyes sparkling.

"Told you this was a good decision," I whisper to Dandelion.

"Girls, you'd better eat your eggs before they get cold and stiff! The boys will be playing all afternoon. You'll be able to watch them after you eat."

A surge of love for Sandy gushes from my chest so hard I can feel it. She's like the mother I was supposed to have. And, she's going to bring us to the clubs on Sunset. Wow, did we ever hit the jackpot.

The sun is setting when Marty picks us up after we call the cab company's dispatcher. It's been a dreamy day of having a new mother and watching a real rock band practice.

"They probably won't even be there when we go back," Dandelion says glumly.

"Don't say that!" I snap, because I don't want to think that Sandy may have been lying to us when she told us to come back to her house the next night so we can all hit the Roxy together.

"This town is full of liars! Daddy says that all the time!" she whines.

"He ain't kiddin', Miss Dandylion!" Marty sticks his two cents in.

"Well, I don't think Sandy was lying to us. Marty, we have to get back here tomorrow night. Twenty dollars if you bring us and pick us up."

"I already told yous girls I don't want your money. And tomorrow night is gonna be tricky cuz Miss Tulip already has me booked for eight o'clock."

Getting back to Sunset is already a challenge, because Dandelion has to lie to her parents and tell them she's at the stupid homework club. And now, another problem.

"Then bring us at seven," I say quickly before Dandelion starts whining again.

"Oh, it's never gonna work! I'm gonna get caught! The Honeys are gonna take revenge on me because I broke rank!"

I don't know what her problem is. We've had such a fun time at Sandy's, eating good food, smoking pot, listening to a band that will probably make it big, and meeting several other party people. She was laughing and bragging about her family tree the whole time and now she's all negative. And what's all this crap about "breaking rank?"

"Are you in the freaking army or something?"

We squabble in the back seat until Marty sticks his fingers in his mouth and whistles really loud.

"Uh, I don't mean to disturb yous girls, but I have to know where yous live, Miss Highway Child. I can't exactly bring Miss Dandylion home with yous in the cab. Miss Tulip will fire me."

Uh-oh. Now Dandelion is going to know things about me that maybe I'm not ready to have her know. How to do this…how to…

Very calm and businesslike I say, "The Ladybug Motel on Grand Avenue, please." I throw one leg over the other and picture myself in the back of a limo asking the driver to take me to the Beverly Hills Hotel.

I read somewhere that if you look and sound professional, even if you're saying the weirdest thing in the whole world, people will take you seriously.

"The Ladybug Motel?" Dandelion is looking at me like I have the little orange bugs crawling all over me.

Oh well, I tried to make the theory work.

"It's a convenient location to my job!" I'm on the defensive.

"Highway Child, you're gonna get yourself murdered!"

"I don't have a home and a mama and daddy like you, so shut up!"

Pretty soon we're sitting back to back and both have our arms folded. It's deadly quiet as Marty struggles through nighttime traffic to bring me home. He puts on an old radio that's just a whole lot of fuzz and the occasional bit of music that may or may not be recognizable. Dandelion loses her attitude before I do as Marty drags down the mostly deserted streets of central L.A.

Los Angeles must have the only downtown area I know of that isn't bustling with activity. I've known a lot of downtowns in my short life and L.A. definitely has the weirdest one. No one of any virtue hangs around here.

The Ladybug Motel has a lighted sign with a hole smashed through the namesake bug depicted on it. The squat, depressing, one-story lodge even looks frightening at night when you can hardly see it.

"I wish I had somewhere you could stay," Dandelion murmurs, touching my arm as I reach for the door handle.

I desperately want to lay my hand over hers and feel her warmth, both the physical and the caring kind that she's projecting at me with her gaze and her heat. All these weeks we've spent apart I've been thinking about this girl who showed some concern for me when no one else has in years. But I'm so irked by some of the things she's said to me on the way here that I have to launch into self-preservation mode. She really must not care about me but needs me for something, which I'm used to.

"I don't need anywhere else to stay. I'm fine right where I am," I toss over my shoulder as I step out of the cab.

Dandelion doesn't need to know that what she considers a place that I'll get "murdered" I consider the best place I've ever lived in my entire sixteen years.

"We'll be here at 6:30 tomorrow night so Marty can pick Mama up after us! I'll make sure Mama and Daddy think that I'm at Cherry Red's house for the homework club!"

Dandelion is calling out to me in an annoying sing-songey voice like everything is rosy. This, after she screwed up my whole happy mindset! I ignore her and keep trudging through the gravel parking lot in my heels, which is no easy task. Thankfully, the cab rolls out and I'm safe to continue to room 13, which never struck me as ominous until now. Before I deadbolt myself in I turn and look down the street at the sign for the One Grand Evening Club and think of the complete irony of the name. I'm still waiting for my one grand evening there but don't have much hope that it's ever going to happen.

I'll be seeing a lot of the inside of the club for the next month.

I don't know why I make the decision that I make. All it really does is hurt me and hurts someone I really care about. But that's me. That's my life. I don't know how to get out of this ugly cycle yet.

Mommy used to tell Dadda to "sleep on it" when they had a problem, which was basically every day. In fact, she probably told him to "sleep on it" the night before they decided to give me some sleeping pills and leave me on the corner of Sunset and Vermont in a dangerous part of East Hollywood.

Their fifteen-year-old daughter. Those are the kind of memories I have to contend with. The kind of odds I have to change.

I sleep on my pain and wake up with a verdict: screw Sunset Boulevard. Screw Dandelion. Screw my dream of being a groupie. Screw the human race. I'll just keep on keeping on the way I have been since that day I woke up on that street corner and had to fend for myself.

I call Chico, my boss over at One Grand Evening, and tell him I want to put as many hours on the clock as he has the club open, which is from noon every day until four in the morning. Sometimes the guys want to watch the sun rise with the girl of their choice but Chico usually kicks them out at four because already he's paying the L.A.P.D. off to let him go two hours past the usual last call for alcohol. Anyway, it's us girls that have to entertain the cops as payment. And let me tell you, the fine upstanding men in blue are some of the biggest lowlifes at the club.

"Chiquita, they don't call them pigs for nothin'," Chico reminded me when I complained about one of the cops and how rough he was with me on the dance floor. And that was the end of that conversation. He waved his hand at me in dismissal, told me to get back to work because he wasn't paying me to tell him what he already knows.

Now, on the phone, I can't say anything wrong to Chico. He's been wanting me to work more hours since I arrived on the downtown scene. I make lots of money for him and I'm considered a "top girl" because as soon as one guy is done with my services another wants me. I keep my tips but Chico and I get a fifty-fifty split on the hourly charge, which goes up the more hours I sit on the couch with the other girls and wait for the next customer and with each new guy that asks for my services.

"You'll be in at noon today, Chiquita?" he asks in his Mexican accent that I could almost fall in love with over the connection, though face to face Chico isn't nearly as endearing.

"I'll see you then, Rico Chico," I promise.

Noontime comes too quickly, especially since I'm trying to talk myself into changing my mind and going back to Mother Sandy's with Dandelion the whole time. But I put on a hot fishnet and leather outfit and head out the door to the club.

My decision to change course seems to haunt me from the word "go."

Before I'm hardly out of the motel parking lot, some bottom-feeder that has probably already rubbed up against me in my professional life rolls up next to me in a trashed car that doesn't even have a decipherable color of paint and has piles of dirty clothes strewn all over the back seat.

"Hey baby, how about some love and I'll give you a twenty and a free bump?" The monster can barely speak English. I swear some of these foreigners just learn how to pick up a girl in English but don't know how to say anything else.

Furthermore, I'm insulted by his offer of a tiny amount of money and a tiny amount of drugs. I'm feeling totally worthless, like when I woke up on the street corner in East Hollywood after Mommy and Dadda got rid of me. I try not to pay any attention to him but he's persistent, driving at the same speed I'm walking.

"Come on, bitch. Forty is my final offer for you to suck my-"

"Hey!" Chico is out in front of the club waving his hands and is ready to start charging. He's lifting up his shirt to show that he's locked and loaded. I see the butt of his gun. It's made of polished wood. He's reaching for it and yelling something in really fast Mexican Spanish. All I can decipher are the words *el gallito*. His eyes are really wild. Uh-oh.

The car takes off after a rubber-burning screech.

"Stay away from *El Gallito*, Chiquita," Chico warns.

"I was trying to, Rico Chico, but he just kept following me."

"I'll have Tito walk you home later on."

Tito is the bouncer. He has to bounce plenty of guys out and an occasional girl too.

"Thanks," I say as I follow him up the steep, dark staircase that has worn carpet that doesn't look like it could lead to anywhere nice.

And it doesn't lead to anywhere nice.

One Grand Evening tries to look like a happening place and sometimes at night, when the flashing colored lights are on it may partly succeed. But in the light of day the threadbare couches and chairs and the haphazardly painted walls with crooked pictures on them tell the real story of depravity.

Only two other girls are on the couch and a few skinny guys are standing together looking like they're trying to get up the nerve to ask them to dance while they twirl their little red straws in their watery drinks. They make immature noises when I walk by, trying to get my attention. I resent this breed of customer. Just be bold and take me onto the dance floor and give me a tip, I want to tell them. I hate beating around the bush.

It's going to be a long sixteen hours.

Things don't start to pick up until the clock reads seven, around the time when Dandelion and Marty are supposed to pick me up and whisk me away to the Groupie Promised Land. I feel every tick of the large-faced wall clock as I watch the second hand move from over the shoulder of this guy or that. I have to watch the clock hands move. That way I can block out what the guys are doing to me with their hands.

I have a record-breaking night. My would-be groupie wardrobe works well in the club with the guys. But I find it beyond sad that I'm working for all these cool clothes and I'm wearing them at One Grand Evening for the slugs of the earth and not for the long-haired cuties moving and shaking out on Sunset Boulevard to the new metal sound.

This is the choice I've made and I have to stick with it.

Tito walks me home after I wait around for him to get his tips from the rest of the girls. It's nearly five the next morning now. I'll be back at the club in seven short hours starting the whole routine over again.

"Tito, what does *el gallito* mean?" It doesn't occur to me until now that I don't even know what Chico was calling the awful guy in the car seventeen hours ago. I'm kind of glad that I have something to say to make conversation with Tito, because he's just too quiet.

"*El gallito* is a rooster, a troublemaker," he says stiffly.

"Oh, okay. Thanks." I feel so stupid and uncomfortable.

The Ladybug Motel never looked so good. I can see my door from the edge of the lot and tell Tito I can walk myself from there. He follows me anyway.

"You want some company, baby?" he asks at my door, which looks like it's been kicked in several hundred times. The fact that it still locks is a miracle.

Tito is short, fat, and has a terribly pitted complexion. His arms are loaded with faded tattoos. He spends his nights and mornings at the club going girl to girl and complaining about his "*puta*" wife and their five hyperactive children. In short, he's just another example of what I've chosen over going to West Hollywood and trying to elbow my way into the "in" crowd.

"Sorry, Tito. I can hardly keep my eyes open," I say with a yawn.

He grunts a "good night" and leaves. I wonder if he'll go

home to his *puta* wife. The Mexican girls at the club, which are most of them, tell me that *puta* means prostitute. I wonder if Tito and Chico call me *puta* behind my back.

Because the lighting in the parking lot is so poor, I don't even realize until I open the door that a pink "While You Were Out" note from the office is taped under the peep hole.

I've been at the motel for two months now and I've never gotten a "While You Were Out" notice. I feel like I've just won the lottery. My hand is shaking as I bolt the door and do my customary safety check in the closet, under the bed, and behind the shower curtain to make sure no riff-raff is waiting to make me L.A.'s next nameless murder victim.

The coast is clear.

I put the pink piece of paper under the chipped fake crystal lamp next to the double bed that I wake up itching from every time I sleep in it. The overnight shift motel desk woman, Olga, has scribbled a few things with a pen that was clearly almost out of ink and checked off all six boxes on the form: telephoned, came to see you, returned your call, please call, will call again, wants to see you. The "wants to see you" is circled in black marker that actually worked. Olga has written: "Lot of call and visit from Daddalon" which I translate as "Dandelion Dagger is desperate to find you."

My face is burning with pleasure.

Over the next month, I receive so many pink slips from staff on all three shifts that I have to go to the nearest department store and buy them a package of new pads. I also have to pay them off to keep them from telling Dandelion what room I'm in and when I'm there, though hiding from her is fairly easy because I'm working sixteen hours a day every day. But one day she must just decide to go down the row of battle-scarred doors and knock on every one, because I look out my peep hole three weeks after I stand her up and there she is. By now I know, from handwritten notes she's left me almost every day, that those girls she's hanging around with at school are ready to turn on her, thus leaving her with no escape from her parents. And her father is just barely holding onto his post on Saturday nights at Holly Woods, which leaves her mama hanging around home comforting him and throwing endless parties. All of this knowledge makes me want to toss open the door and start rehashing The Way Things Are Going To Be. But now my anger has turned to embarrassment. I know I'm not good enough for that life. I've already found the only life I'm good enough for.

Dandelion Dagger moves on to door number fourteen.

My eyes fly open after a wild Memorial Day weekend at the club. My mind is working overtime when it's usually my body that's doing double time.

Summer is almost here. The school year is almost over. Once the school year ends, I have no way to track down Dandelion unless I show up at her house, which is a bad idea because she already told me that her parents have their radar out for me, or at Holly Woods, which is a worse idea for the same reason. Going back to school makes no sense when it's nearly June. Which means, I'm really stuck in this life. The two thousand dollars in my checking account and additional three thousand on my bank book are about the only bright spots, at least until I consider what I had to do to earn that money.

The fun that Dandelion and I could be having on Sunset with that cash!

Another week goes by and now it really is June and the summer at One Grand Evening holds no thrill for me. Nothing holds any thrill for me. Maybe I'll disappear. Other than being a dance hostess, vanishing is about the only thing I'm good at. Maybe I need some of those drugs my dance partners keep offering me.

"Chiquita, you have a customer waiting in the back room," Chico tells me, a routine reminder on the first Saturday night of the new month.

I've just spent an hour dancing with a regular customer that is really nice but has a habit of rubbing his calloused hands up and down my bare arms and making me itch and turn red. I want to take a short break and put some cheap cream on my arms in the bathroom to look better for Mr. Next Guy, but Chico growls that the man has been waiting and I need to go and do my job.

"On the blue couch," Chico orders, pointing toward the spacious room beyond the "dancing room" that has several different couches facing several different directions that are no doubt harboring any number of diseases in their fabric.

My next money man has his back to me and all I can see is a Dodgers cap turned backward. I straighten my leather skirt, give my red fringed bustier a yank up, and lay on the strut as I round the couch.

"Hi honey, thanks for waiting!" I offer my typical line in a bubbly voice that always sounds fake and ridiculous to me considering the surroundings. The fact that it works every time is even more ridiculous.

My eyes focus on the load of flesh on the couch, the eyes popping out from the flabs of skin on the pudgy face.

I feel my eyes popping out of my firm skin.

Holy Jesus, it's Marty, Tulip Dagger's cab driver!

"Miss Highway Child, it's yous! I found yous!" he breathes, the extra *s* on the end of *you* confirming his identity. I don't know anyone else who talks like that.

Knowing someone outside of the club renders it just about impossible for me to relate to them inside the club and Marty, as little as I know him, is no exception. He's part of a different life. I guess it's that mixing business with pleasure thing. I'm rooted to the floor, looking down at him on the couch from my high, high heels, not being able to do much of anything. I'm caught between a fat guy and a hard place. I can either play it cool and act like it's no big deal that he's found me or I can move in and make it look like I'm doing my business, meanwhile pumping him for information about my cosmic twin who's been stalking me for weeks now.

I toss another option around in my head. I can have the cabbie thrown out. An enemy, like *El Gallito*. But I see how he's struggling to be decent, to not look at my chest the way other men do without a second thought. And he has a sealed envelope on the couch next to him with my name on it in handwriting that I recognize.

Dandelion.

Through the doorway I just came through I can see Chico

looking at me with suspicion, so I sit down next to Marty and slide closer.

"Miss Highway Child, please don't start doing all those nasty things to me. I'll never forgive myself," he pleads, trying to ease away from me.

I've never had a man beg me to leave him alone.

"Then what are you doing here if you don't want me to touch you?" I try to act annoyed but a calmness is seeping into me, a relaxation that I've never felt under the roof of One Grand Evening.

I have two friends, not just one.

"Miss Dandylion made me come here cuz we saw yous walking in here the other day. She's been lookin' high and low for yous every day. I have to bring her down here once a day lookin' for yous. She's makin' me crazy!" Marty has droplets of sweat pouring down the sides of his face even though the air conditioner is working particularly well today, a miracle in the old building.

"Listen put your arm over the back of the couch. And I need to smile while I talk to you because we're being watched," I order.

Marty reluctantly lifts his chubby arm and puts it behind my head.

"I don't like this, Miss Highway Child. But I had to do it for Miss Dandylion." He pushes the envelope toward me, saying, "Here."

"I'll read it later," I snap. "Do you realize how much money I cost?" My high fee usually fills me with a strange sense of accomplishment, but in real-world company I'm not quite so proud. In fact, my stomach gets queasy.

"Miss Dandylion gave me some money, but I'm gonna give it back to her. She's worried about yous and so am I. This is no place for a nice young girl like yous."

"What you and Miss Dandelion don't realize is that I don't have anywhere else to go. I have to survive somehow." It's hard for me to keep up the hard-ass act when people are showing concern for me.

"Listen, Miss Highway Child, I have a friend who works in a shelter that takes in runaway girls and treats them real nice so they can go to school and make something of themselves. I told her about yous and-"

His words almost have me jumping up from the couch. But I know if I do, Chico is going to send Tito in to bounce Marty out. Tito might even hurt him. My frozen and fake smile is harder than ever to hold.

"Thanks so much for your concern, but don't be telling people about me." I can just imagine living in a shelter and having curfews and dress codes and codes of conduct. Someone named Highway Child is not going to be able to tolerate such nonsense!

Marty takes out a faded blue kerchief to mop his face. The cloth has been through the washer one too many times. Come to think of it, so have I. Maybe it's time to get out of the rinse cycle now that I have the chance.

"I'm sorry, Miss Highway Child. I won't do it again," Marty promises in a whimper.

"Uh-oh. Here comes the bouncer. Just play along with me." I swing a leg over Marty's stubby sticks as Tito comes over with his arms folded and his eyebrows almost touching in the middle because of the scowl on his face.

"Everything okay over here?" Tito growls.

"Oh sure, baby. Everything is fine. Johnny is just a little shy. Just warming him up a little for the back room," I say flippantly as Marty puts a sweaty hand on my knee but can't seem to bring himself to do anything else.

Well, he does offer Tito a pained smile that makes him look like he's constipated and trying to make the best of it before his laxative starts working. "She's a real nice girl," he says stupidly, and I want to pinch him so he doesn't say anything else.

"You sure I don't need to show this guy the door?" Tito booms, agitated.

"No really, honey. We're doing just fine and Johnny says he's got plenty of money that he wants to spend on me." I giggle and run my finger down the side of Marty's face. It's wet with sweat when I'm done.

Tito nods, narrowing his eyes to slits.

"I'll be watching," he warns.

But he walks away.

Marty's bottom lip quivers. "This is pretty awful, Miss Highway Child. I can't stay here for much longer and I definitely ain't going in no back room with yous unless we can have a real private conversation and I can talk some sense into yous," he assures me.

"I just said that to get him off my back. The rooms have two way mirrors. They can see everything we do and don't do." I sigh, knowing I have to think of something to relieve Marty of his misery, but also knowing that if I let him leave I could miss my last ticket out of hell. So I make a snap decision and continue, "Listen, my room number at the motel is thirteen.

Can you come around midnight? I'll tell Chico I'm coming down sick with something and we can talk there."

"That's the best thing I've heard yous say since I got here. Miss Dandylion will be a little bit happier, even though she told me not to leave here without yous and until yous read the letter." Marty looks relieved as he pulls some crumpled money out of his pocket and gives me a fifty.

"I can't leave with you and I can't read the letter with everyone watching, so meeting you is the best I can do. I'll give you the money back when you come to the room. Don't forget to pay Chico for the time off the clock on your way out."

As he stands up I shine another stupid smile on him, pat his cheek, and give him a smacker on the lips like everything is jolly good.

"Oh, and one other thing. Don't bring Dandelion to the motel with you. I'm not ready to see her yet," is my last request of him as I struggle to have some kind of power over the situation.

After Marty makes an uncomfortable exit and Chico and Tito stare after him with curiosity, I approach my boss at the front desk with a giggle.

"Wow, I think that poor sap took a wrong turn somewhere, but he gave me a good tip for doing nothing." Strange things like that happen once in a while. And I'm a damn good liar.

Chico laughs and shakes his head. "*Loco*, Chiquita, *loco*." He spins his finger around near his head.

I giggle with Chico, fake and stupid.

But the truth is that Marty is the least crazy guy I've seen in the club in months.

I need to get through a few more hours before I feign illness and meet my unlikely savior at the Ladybug Motel.

My much-considered ploy for getting out of One Grand Evening is to play up my sickliness so well that Chico actually tells me to go home without me having to ask. I have to want this pretty badly if I let one of my customers buy me the disgusting wine that Chico sells for way too much money. I never drink at the club, and after three glasses of the deadly potion I know why. By ten o'clock I'm hurling in the bathroom and holding my gut outside of the bathroom. Chico notices pretty quickly, because he has an eagle eye for a girl who isn't going to make money. I've never been that girl before. He zeroes right in on me.

"Chiquita, you don't look very well. Bonita said that you just got sick in the bathroom, yeh?"

"Yeah, I did, but I think I'm okay now," I say, because I figure it's better if I act like I don't want to leave.

"I don't know about that. The guys aren't gonna want to dance with a girl holding her stomach no matter how big her *chichis* are." Chico doesn't even crack a smile even though he's being crude. This is the nature of the business he knows so well.

I wince and sigh, holding my head now. "I'm a little dizzy, too."

Chico comes out from behind his counter and waves to Tito, who looks like he's dumping his usual problems on one of the new girls on the couch.

"No gettin' sick on my carpet! Tito, bring her home. Come back when you feel better."

Chico leaves no room for disagreement. I've pulled it off so perfectly that now I have over an hour to feel better before Marty arrives.

Tito leaves me at the edge of the parking lot this time because Chico has told him to come right back or else his pay will be docked. When I get inside the door I flash my outside light as he asked me to, the sign that all is safe. But all is not safe until I've done my own check.

Although I've received several messages from Dandelion and even a visit, there's something much more exciting and urgent about the letter sent through Marty. There's something final about it, too. I jump on my bed and tear it open even though I really need a shower and to get into some regular clothes before Marty arrives.

Dear Highway Child,

What the hell is going on with you? West Hollywood is waiting for us and you won't let me find you? Well, you can't hide from me forever. Marty and me have been riding around downtown every day and I finally saw you walking into that club looking like you should be surrounded by rocker boys in the Roxy instead of those grosso guys you dance with. You come back to me right now. Marty will put all of your stuff in the back of his cab and move you out of the Cockroach Motel. Mother Sandy said that you can have a room in her house and can stay as long a you want. It will be perfect, can't you see? With Gazzarri's and the Roxy right down the hill? I have it all set for you so you don't have any reason to say no anymore. If that isn't enough for you, then listen to this: I LOVE YOU. Did you hear that? I LOVE YOU and we have work to do and summer is almost here and rock and roll won't wait any longer.

Pretty soon school will be over and I won't have to put up with those three stupid girls who are waiting for Hall Pass to be stars when they aren't ever going to be anything. They practically hate me now and have just about kicked me out of the fold, so the timing is just right for us to take over the world.

Mother Sandy tells me about Mama all the time and how the hair metal boys are starting to prefer her to the younger girls like us. We can change that. We have to change that! You call me right now! I have the ringer turned off on my phone but a little red light goes on when someone calls so you can ring me at any time, day or night and I'll answer.

You can run but you can't hide! I won't ever give up on you so you'd better just surrender!

Love, Dandelion

Like I have with every letter and note she has left me, I admire not only the prettiness of her handwriting, but the perfection of her spelling. Dandelion is school smart, a lot smarter than me. If I wrote something to her she might not be able to understand it, kind of like when I get notes from the motel office. I decide that I need to go back to school in the fall. But first, I have the whole steamy summer to look forward to.

I want to toss the note aside and call Dandelion before I can talk myself out of it, but I have to reread a few special parts of the letter first.

I LOVE YOU. I LOVE YOU. I can't run my eyes over those words enough. And I have to read the part about Mother Sandy taking me in again just to make sure that I got it right the first time, that it wasn't just a figment of my over-active imagination. Lastly, I'm a big fan of *I won't ever give up on you.* Because everyone gives up on me, or at least it seems that way, because if your own parents drug you and leave you on street corner, who else is there to trust in the world?

But there is someone.

I dial Dandelion's number in Hollywood, as something crashes against the wall in the room next door. A hooker named Britt lives over there and chances are fairly good that it's her body making all that noise. Every time I see her she's black and blue from being beaten up and so far gone that she tells me she makes enough money to keep her in drug heaven by letting men toss her around. It's people like Britt who make me feel like I'm not doing so badly for myself. But I need to lift the bar before it gets dropped on my head.

A whispery voice comes through the receiver like a violin in a symphony might. Not that I've ever heard a symphony before, but I can imagine that it might sound this good.

"Ricky?" the voice asks.

I almost hang up. Is that who Dandelion is waiting to hear from? That scrawny Hall Pass drummer she says is a cheater? My ego falls several notches, but my anger amps up several degrees.

"No, it's not Ricky, you ass!" I shriek.

"Oh my…Highway Child…is that you?" She's clearly in disbelief. Now that's the kind of reception I was looking for.

"Sorry to disappoint you. I know you wanted Ricky, but it's just me." Time to lay on the guilt trip over her goof.

"He's been calling me all night and won't leave me alone. I can't wait 'til the end of the school year, so I can get away from all of them."

I feel silly now for giving her the Highway Child attitude. That ploy never seems to work with her.

"Well, sorry. Only a few more weeks of school then you're free of them," I mumble.

"Yeah, but then I'm gonna be stuck here being bored unless you come back to me."

A cab driver is my savior. And a girl without a real name is Dandelion's. The world sure works in funny ways sometimes.

"Well, I don't know if I want to leave my life here," I suddenly blurt.

"Highway Child, I have it all set up for you. We can meet at Mother Sandy's whenever you want and you can move in," she whines.

"Oh, I was just kidding. Marty is coming to my room at midnight and I'm gonna leave with him as soon as we can get my stuff in the cab."

"Ohmigod, do you-" a shuffling sound breaks up her voice then all I hear is "Oh, shit!" and the connection goes dead.

"Dandelion!" I say desperately, but all I get is a buzz.
Now what?

I stare at the phone. Give her a chance to call back. Maybe she did something as simple as dropped the receiver. No call. I try to call her back. Busy signal.

Hope sure does come and go fast around here.

"I'll bet you won't even come, Marty," I say aloud to the empty room, and start to sob.

I want to start packing my clothes and toiletries into the two suitcases and beat-up trunk that I brought here half empty two months ago, but the silence from the phone forces me to rethink my actions. Maybe Dandelion and Marty are messing with me the way I've been jerking them around. Maybe the letters and visits are all a lie.

It's 11:30 p.m. and I still smell like I've danced with four-teen different men since noon. I step out of my clothes and into the shower. A long-legged bug keeps me company from the ceiling. I'm just pulling on a camisole and shorts when I hear the knock on my door. I'm relieved that Marty is there. In the background, his old yellow cab looks misshapen through the peephole.

"Quick, come in," I say as soon as I throw open the door.

"Yes, Miss Highway Child. It's kinda spooky out there."

Precisely why I want him to come in without hesitation. The clicks and clanks of the three locks on the door echo through the desolate room.

Marty takes off his Dodgers hat and looks around. His face falls. Is it the water stains running down the walls? Or the bulge in the ceiling where the toilet upstairs is ready to dump a leak square into the center of my bed if the drug dealer up there flushes it too many times? Or maybe it's not even the way it looks, but the stale odor of smelly bodies of days past that permeates everything. Whatever it is, I have to distract him.

I toss up my hands. "Well, I tried calling her and our

connection got cut off! So, now what? How is Mother Sandy gonna know I'm coming?" I ask hopelessly.

"Yous called Miss Dandylion?" Marty's dark eyes, that have noticeable circles under them, widen and gain a sparkle.

"Well, what else can I do? Stay here?" I sniff, folding my arms.

"Know what, Miss Highway Child? Yous is such a pretty young lady. But yous ain't gonna stay that way if yous hang around here for much longer." Marty speaks sincerely, but like any man, he can't keep from running his eyes up and down me. Then, it must hit him that I've mentioned someone he doesn't even know about because he asks me who Mother Sandy is.

I tell him about how we met Mother Sandy, how Dandelion put in her letter that I could move into the house just north of Sunset Boulevard and all the hot rock and roll clubs.

"Well then what are we waiting for? Let's get yous packed up and out of here." Marty hauls his bulk out of the rickety chair he tentatively sat down in just a moment before. I'm surprised it even holds him without coming apart.

"Wait! I just told you that I lost the connection with Dandelion and I don't know how to get in touch with her or Mother Sandy. I can't just knock on Sandy's door at three in the morning and start moving in."

I'm being logical but I guess I'm still kind of stalling. This is a big change for me. For everything that it's not, the Ladybug Motel has been the most stable place I've ever lived. I have a job. I have money. I have people to keep me safe, at least as long as I continue to make them money.

Chico and Tito's faces flash in front of my eyes. I like to deceive myself that these people care about me. What's wrong with me!

"We'll take care of that tomorrow with Miss Dandylion. Until then yous can just stay with me. My place ain't too great and it's pretty small but it's a lot safer than this."

I throw my finger at him. "You'd better not touch me! Just because I work as a dance hostess doesn't mean-"

Marty's face sags even lower than it did when he saw how I'm living.

"Miss Highway Child, did I even touch yous in that club?" he moans as if he's in physical pain.

I let my hand drop to my side and retract my finger into my palm, trying to hide it, ashamed that I'm treating my savior like this.

"No, but you are a man," I say lamely.

"And any man would love to look at yous because yous are so pretty. Maybe I'll even flirt with yous. But that don't mean I'd do anything else. Give me a damn break, Miss Highway Child. I ain't no pervert, no matter how much yous wanna think I am."

He's ready to sink back into the chair, he's so distressed. I picture the chair collapsing and adding further stress to the poor sap. Marty in a heap of simulated wood is not a pretty vision. So I say, "No, don't sit down. Let's pack. We really have to be out of here before someone notices I'm leaving and we can't come back."

"Well, I kinda thought that, too," Marty says with a sigh.

"It's just my clothes and supplies. Everything else belongs to the motel."

The need to disappear before daylight suddenly hits me. We have to get a move on. I rush to the closet and pull out the suitcases and trunk I came with and unceremoniously start taking the hangers full of my clothes off the bent pole in the closet. Into the trunk they go.

"Marty, can you grab one of these suitcases and just take everything off the bathroom counter and sink and pack it?" I ask when I see he's not sure how to help.

"Sure, Miss Highway Child. Whatever yous want."

Because time is of the essence, I shove all my precious clothes into the trunk like I'm packing useless rags and slam the top closed. Afterward, I pop into the bathroom because I don't hear much coming from Marty. I can't believe that he's in there handling my dollar store shampoo bottles and cheap perfume like I bought them on Rodeo Drive; he's tightening caps and making sure they're neatly in the suitcase. The perfect order they're in makes me stare from the bottles to Marty. Things just aren't matching up. Is Marty some kind of neat freak? He certainly doesn't dress like he is!

"Well, I guess I'm a little OCD," he admits.

"Do you realize that when you pick up that damn suitcase by the handle all of those bottles are gonna get messed up?" I ask testily, looking at my watch in hopes that he'll get the hint that we don't have the rest of our lives to obsess over plastic bottles.

Marty starts busting out in sweat again, like he did at the club.

"I wasn't gonna carry it by the handles."

I make fists, hoping to absorb some of my attitude in my hands so I don't start being mean again. I have to be nicer to this odd character but he's really pushing my buttons.

"However you carry it, we kind of have to get out of here," I remind him.

"I know, Miss Highway Child." Even though he claims to "know," he's still lining things up exactly right in the suitcase. He's just doing it a little faster.

"The trunk is ready, Marty. I'll finish packing in here."

Marty looks mournfully back at his handiwork as he exits the bathroom to pull the trunk out to the cab. I can't help but pack the rest of my toiletries as neatly as possible so Marty doesn't think his hard work is all for naught. He doesn't carry it out to the cab by the handle.

Pretty soon we're ready to go. Just as I'm about to close the door on my little one-room home the phone rings.

"I'm not answering that," I tell him.

"But what if it's Miss Dandylion?" Marty questions.

"But what if it's not? What if it's someone I really don't want to talk to?"

"Do yous get a lot of calls at two in the morning?" Marty's eyes are wide and he has to be thinking the worst of me. He starts scratching the back of his neck nervously.

"Actually, I don't. So it must be Dandelion." I barely catch the door before it slams with the key on the bedside table.

"Are you leaving with Marty?" Dandelion is whispering breathlessly on the other end the second I pick it up.

"What the hell happened earlier?" I yell.

Someone upstairs starts stomping on the floor and demanding that I shut up.

"I'm taking a big chance calling you right now. Mama stole my phone out of my room again because she caught me talking to you. I'm on the house phone, so can you please just answer my question?"

She is taking a big chance. For me. She already told me how she's getting grounded every five minutes for something new, anything that her mama can use against her to keep her in the house. If we're not careful she'll be so grounded she won't be able to leave the yard all summer and there goes the groupie dream. Again.

"We're trying to leave now but I had to come back in to answer your call. The cab is all packed and I'm staying with Marty until we can talk to Mother Sandy about me moving in."

"Holy shit." She's spellbound. "I'll see you after school at Mother Sandy's. I'll call her from the pay phone in the hall in the morning. Meet me there at three?"

"Deal. Now hang up before you get your ass grassed."

I can hear her giggle on her end. I join her. It's a beautiful sound.

I feel like a teenager again instead of the practicing adult I've been forced to be for months now for the sake of survival.

We're standing in Marty's living room an hour later.

"It ain't much, but yous will be comfortable here until yous can talk to that Sandy lady." Marty is motioning toward a couch that has a fold-out bed. It's the best thing I've seen in my life. It looks brand new. Marty mumbles that his parents bought it for him for his last birthday because he didn't have anywhere for them to sit when they visited.

Marty's pad is a studio apartment in Hollywood on the third floor of a privately owned apartment house. He says the apartments on the first two floors are really big and nice and he has the small one. It's plain and his furniture is nothing special, but the two connected rooms reflect his obsessiveness with order.

I get the best night of sleep that perhaps I've ever gotten.

Marty is gone when I wake up at eleven the next morning but he's left me a note that he'll pick me and my stuff up at two to take me to Mother Sandy's. So he wouldn't have to carry my heavy suitcases and trunk up to the third floor, he's left them with the landlady whom he's told me is trustworthy. At least that's what I think he's trying to get across. His spelling and grammar are about as bad as mine.

Marty has left a blueberry muffin and a banana on a paper plate for me under some plastic wrap. I'm so hungry I practically inhale it. Then I head down to the first floor to meet the landlady and make sure she really isn't going to rob me of my hair metal wardrobe. Turns out she's pretty old and in a wheelchair and probably isn't going to Holly Woods picking up rock stars anytime soon. But Marty is right that she has a really nice apartment that takes up the whole floor.

"Aww, you and Marty make such a cute couple!" she chimes when I agree to sit down and join her for a burger. "He's such a nice boy!"

Mrs. Dellmar has to use a walker to fry the burgers on the stove for us and I'm so grateful for more food that I let her think I'm Marty's new girlfriend. She packs me full of fresh food. It's been a long time since I ate anything but fast food from some dirty downtown joint.

True to his word, the "nice boy" shows up a few minutes late to bring me to West Hollywood. I'm still downstairs looking at photo albums with Mrs. Dellmar, whose two daughters and son have deserted her. Her husband died five years ago. The old lady and me aren't as different as I first thought.

"Yous ready, Miss Highway Child? I have a busy afternoon. First I have to pick Miss Dandylion up at the corner of Highland and Sunset then I have to bring Miss Tulip somewhere, so we have to go."

"Aww Marty, you picked such a nice girl!" Mrs. Dellmar bubbles, missing the anxiety in his tone.

"Aww, Mrs. Dellmar, Miss Highway Child-" Marty is looking at me worriedly.

"I'll come back again soon to look at pictures, okay?" I promise the kind lady before Marty can finish.

"I'll leave the album open right where you left it," she gushes.

I lean over to hug her before I help Marty bring my things back out to his cab.

"We're picking up Dandelion?" I ask, my voice shaking.

"Yeah, she's hiding somewhere until we get her."

That Dandelion sure has a lot of tricks up her sleeve. We're going to be a great team.

We pull into an alley between two squat buildings on the southeast corner of Highland and Sunset. A head pokes out from behind the right side dwelling. The rest of the body makes an appearance. She's back to wearing dresses and sandals. I'm too excited to see her to care. And she's beautiful and has an attitude apparent in her gait. When we embrace in the front seat it's more like a death grip for both of us.

"Don't you dare leave me again," she barks, slamming the door.

We have to share the passenger seat because my stuff is in the back. She throws her book bag over the seat and settles in.

"Where are your clothes?" I demand.

"I'm wearing them," she says sarcastically.

"You know what I mean." I roll my eyes at her.

"I'm sick of those bitches at school so I gave their clothes back to them. I've had it with Ricky too and we're done. Plus, Principal Paulson called Mama and told her how I'm dressing and that was that. The fat asshole. Wonder why it took him so long."

"Miss Dandylion, I know I ain't supposed ta be nosing into stuff, but it don't sound good when a pretty young girl like yous is cursing," Marty warns.

"Mind your own shit, Marty," Dandelion sneers.

Personally, her cursing is like music to my ears. It's so rock and roll.

"No worries. I have plenty of clothes for both of us," I assure her. "And I have lots of money in the bank, but we have to go downtown and get it out one of these days." I hit

Marty with a look because he'll probably be the means of getting there.

He gets the hint and says, "Yous let me know when yous want to go."

"Marty, there's no 's' on the end of you," Dandelion nags. I wonder what her beef is with him. He's been good to me. But he is that kind of person who's fun to mess with.

"Miss Tulip tells me that all the time," Marty says with a sigh.

"Anyway…" Dandelion looks pointedly at me and reaches into the top of her dress, under which I see the hint of a strapless bra. "Mama and Daddy have been throwing a zillion crazy parties lately with lots of stoned people sleeping over. Lots of open purses. So, I've been doing pretty well." She produces a roll of money of which most of the bills look like big ones.

Marty is turning red. But when he opens his mouth to speak Dandelion stops him with a "Don't even say it!"

"Parties?" is what I want to know more about.

"Parties almost every night. They don't have much of anything else to do. Daddy is ready to lose his two Saturday nights a month at Holly Woods," she answers frankly.

"And what do you do while they're partying?"

She shrugs. "Wait for the perfect time to steal money."

How could I ever leave this girl after I met her the first time?

"That's gonna get boring after a while," I decide.

"It already has. But I've only been doing it since I stopped going to Cherry Red's house all the time and that's been less than a week." Dandelion is putting the money roll back in her bra. From what I can tell she doesn't have much else in there. Poor bitch. At least I have boobies.

But wait...did she just say...

"You stole all that in a week?" I howl, making both of my car mates practically jump out of their skins.

"Sure. When your parents won't let you out of the house because the overweight principal tells them you're wearing fishnets to school you have to invent new ways to pass the time."

I want to tell her how her parents could leave her drugged and on a street corner in East Hollywood, but I'm not quite ready to fess up to that. Instead, I murmur quietly, "We'll have to hit the shops on Hollywood Boulevard soon." I silently lick my abandonment wounds while my friend chatters about how she finally went back to Mother Sandy's last week without me and made herself at home when she was supposed to be at Cherry Red's.

"She said we can both move in and believe me, I'm thinking about it!"

How perfect would that be?

"Let's do it!" I gush.

"Well, let's see how things go," she says, avoiding my excited eyes.

I let the subject drop, because I know she's not ready to make the change. I can understand that, having just left whatever safety I'd found in life.

We're quiet as Marty starts to roll through West Hollywood. I've been back here a few times since we discovered those greasy boys in front of the Whisky, but the effect is the same: as the notorious clubs loom up in front of us a pleasant quivering takes over my stomach. I picture the lights of Sunset flashing and throbbing with rock and roll energy, boys and girls in leather and studs and eyeliner competing for the biggest hair, Dandelion and me, arms linked, taking over the scene. When Marty makes a right on Hilldale and approaches Mother Sandy's house it's like looking at a castle. Still, I wonder if she's really serious about taking me in or if I'll have to go crawling back to the Ladybug Motel and Chico and Tito at One Grand Evening. The lovely feeling coursing through me temporarily changes to a creeping disgust.

I remember how the last time we came here the first smell we encountered was puke. As Dandelion and I get out of the cab and tell Marty we'll be back momentarily, the aroma that wafts from behind the house is much more pleasant: food on the grill. We ring the doorbell and hear some shrill sound that echoes from the back yard. Then, "Come on back!" and it's Sandy's voice.

Dandelion and I look around until we discover a way to get into the high iron gate that's connected to both sides of the house. We follow a narrow walkway around to the back and find Mother Sandy, the three boys from Smut, and a few other people with nothing to do on a late spring afternoon in L.A. draped over lawn chairs, drinking beer and smoking pot around the grill. Sandy is doing the grilling but puts down her spatula when she sees us and opens her arms.

"You finally found her! Did you bring your stuff with you?" She pulls us both into her. Her scent is surprisingly good. Not perfumed. But fresh, like she just got out of the shower.

"I brought my stuff, Mother Sandy," I murmur, making her hug last as long as I can. "It's out in Marty's cab."

"Well, bring it right up. You can have the small room all to yourself across from Diesel and Bullshit."

Said boys are too drunk to do anything but wave, wink, and drool. I had no idea that they lived here now. I vaguely remember them saying they lived in Van Nuys in a place they referred to as Smut Central, but I don't ask and they don't tell.

"Thank you, Mother Sandy. I'll try not to impose on you for too long." I've been practicing this line because I have to know how long I can stay.

"You're not imposing and you can stay as long as you want. It's about time we hit the clubs!"

Wow, can it get any better! Everything I want to hear!

But it can get better if Dandelion moves in, too.

We'll have to work on that.

"We'll call it the summer of spandex and hair," Dandelion says, her eyes sparking as she pulls on her very own black liquid sex pants bought on Hollywood Boulevard with her stolen money. Her hair is poofed up toward the second floor ceiling and she looks ridiculously rock star ready, a total little groupie slut ready for action from boys in groups with names like Here Kitty Kitty, Jack Rabid, and Scarlett Rouge.

We've been looking hungrily at the marquees on Sunset for the past few days, waiting for this night, this Friday night when Hollywood High and One Grand Evening are both far from our minds.

Earlier in the day, while Dandelion was at school, Marty brought me downtown to withdraw my banked money from One Grand Evening and close my accounts. Now it's comfortably in a new bank on Sunset and Dandelion and I enjoyed a shopping spree today for our inaugural weekend as the new groupie street team.

"It's leather and hair for me," I proclaim, checking myself from every angle in the full-length mirror I bought for us in Another Man's Treasure, the second hand store on Hollywood Boulevard that's quickly becoming the aspiring hair metal groupie's and rocker's paradise for clothes and furnishings.

I'm damn proud of myself for scoring not only the mirror but the dress I see hugging my body in the glass, a short black and white zebra striped leather spaghetti strapped mini dress. I've put a neon pink bra underneath it and it looks like part of the dress. My shoes are silver and Lucite platforms from Frederick's of Hollywood. My four-day transformation from downtown dance hostess to Sunset groupie is dizzying; I can hardly believe I'm standing here about to burst onto the scene that I've been craving for months now.

"Isn't this all a dream?" I ask Dandelion in the most carefree voice I've ever heard myself use.

That's when Diesel and Bullshit, the two trashy boys from Smut, Mother Sandy's hard rock house band, fall through our bedroom door drunk.

"Spoke too soon," Dandelion deadpans, rolling her eyes at the two dirty rockers on our floor.

I strut over to them and give Diesel a kick in the side with my Lucite heel.

"Nice panties to match your brassiere. Be my Valentine?" he slurs, not ashamed to be looking up my dress.

"It's June, you dickwad. Get the hell out of our room!" Dandelion screeches, whacking both of them with one swoop of a tiny velvet bag that she'll sling around her body.

"You're gonna treat us different when we're big rock stars," Bullshit offers a cryptic warning, flat on his back the way he likes it, and pointing a crooked finger at Dandelion then me.

"Sure, Bullshit. In your wildest fantasy," I say with doubt.

How could these two ever make anything of themselves? The third Smut member probably isn't on our floor because he's knocked out on some illegal drug. But who has time to worry about losers at a time like this?

A set of boots is pounding up the stairs. The rhythm is familiar and I know it's Mother Sandy. For our big night she's decked out in jeans, a Harley camisole, and red bandana around her neck. Quite a chaperone.

"Are my children ready for some hell raising?" she bellows.

"Born ready!" Diesel gurgles.

"Wow, you girls are gonna get some long-haired action tonight!" Sandy whistles under her breath.

That's all we need to hear to make us forget about the creeps on our floor.

Dandelion runs to the mirror and gives her hair one last tease with hairspray. I grab a bottle of greasy body lotion and slather it generously on my arms and legs so that I glow. She grabs it from me and makes her skin glow, too.

It's time for our Sunset debut.

Dandelion and I are anxious to get to the Roxy, but Mother Sandy scolds us.

"There's an order to all this. First, dinner at the Rainbow. Then, we hit the clubs. The Roxy, Gazzarri's, and back to the Rainbow. And we won't even walk a mile all night," Sandy tells us proudly. We already know that she considers herself a genius of sorts for buying the house on Hilldale before living on Hilldale was cool, and this is just another one of her brags. We really couldn't be any closer to the action. What crazy luck we've had, and yet it has taken us so long to get to this moment.

Mostly because of me.

But when something is meant to be it has to be even if the likes of a stubborn bitch like me tries to get in the way.

Diesel, Bullshit, and Little Drummer Boy, as the third member of Smut is referring to himself as of today, are suddenly wide awake and looking somewhat clean, maybe even a tad desirable as they lead the way to the Rainbow like their names and handprints are in the concrete in between Mother Sandy's house and the fabled restaurant.

"The boys know how to make a statement. Just watch them and you'll be fine," Sandy assures us.

"Them? Making a statement?" Dandelion asks incredulously. "They can hardly stand upright most of the time, Mother Sandy!"

"Get used to something, girls: you don't have to be upright to make a statement in the world of rock and roll. In fact, if you think that you're going to be better groupies than Tulip in the upright position, you have another thing coming." Sandy winks at us. I get her meaning right away but it takes Dandelion an extra few seconds to understand what she's saying. She looks at me and grins when the light bulb finally comes on.

Picturing myself as the new sought-after girl on the scene, I squeeze my pelvic muscles sharply and hope that it's finally time for me to learn what sexual pleasure is. My mind makes a fifteen-second collage out of the unpleasant experiences I've had in the club with men who paid me extra money to stick their nasty fingers into me and even before that, a few episodes in the backseat of Dadda's car when my parents said we needed money for food and gas. All those times, at the mercy of some nameless man whose face I made a blur of because I didn't want to remember them in the dead of night when I'm alone in bed and trying to fight insomnia. The time has come for me to be the one in control and to love every moonlit feature of the gloriously sexy rocker boy who I'm grooving with to the driving beat of hair metal.

I'm not looking for love. I'm looking for lust. I want to know what lust is and not just see it happening to someone else in a movie.

Outdoor tables under an awning on the side of the Rainbow are packed and Mother Sandy waves to some friends.

"The real action is inside," she tells us.

As the Smut boys open the door to the Rainbow the force of our much-anticipated dream world pulls us in. A sacred light pours out and shows us the way. Dandelion grabs my fingers and squeezes. Heads turn. Elbows poke arms and more heads turn. Stunning women rush to wrap their arms around the three musicians who were half knocked out on our floor and looking not the least bit attractive just minutes ago. Stunning men suddenly jump to attention when they sniff the new flesh encased in spandex and leather entering. Bodies are tight. When I start hearing "hey baby" as we join the crush it's a way different "hey baby" than the one I'm used to at One Grand Evening. The same greeting there elicited dread and discomfort. The two words spoken at the Rainbow open several doors to the quenching of my middle-of-the-night fantasies and I merely have to pick the one that I want to open further. It's like playing *Let's Make a Deal* for the best guy with long hair. They all look so good it's going to be a tough decision.

I mouth the word "wow" to Dandelion, who looks as wowed as I feel.

"Remember, we own the place," Dandelion reminds me of what Mother Sandy said was her finest advice.

Act like the scene wasn't a scene until you showed up.

My back straightens. Lips purse. I flip my long black curly hair around. No one could know how intimidated I am by the heady hedonism swirling around.

Mother Sandy and Smut seem to know everyone in the place and even though the main dining area doesn't look like it could fit six more people, much less cough up a table for us, we're nevertheless shown to one of the red horse-shoe-shaped booths that I've seen only in pictures up until now. Everyone I see at the other tables and booths look like they're either rock stars or someone connected in some way to rock and roll. I swear that I see faces that I've seen on magazine and album covers, though it's hard to stare without looking like a "fan." Dandelion and I have already figured out that we don't want to look like fans but like girls serious about being "backstage fixtures," a term that she coined.

"Mama doesn't like that term, but I think it's just fine," she'd snorted when she told me.

No sooner do we sit down than two really young and really pretty girls get down on their hands and knees and crawl under the table. I can feel their presence around my shiny legs but obviously they aren't there for my benefit. Diesel and Little Drummer Boy soon have their heads back and their eyes closed. Bullshit, not to be outdone by his buddies, snaps his fingers at a pubescent blond eyeing him hungrily as she walks by, points down at his manhood, and is soon enjoying what the other two are getting. Mother Sandy is taking it all in stride.

"What the hell?" I shrug as Dandelion and I make eye contact.

"That's not us. We're not doing that," she states firmly.

"I wouldn't even think of it!" I agree, but what I'm really thinking is that maybe these Smut guys are going somewhere besides falling in and out of our room and we need to discuss giving them more positive attention.

The Rainbow is chock full of rock memorabilia and soft, colored lights, giving it a busy and important but relaxing and dreadfully cool vibe. The girls under the table prove to be the norm and not the exception, as I notice other male diners enjoying the pre-appetizer warm-up. When the girls are done they emerge from their posts and disappear, seemingly into the unknown but more likely to the next table, the next bar, the next finger-snapper. As for our tablemates, they casually zip up and pick up their menus as if nothing out of the ordinary has happened. I'm guessing this is all perfectly normal.

Two yummy hair guys come to our table to greet Mother Sandy with cheek kisses. Then they slap hands with the Smut trio and talk rock: what gigs they're playing, what songs they're writing, what record companies they're gracing with their demos. It's all ridiculously exciting. I want to digest every word and I can tell Dandelion is enraptured even though she's trying to keep a calm demeanor. If I'm ready to burst from the thrill there's no way she's not!

Diesel graciously introduces Dandelion and me, as the boys make it clear that they want to know who we are. Frenchie Dane is the bleach blond and Danie French is the lanky brunette. Upon closer inspection, they're brothers if not actually twins. Frenchie just looks like he spends more time in a gym than Danie, who looks like he does drugs to keep his slim rocker figure.

"I'm Derek Dagger's daughter. And Tulip is my mother," Dandelion sings as she gives them a flirtatious little wave.

How the hell do I follow that up?

"I'm not Derek Dagger's daughter and Tulip isn't my mother, I'm just fresh Grade A hair metal junkie," I bubble, sitting up nice and straight, so they make no mistake that I have the best set of boobs this side of Laurel Canyon.

Dandelion rolls her eyes.

"So, you girls will be at the Roxy later on?" Danie tickles me under the chin and croons, "Here kitty, kitty!"

I catch his drift: Here Kitty Kitty is the name of the band playing at the Roxy tonight.

"We're working our way over there!" Dandelion vies for attention, throwing her hair around.

Frenchie, who has sexy black and pink streaks in his tousled blond mane, extends an invite backstage.

"Ohmigod, are you in Here Kitty Kitty?" I shriek, sounding way too much like a fan. Dandelion glares at me from across the table.

"They're the hottest band on the Strip!" Mother Sandy assures us, while Smut, who is still only a living room band, insist that they're the hottest band on the Strip, or will be when they start playing in public.

The banter between the two bands continues to be fun, though the two hot guys are ribbing our housemates about not having any paying gigs.

"Just cut an album girls, signed to Rude Boy Records in a pretty nice deal," Frenchie gloats, thus making our Smut friends cringe.

"Don't you worry, Frenchie. We'll have a deal soon enough," Diesel, who seems to be the Smut spokesperson, assures the Here Kitty Kitty boys with a wave of his hand.

Danie returns to the original subject: "So, we'll see you backstage, right?" he asks, making eye-contact with me then Dandelion.

"Sure, honey. We'll be there," Dandelion answers coolly for us.

Diesel is incensed now and squirming in his seat. Good thing Frenchie and Danie swagger away. They're garnering big attention from the Rainbow girls and have four under their table as soon as they sit down.

"Two apiece. Hmph!" Bullshit, who is rarely coherent for

any other reason, sniffs jealously.

"Oh my god, they're gorgeous!" Dandelion, who was so smooth a moment ago, is a shivering heap now.

Even though his drummer is now snoring and drooling next to him, Diesel is all business.

"You girls need to stick with us, not those sissies with make-up and hair dye. We'll show you the real way to rock," he growls.

"Sure, Diesel," I say, liking the fact that he's jealous and suddenly there are rockers fighting over us.

And it's only our first night.

We show up at the Roxy a half hour before Here Kitty Kitty goes on. Mother Sandy doesn't even take us through the front door; it's straight through the back, no questions asked.

"Can you believe how easy this is?" I marvel. "And Frenchie and Danie asked us to come back here?"

"It's because I told them who my mama and daddy are. It works every time." Dandelion nods confidently.

I feel the expression of joy and wonder on my face melt off and I shoot back, "Personally, I think it was my boobs that did it."

She peers down into my bust line and raises her dark and feathery brows.

"Well, you certainly have it in that department. But they see boobs every day. It's not every day that they get to hang with a rock star's daughter."

We start squabbling about who Frenchie and Danie want

to see more as we go through a small, dark area. When we actually get backstage the fight is over; we're two of many wild girls jockeying for position with Frenchie, Danie, and their two equally scrumptious bandmates who are all tricked out in outrageously sexy leather and fishnet with animal print and stud accessories.

"Well, do your thing, miss daughter of Derek Dagger," I spit.

I can see Dandelion steeling herself for a big move.

"Believe me, I have an excellent teacher," she tosses back, and I know she's talking about her mama, who has yet to appear.

Before I can make some other smart-ass comment, Dandelion focuses on the members of Here Kitty Kitty and starts bulling her way through the throng of girls. Mother Sandy is chatting with all these people she knows and being that I don't want to be left alone with Diesel, Bullshit, and Little Drummer Boy in my really short dress, I fall into step behind my friend.

"Excuse me, you're in my way. I'm trying to get to my boyfriend," I hear her say on the way to our pretty new friends.

"Stop pushing, bitch," is a typical reply.

"Then get out of my way, bitch," is Dandelion's typical comeback.

I guess she wasn't kidding about that excellent teacher. Maybe I should've paid more attention to her mama while I had the chance!

We're suddenly standing in front of Frenchie and Danie, who snicker when they see us.

"Well if it isn't Derek Dagger's little girl. Didn't take you very long to show up, did it? Does your daddy know you're here?" Frenchie croons to Dandelion, pulling her into his embrace.

I don't hear her answer because Danie informs me that "You're one hell of a nice kitty, baby." He has wine on his breath and it's the best smell I've ever sniffed into my nostrils. Overcome with desire, my hands sink into his wavy, shoulder-length hair that looks like he just had it done in a salon. He has the most full and luscious lips I've ever been so close to.

"You're a pretty nice kitty yourself," I tease.

"Maybe after the show you can show me how nice of a kitty you really are." Danie's smile is infectious, his teeth taking my bottom lip between them.

"I can't wait," I assure him.

My reward for my willingness to be a compliant pussy is to watch Here Kitty Kitty from the side of the stage. Dandelion is right there with me. Our Smut anti-heroes stalk out into the crowd with a line of girls following them.

"Whatever it is that makes the girls chase them I haven't figured it out yet," Dandelion says with a shake of her head.

"Who needs Smut? We have Here Kitty Kitty!" I whoop.

"And I don't need Hall Pass either! Ricky Rude is really small potatoes now!" she hollers back.

And we jump around hugging each other.

Here Kitty Kitty puts on an eye-popping show that has several females in the audience flashing their bare bosoms if not completely shedding their tops and letting them shake unabated. Danie, who is the lead guitarist, comes over to me several times and drinks Jack Daniels, the liquor of choice for all rock stars young and old according to Dandelion, or drapes me with some crazy piece of clothing that he's too hot to wear. He's coated in sweat but he's so gorgeous that he still looks edible even while shiny and dripping. He's down to black leathers that slip down to his narrow hips and a leopard print scarf wrapped around his neck.

"Whattcha doing after the show?" he asks some variation on this line before he hands the bottle of Jack back to me and leaves again. I try to come up with something witty to answer the first few times, but pretty soon I'm so crazy to be with him that I don't know what to say.

After two encores, Danie slips off the stage and grabs my hand. I wave to Dandelion as I skitter away on my giant heels.

Destination: broom closet.

"Danie, a broom closet?" I say with a curious giggle that hides the fact that I'm totally intrigued.

"Sure, baby. The brooms won't tell what I'm gonna do to you," he moans as he feels around inside the door for a light.

We don't have much room, but when he expertly unzips my dress and peels it down me, the feel of his supple hands on my bare flesh tune me into the reality that it isn't where we're doing it that counts, it's all about how good it is.

And there's no doubt in my mind that my fantasies are about to become reality.

"These are the most amazing traffic stoppers I've seen in a long time," Danie whispers after unhooking my bra and burying his nose in my cleavage.

I knew it! So much for Dandelion's theory that her daddy's fame got us in so quickly with Here Kitty Kitty.

"But you see boobs all the time!" I echo her earlier comment.

"Not like these! And I'll bet that little kitty is just as pretty. C'mon, baby, bend over real nice for Danie and let him have a taste."

I think I'm going to die, cry, or both. A rock star is going to do to me what I've been wondering about since I first saw it in one of Dadda's porn magazines.

I'm naked now other than my tiny panties and big shoes. Danie is on his knees behind me and pulls my string bikini down with his teeth. I feel his breath on my thighs and already I'm about to scream. When his lips and tongue start working on my pleasure center I do scream. A joyful chant circles round and round in my mind as he brings me to my first orgasm in a matter of seconds:

I love being a groupie. I love being a groupie. I love being a groupie.

"Nice, kitty. Now how about a little for me before I finish the job?"

Danie is back on his feet and already has his leathers around his knees. From that same porn tome I already know what he wants, another first for me. I close my eyes and make like the models in the magazine. I must be doing something right because before long he's telling me to bend over again, and put my hands around my ankles.

"Look at those beautiful shoes," he instructs.

The floor is gross, spotted with cleaners and scum, but my shoes, well, they are beautiful. But not nearly as beautiful as the feeling of my first rocker sliding into me smooth and easy because I'm so ready. I love to hear the sound of his supreme passion and know that I have something to do with it. I love the new and real sensations of my own weak-kneed ecstasy. I love it that I can give and receive. Because before now, I've done a whole lot of giving without getting anything back.

I love my new life.

I love being a groupie. I love being a groupie. I love being a groupie.

"Baby, you're the best ever. There's no one like you," Danie laughs, one hand on his zipper and the other on the doorknob after he fastens my bra and helps me step back into my second skin dress.

Danie lies. But that's okay.

"I'm gonna remember this for a long, long time," I gush.

Because I lie, too.

"Next up, Scarlett Rouge!" Dandelion giggles the following evening, when we get ready to hit the Rainbow again with Mother Sandy and our Smut tour guides.

The trail to Scarlett Rouge is paved a little differently: we don't meet them in the Rainbow, but smoking grass behind Gazzarri's with their manager, a guy named Stephen Gant who must weigh a half a ton. Naturally, Mother Sandy knows "Shark," as she refers to the big man. As for the talent, the result is the same: an invitation backstage. But the boys in the band want to double team us before the show, before we even know what they can do onstage, and they want to do it all in the same dressing room. Dandelion and I look at each other, shrug, and say, "Sure!" Because a big part of being a groupie, let's face it, is being agreeable.

And what fun we have. Four boys in lipstick and eyeliner, two girls in leather and spandex, two feather boas, eight cans of whipped cream, three jars of smooth peanut butter, and a whole dressing table full of make-up and hair products.

"You girls are fun chicks. How about meeting up with us at the Troub in two weeks?" Kenny Pride, the bass player, suggests.

"We'll try to make it," Dandelion decides, with the hair flip that is becoming her signature move.

We prance out the door and take our places at stage left. Because we won't settle for anything less, two nights into our groupie careers.

Marty brings us shopping during the week. Dandelion only has a few more days of school and the Summer of Spandex and Leather has gotten out of the starting gate like one of the championship race horses that Dadda used to bet all of our food money on when we were living in our car.

"I can't believe we've made it through a whole weekend on Sunset without seeing Mama," Dandelion marvels as we sit in the back seat of the wobbling cab like we're celebrities in a long black limo, our gleaming legs poking out from beneath our short black skirts.

Marty's eyes appear in the rear view mirror like he has something to say. He probably knows, however, that he has to choose his words carefully, else Dandelion will bite his head off his shoulders!

"Uh, Miss Dandylion?" he says tentatively.

"Yes, Marty?" she replies in an annoyed tone.

"I knew where yous girls were gonna be this past weekend so I suggested the bands at some other clubs and she agreed to see them. That ain't gonna last forever, but I'm tryin' to keep yous two from clashin' with her."

Dandelion loses some of her uppity posture as she meets eyes with me. I know what she's conveying: Marty was being a pretty good cover for us and we didn't even know it.

I lean forward and pat Marty on his well-padded shoulder. "That's great, Marty. We appreciate it," I tell him softly.

"Yeah." Dandelion's voice is even softer than mine.

"I'll keep doing what I can. I'm doin' a hell of a lot of lyin' for yous two, but I guess yous are my customers now, too."

Marty still hasn't accepted any money from us so I don't know how we can be customers in the true sense. It's a good time to offer it again so I do, but he waves his hand at me as he pulls up to our favorite store, Another Man's Treasure.

"If I start goin' broke yous can help me out. But I ain't goin' broke. I'll be back in an hour to bring yous girls home," he says as we get out of the car.

"I so don't want to go home. My lies are gonna catch up with me any minute now," Dandelion worries as he pulls away.

"Listen, if you've fooled your parents for this long now, you can keep doing it. And remember, you can always come live with us," I remind her, because she just seems to be putting off moving to Mother Sandy's and making things completely perfect.

"Look, new stuff in the window!" she shrieks, pointing toward the hair metal display in the large glass storefront window.

Hmph. Put off again.

I go on a personal crusade to get Dandelion out of her parents' house and into Mother Sandy's.

"I so don't want to live with those creeps in the next room," she whines, referring, of course, to Smut.

I know it's just an excuse, but she can't use it anymore when Diesel, Bullshit, and Little Drummer Boy, who is about to change his name because that's what he does, pack their filthy belongings in garbage bags and move back to "Smut Central" in Van Nuys. The story from Mother Sandy is that the small house was condemned, thanks mostly to them, but the landlord lets them back in because they manage to pay their rent on time every month. No aspect of this transaction seems possible to me but pretty soon they're gone and calling Mother Sandy's begging Dandelion and me to come visit them and play some "fun games" they've made up. They're easier to ignore when hanging up is an option. But I can't ignore the empty room that I want to be filled with Dandelion and her new wardrobe bought with all the stolen money from the drugged out weirdoes at her parents' all-nighters.

I'm pretty sure I just about have her worn down when she makes a frantic call to Mother Sandy's and tells me to get ready to take a ride with her and Marty. I fully expect that she's playing a trick on me and that she's going to show up with her belongings to move in, but she's empty-handed and in distress when I slide into the back of the cab with her.

"Things are really bad with Mama and Daddy now!" she cries.

"Where are we going?" I demand.

"You'll see," she says ominously.

Marty drops us off across from the main concert entrance of Holly Woods.

"Daddy is so depressed I couldn't even think of leaving him now," Dandelion drones mournfully.

We stand and watch as Derek Dagger's name is removed from the marquee. Dandelion's daddy has lost his last gigs at the Woods. In place of his name go up the monikers of bands that we have already started to conquer and those we are looking to conquer. A meeting of the hair metal minds is coming up in a week at the Woods. Scarlett Rouge is near the bottom of the bill while Here Kitty Kitty is in the middle. The other names, like Flame Game and Lipstick Loves Mascara, are on our tongues. We want our names on theirs and that's not all. It's a bittersweet and confusing moment.

"Well, the only thing we can do is get ready for Scarlett Rouge at the Troub on Saturday night," I say with a sigh.

"When the chips are down, get ready to rock," Dandelion agrees, a look of grim determination on her tanned face.

After further discussion, we agree that we really don't like Scarlett Rouge all that much. We've been seeing some pictures of them in local rock magazines. They're a bit pudgy and don't look nearly as good as the Here Kitty Kitty boys in their bright and tight clothes. They even seem a little, well, *old* to be touting themselves as the new glam boy quartet poised to rule the scene. Heaven help us, they're almost thirty!

"Why don't we go somewhere else?" I suggest as we put the finishing touches on our latest fashion creations bought at Another Man's Treasure.

Not even turning her eyes away from herself in the mirror, Dandelion shrugs and says, "I think we should go anyway. I just have this feeling that we should be there."

I wave my hand at her. "Sure. You and your feelings." I've heard this line before from her.

"Wait. You'll see," she predicts, but I know she's joking and isn't concerned about my doubt in her "feelings."

Even though we won't honor the invitation to "play" with Scarlett Rouge again, we show up at the Troub with our now-usual posse of Mother Sandy and Smut plus Lon, a friend of theirs. Lon is more of a loser than they are. And we didn't think that was possible.

"The girls won't come over and play our new games," Diesel boo-hoos when Lon is equally unsuccessful at attaching himself to us. "They want to share lipstick with their conquests."

"If you talk about lipstick one more time-" I ball my fists and get ready to sock Diesel in his unshaven chin but Dandelion drags me away.

"C'mon, Highway Child. Let's check out the prospects."

The club is full of lookers who are no doubt movers and shakers we don't know yet.

"Wow, everyone is beautiful," I comment before I notice that a not-so-lovely human is making a beeline toward us: one of Scarlett Rouge's roadies. "Here comes Freak," I warn Dandelion.

"Hey, girls! The guys are gonna pay me good money to bring you back to them," Freak mumbles, trying to sound smooth but instead sounding like a stalker.

"I think I'll pass on the peanut butter tonight," Dandelion speaks for both of us as Freak grabs our arms and attempts to move us backstage.

As much as we struggle he's doing a pretty good job until a sudden giant shadow falls over all of us.

"What the fuck are you doing to these girls?" a voice that matches the shadow booms from behind us.

I'm almost afraid to look around, because Mother Sandy's friend "Shark" Gant, who is Scarlett Rouge's manager, is behind us. All I see is a pair of pissed-off orbs staring out of some facial hair covering the head of a massive human being. Freak lets us go, trying to tell Gant that the band wants us backstage.

"I don't give a rat's ass what they want. No girls are gonna be forced backstage as long as I'm running this shit show."

The power of this man's glare not only has Freak backing off, it has Dandelion and me doing a nervous little curtsy that must look ridiculous. I for one am really happy when he follows Freak. I stare after them, temporarily speechless. When the shock finally wears off and I turn back to Dandelion, her gaze is locked on someone else.

"Look, Highway Child. I saw those four at a party at

Cherry Red's house once before." She nods toward a tall and glamorous blonde who couldn't be anything else but a model she's so perfect, and three young men whose faces I can't see. Two of them are blondes and the same height as the woman, the other is taller than she is, even though she's six feet or better in heels. They must have just arrived because I didn't notice them before, and I would've remembered a woman that stunning.

I'm ready to say, "Whoop-di-do!" when the lofty fellow turns his head and I see the most amazing face ever to grace a man. And the hair…the hair is dark and full and long and falling over his forehead with a part to the side. He smirks at the model and his teeth are just as fine as the rest of him. That grin does it for me. I can tell he's a bad boy. I can't speak for another reason now, though Dandelion is babbling about something and I can't even pay attention to her.

My daydream is interrupted by the opening band taking the stage. They're pretty cute too, a lot cuter than Scarlett Rouge, though they don't quite compare to Mr. Tall and Beautiful, whom I make sure we walk by and who doesn't even turn his eyes in my direction. Dandelion is staring at the model even as I'm trying to get his attention.

"She makes me feel short and ugly," is her comment, even turning to look at the woman after we pass.

"Oh, she's probably a groupie like us anyway," I blurt, trying to make my friend feel better and to soothe a jealous ache I get in my gut.

"Oh sure, Highway Child. She's really a-" Dandelion's feet stop moving at the same time her voice does.

"Come on, let's keep checking out the prospects!" I bark,

suddenly emotional over that guy who won't even look at me. I catch another glimpse of him when I turn to Dandelion, who is once again watching someone.

"Highway Child, look!" Dandelion pulls me back a step and cautiously points toward the front of the stage. "Do you see who I see?"

"Oh…" is all that escapes my lips.

I indeed see who she sees. Decked out in a sweet little sundress and heels, with bows in her long, thick blond pony tails, it's the girl from South Carolina who beaded the jacket for Dandelion's daddy. The blonde with the jewelry. The one I want to round out our little groupie group. She's standing with two other girls that look like they just got out of diapers and put away their rubber duckies. She at least looks potty trained. One of her cohorts has on a set of bunny ears that light up in rainbow colors.

The blonde meets eyes with me then from across the Troub and a look of panic crosses her darling face.

"Let's go recruit her," I say, but once again we come into contact with Shark Gant. And at precisely the wrong time. The beast steps into our path.

"Girls, I just want to apologize for what happened with Freak." His voice is calm now and he seems like a nice, normal guy, not the grizzly bear that made us shake in our platforms just moments before.

Dandelion and I are smiling in fear and doing that weird curtsy again as we're surrounded by the smoke from a cigar he's puffing on. It smells just like the Cuban kind that some of the guys with more money would smoke in One Grand Evening.

I don't want to think of One Grand Evening.

When Shark Gant moves his bulk out of our line of vision our Southern girl is gone. And so are her two juvenile friends.

"Where the hell did they go?" Dandelion curses.

"C'mon, let's see if they're running down the street," I suggest.

We bolt out the front door and onto Santa Monica Boulevard, which is so crowded with people that we couldn't possibly spot the three teenagers if they were running away from the Troub.

"Damn, missed her," I hiss, punching my fist into my palm.

"We'll get her next time. Didn't I tell you we had to come here tonight?" Dandelion has a silly grin on her face. "Told ya so," she gloats, giving me a friendly shove.

I giggle as we turn to reenter the Troub.

Coincidently, we come face-to-face with the blonde goddess, who is on her way out. Mr. Tall and beautiful and their blond friends who are no slouches in the looks department, are with her, and so is Shark Gant. He doesn't even acknowledge us now, nor do any of the pretty boys.

I have to see the face of that perfect man one more time so I reel around and stare.

I'm saving you for another day, I think. And I mean it.

We have been warned.

"Yous girls have to beware. I tried to tell Miss Tulip about a concert at the Long Beach Arena but she ain't goin' for it. She's gonna be at Holly Woods at the same show yous are gonna be at this weekend," Marty tells us the Thursday before the six-band Hairspray Hoopla at Holly Woods.

As has already become habit, Dandelion and I are shopping for cute new clothes on Hollywood Boulevard before we go.

Dandelion comes crashing down from the numbing excitement we're feeling with such a big show so close at hand.

"Gee thanks, Marty. You sure know how to rain on someone's parade," she mutters.

"Miss Dandylion, did yous just wanna run into her without being prepared?"

Sometimes Marty just seems too sensible. He's a lot easier to deal with when he's an overweight pushover.

Dandelion folds her arms stubbornly across her chest and decides, "No, I suppose not."

And from here on in I can't bust through her pissy mood. Not with shopping. Not with swooning over pictures of the pretty metal studs that we'll meet at Holly Woods. Not with talking to her about moving out on her parents, thus rendering any meeting null and void of meaning.

"I get this feeling that Mama knows I've been lying to her for a really long time now. I just don't know why she hasn't ratted me out yet," she finally says with a shake of her head as we're preparing for a night of lots of boys with lots of hair.

Clearly, this is doing more than raining on her parade. It's pouring on it! And I don't like getting wet. So I remind her what we've talked about more than once now.

"If she rats on you, you'll rat on her. Remember?"

"Maybe so. I hope you're right. But I still want to get our meeting out of the damn way."

"Let's make the meeting work to our advantage, not hers," is my brilliant idea.

At first Dandelion just stares at me. Bu then she picks up on my energy and starts to nod.

"Yeah, our advantage, not hers." She stares off into space then and must be having a pretty good vision, because before long she's sticking her hand out to me. We squeeze each other's fingers.

Deal sealed.

Two birds, one stone, six bands, no Smut. Mother Sandy is at that Long Beach Arena show with my dirty former housemates so we're on our own for the first time in our groupie pursuits. Maybe we'll finally figure out whether it's my boobs or Dandelion's borrowed fame that gets us through the door. We're still having that dispute, though it's more friendly and jokey than anything else now.

We're a little late because Tulip Dagger had Marty booked ahead of time to arrive at the Woods at the approximate time that the bands finished up with sound checks. We have no choice but to show up after she's already been making the rounds.

"She's probably had her way with every member of every band by now," Dandelion huffs as we clomp through a dirty alley behind Holly Woods to a rear entrance that's full of girls like us vying to get through a garage door. Trailers and trucks and equipment and tons of roadies are congregated in the back lot.

"Let's worry about getting through the door first." I can hardly keep up with her because she's walking fast, anxious to get her face-to-face with her mama out of the way. I can't blame her I guess, but this is supposed to be fun too.

"Oh, don't worry about getting through the door. I just have to see someone who knows Daddy." She's perusing the guys with "crew" and "Holly Woods" shirts on.

We're already attracting attention from the swarm of sweaty men who are mostly standing around and smoking or drinking. Only a few are actually working and a few more are tossing around a football.

"Come on, I just spotted Coot. He knows Daddy. He's a regular here," Dandelion says firmly.

"Coot? Freak? Why don't these guys have normal names?" I half joke as I follow her over to the garage door.

"Rock and roll isn't normal," she reminds me snootily.

I give her hair a yank because it's the first thing I can grab. "You're such a bitch," I hiss.

"Bitches get places. You should know that by now." She flips her hair.

Coot looks like his name: he's old, hairy, and not afraid to zero in on the body parts of girls one quarter his age.

"Woo-wee! Baby Dagger is all grown up since the last time I saw her!" he guffaws.

"Coot, we want to meet the bands. Bring us back, will you?" is all Dandelion has to say and Coot is ushering us in with a grand sweep of his hand.

Hmph. Must be the borrowed fame after all.

Coot's breath stinks from something I don't even want to guess at. I get a too-big whiff when he leans into me behind her back and whispers, "That's some set of knockers you have there, little girlie. They can get you through any door, can't they?" And he laughs like the boogie man.

Score is tied again.

Those two birds are about to meet the one stone.

The melee behind the scenes at Holly Woods is like the Roxy times ten. We quickly understand the full story of needing to rise to the top of the heap, because the heap is huge. But Coot escorts us right by most of the hopeful girls and to an area that has lots of food, lots of incredible guys, and…Tulip Dagger in the midst of it all. She looks amazing in a black patent cat suit that has a deep scoop neck and laces all the way down the front before continuing down the left leg. She's hardly the only woman there melting into the boys but she's the most obvious one. A cutie that we've seen in magazines named Sky Phillips has her in a lip lock and appears to be sharing a strawberry with her. She has to be fifteen years older than him, but he doesn't seem to care. They're oblivious to the party raging around them so Tulip misses our entrance.

"Hey, why don't ya show your mommy there's a new kid in town," Coot chuckles, too close again, but this time Dandelion gets a whiff of his breath and looks at me, horrified.

"I think we will," Dandelion agrees. "Thanks, Coot. I owe you one."

"You could always blow me," Coot lobbies for action.

"I could always tell my daddy you said that," Dandelion bites back.

Coot disappears quickly.

"Whoa! Hi girls, when did you get here?" Frankie Flame, lead guitarist of Flame Game, the top-billed band on the marquee, reels around to greet us and accidentally steps on my toe. I bite back the pain, grinning and grimacing widely.

"Actually, honey, we just arrived and we're here hoping to see you," Dandelion, always quick on her feet and with a great line, gushes with a teasing flip of her dark brown mane.

"You two must be Dandelion and Highway Child," Frankie guesses as he pulls us both into an embrace, thus leaving behind three giddy girls who were red-faced over him and no doubt pretty close to a foursome with him as the subject.

"How did you guess?" I giggle, catching the hair-flipping fever.

Dandelion glares and curls her lip at me as she looks at my chest. I arch my back to piss her off further.

"Word on the street travels at the speed of sound," he answers. "How about coming to the tour bus and having a little bit of fun? I can borrow some peanut butter from your friends Scarlett Rouge."

"Gee, Mr. Flame, you sure work fast," Dandelion croons, ignoring the peanut butter reference. Word does get around, doesn't it?

"Wouldn't want anyone else to get you first," Frankie reasons. "Besides, the party has been going on without you for an hour already. It's almost time to rock."

I wave my hand at him and remind him, "But Mr. Flame, you go on last. You have all the time in the world for fun!"

"Not when you consider my wife is showing up in an hour." Mr. Flame is dead serious now.

"Well, in that case, let's go!" I agree.

"Honey, you'll let me say hi to my mama first, won't you?" Dandelion asks innocently as Frankie is leading us away and in the opposite direction of Tulip.

"Well, she looks a little busy with my drummer over there. You sure it can't wait 'til later?" Frankie glances toward Tulip and Sky Phillips

"Oh no, it can't wait." Dandelion is shaking her head confidently.

"Maybe we should invite them to join in the fun?" Frankie suggests.

"Let's keep it outside the family if we can, Frankie, okay?" Hair flip.

Gosh, Dandelion is smooth.

We must be quite the picture of youth and nuttiness as we approach Dandelion's mama and her much younger conquest. Tulip has her hands on Sky's face and a pouty grin on hers. Sky spots us with Frankie first and his eyes widen. He seems to forget about the woman pressed against him, his arms falling away from her sides.

"Look who I found! The girls we've been looking for. Dandelion and Highway Child!" Frankie brags.

Tulip suddenly goes still upon hearing our names. At first she doesn't even look at us; she's in some sort of shock. Dandelion is equally still as she hits her mama with a backstage stare-down, waiting for a response. Tulip's pout, that looked put-on anyway, straightens into a look of disgust and that's the expression she slams her daughter with, but not until her eyes wander over me first. I can almost read her mind from her features: *the party's over.*

And I hope I'm right because I respond out loud, "The party is about to begin!"

"Well, let's round up the troops!" Sky exclaims. Then, he actually turns to Tulip and says, "See ya later, babe. I've got new trails to blaze," before he attaches himself to our little hug line.

As we're walking away Dandelion and I look at each other with our mouths hanging open.

"Could it get any better?" she marvels.

"I don't think so," I assure her, happy for her, happy for us.

We don't even look back.

The first bird of the night is grounded.

Who said throwing stones doesn't get you anywhere?

We have to work fast with the Flame Game boys. As it turns out, the flight from their home town of Miami with their wives and girlfriends is delayed due to weather so being with us is an extra special and unexpected treat for them. They expected to have to pass on the delights of Dandelion and Highway Child until the next time they were in L.A. without their significant others. So we make the most of the hour that we have with them. They're totally cool guys and let us use their make-up and hairspray so we can make a grand exit from their wildly decorated tour bus in the back lot.

"Oh man, we're really the queens now!" I laugh to Dandelion, as we're walking through a crowd of maniacal girls following four gorgeous men back into Holly Woods, flanked by beefy roadies and having our clothes tugged on just like we're rock stars too. I'm dizzy with the intoxicating power of rock and roll.

Just outside the rear door that we use to reenter the Woods stand the girls who have fought their way to the front of the line to get in but have not been able to penetrate the door yet. Through the madness, I see something blinking. Green and pink, pink and green. A pair of bunny ears. I follow the lights down to be sure it is who I think it is before I elbow Dandelion and point toward the prepubescent waif who was with the Southern blonde at the Troubadour the week before. Dandelion catches the drift right away.

"Let's bring her in," she instructs.

The bunny girl is not afraid when I grab her by the arm and drag her through a few layers of girls to get her inside the door. In fact, she's thrilled.

"She's my little sister," I claim, when one of the bodyguards asks me why I've brought her in.

The members of Flame Game leave us behind to continue to their dressing room. We mix into the crowd and find a place against a wall to take care of business with my "little sister."

When we turn in on bunny girl to confront her we don't even have to speak because she blurts, "I know where Carolina is. I live with her."

I roll the name Carolina around in my mind. Suddenly, it's real. The moniker couldn't be more appropriate for the Southern blonde flitting around in her little tie-front gingham shirts, cutoffs, and heels.

"Give us the address. And don't tell her we're coming," I order.

Bird number two: stoned.

CAROLINA

"**D**addy is so depressed!" Dandelion cries.

I shiver every time she mentions her daddy, remembering how he acted when I went into his dressing room so he could try on the jacket I'd made for him. I feel like Dandelion and Highway Child are under the impression that I'm a dirty girl because I was alone with him and that's why they think I'm a natural for being the third girl in their groupie trio. They don't know that nothing went on and I'm too afraid to tell them the truth.

"I'm sorry!" I bawl, thinking that it's somehow my fault that her daddy is so miserable.

"Thank you, Carolina. All he does now is sit around and make phone calls trying to get gigs. And Mama glares at me all day." Dandelion shakes her head.

"Well, she's famous for having sex with rock stars. You would think she'd be able to put a smile on his face," H.C. sneers. She's so mean sometimes, to Dandelion and to me and even to herself. I think some bad things must have happened to her to make her so snappy. Poor Highway Child. And to have to live with that silly name forever.

Poor Dandelion, too. But I'd rather have a depressed daddy and a pissed off mama and to have Highway Child being nasty to me than to be Carolina Clampett. Things aren't going the way I intended. I have to get back on track.

Within a couple of months of Dandelion and Highway Child showing up at Elsa's House, the home for runaway teenagers that I live at, I have two surrogate sisters, a framed picture of my real sister Elly May, and a whole new wardrobe given to me by rock stars either on their way to the top or rock stars who only wish they were on their way to the top. I'm completely confused as to where Carolina Clampett is going. Because it sure does seem like I'm doing pretty good at being a groupie, but that my jewelry is secondary in importance to giving all those horny hair guys what they'll seem to go to any length to get from a fifteen year old girl.

Gosh, my head is spinning! This isn't what I came here for!

Now we're preparing for another steamy early autumn night on Sunset Boulevard. Tonight, a band called the New York Gems is at Gazzarri's. I tell myself that I have to think of it as another new opportunity to hand out my glam-inspired necklaces and earrings and bracelets to the guys. My little Carolina's Creations bag I beaded myself with my name on it, is chock full of my best pieces and they all have little white tags on them with my name and the phone number at Elsa's House.

"Listen Carolina, forget about the damn jewelry and live it up! You're the envy of girls all over L.A. for being on the top of the wish list of rock and roll guys up and down Sunset," Highway Child scolds me.

But if I'm not the envy of me what does it matter? I'm ready to ask. But Dandelion starts talking first.

"Leave her alone!" she shrieks. She always thinks she has to defend me. I guess she must assume I'm too dumb to defend myself.

Everyone thinks I'm dumb because I'm so nervous and jumpy and stumble over words when I talk. But now that I'm enrolled at Hollywood High for the 1983-1984 school year with my new friends, I know I'm going to get smarter. In fact, I'm studying Webster's dictionary to learn new words and I'm even going to take a speech class to talk more confidently.

Now Dandelion and Highway Child are yelling at each other over me. Ma and Pa used to fight over me too and not in a good way.

"Don't say it!" Dandelion warns, shaking her finger at H.C.

"Carolina, we should go to Beverly Hills and recruit Elly May to make us a quartet of groupies instead of a trio!" Highway Child grins with the best set of teeth in the room even though she's never seen a dentist in her life.

I drop my jewelry bag at the mention of my sister.

"Oh, I just can't bear to go back to that place and look for her!" I cry, and start my famous hand-wringing that I got from Ma.

When I first got to L.A., Bunny Baby and I went to Rodeo Drive with a camera I stole from Ma and Pa because we wanted to tell everyone we were there. Everyone looked at us like we were bums and some rich lady walking into the Gucci boutique even called the police on us. We got a ride back to Hollywood in the back of the cruiser! I'm never going back there, so I'm just going to have to find Elly May by accident when she leaves Beverly Hills to run an errand.

"Hey, maybe she'll show up at a concert one of these nights!" Highway Child tosses this out in an offhand way, like she's losing interest in the subject. I hope she is. My heart is aching for Elly May, my better half.

A car sounds out in front of the house H.C. lives in with the nice lady called Mother Sandy who said that I can move in too if I want. I don't think I can live in the same house with H.C. or I might consider it.

"Sounds like fat Marty!" Dandelion says with a roll of her eyes.

She's got it in for the cab guy who picks us up and drives us anywhere we want to go at any time of the day or night. I don't like the way she treats him so I try to make up for it by being real friendly to him all the time. He seems sweet to me and well-intentioned. H.C. was nice to him when I first joined up with them but now she's mean to him too. I'm no expert on reading people's expressions, but something tells me that Marty is really hurt when Highway Child gives him the sass mouth.

I slide into the front seat and lean over to touch Marty's big forearm. "Hi honey, thanks for the ride to Gazzarri's." I add my best Southern smile with the hope that I look and sound soothing.

Dandelion and Highway Child continue some kind of disagreement in the back seat and they're loud, but I can still hear Marty perk up a little and reply, "Yous are welcome, Miss Carolina. Yous look very pretty tonight." His voice has a sadness to it that makes me sad too. Then Marty winces when Dandelion barks from the back seat, "Just drive, Marty. Never mind flirting with a damn teenager."

Funny how they never say that when a rock guy is trying to get his hand under my skirt. These girls confuse me. But they're my sisters and I've always wanted sisters who would drive me crazy and now I have them.

Marty sighs and backs out of Mother Sandy's driveway.

"By the way, Carolina, if we were just going to Gazzarri's we could've walked. It's right down the street, remember?" Highway Child questions me in a voice that sounds like she's trying to make me feel stupid.

I feel my face get hot because I forgot that Gazzarri's is so close. From Elsa's it's a lot farther away. I'm not very good with directions. "Where are we going?" I ask, as this is the first time they told me we aren't just going to Gazzarri's.

"Up Sunset to do a little drive by," Dandelion says with a snicker.

"A drive by?"

"Yeah. You know that redhead bitch in school?" Highway Child interrupts.

They must be talking about Cherry Red, the beautiful hair metal girl at Hollywood High that wants to be part of our group. I think she'd be great, but Dandelion has some huge problem with her, so Highway Child and I are supposed to have a problem with her too. Highway Child plays the game but I talk to Cherry Red sometimes when they aren't looking and she pleads with me to get Dandelion to let her "run" with us.

"We're going by her house? Why?"

I get the "you're so stupid" look again.

"Well, let's just say we want her to know where we're gonna be and who we're gonna be with while she sits in her fancy house with her fancy clothes and dreams," Dandelion spits.

I'm mortified that I have to be a part of this and wish we could just go to Gazzarri's and have fun. So while we're driving up Sunset I close my eyes and let my mind wander.

Maybe tonight will be the night. Not only do I want to get Carolina's Creations off and running, my heart and mind are also set on finding love with a nice rock and roll guy. Someone to cherish me and take me away from Elsa's House and away from being a groupie. Someone who will appreciate my talent as a maker of fine jewelry. Someone who-

"Hey you redheaded witch, you're gonna miss all the fun again! We'll be partying with the New York Gems at Gazzarri's. Sure wish you could be there!" Dandelion's sudden yelling out the window jars me out of my fantasy. I must've fallen asleep for a minute.

"Yeah, and we sure hope that Hall Pass gets that big old contract with Double Take Records pretty soon!" Highway Child adds.

Marty is crawling by this dreamy house, just the kind of house I'd like to live in with my rocker husband. A crowd of people are out front under a fancy porch awning. I sink down lower into my seat so I'm not recognized.

"Gun it, Marty!" Dandelion orders when two dark shadows start moving toward the cab from the direction of the house.

Marty stomps on the gas and the old cab bucks and squeals before getting us out of there. My sisters are proud of themselves. I wonder if Cherry Red even heard them, if she's even there. The whole thing sure seems like a silly waste of time to me.

"Are we going to Gazzarri's now?" I inquire.

"We're near Beverly Hills. Marty, do you know where Elly May Clampett lives?" H.C. is making fun of me again. I clutch my jewelry bag and close my eyes to blot out her jokes.

"Sorry, Miss Highway Child, I don't." His tone is apologetic.

"She's my sister," I lean over and whisper, and he nods with understanding.

A big crowd is piled up outside of Gazzarri's. Marty lets us off right in front. My sisters already know how to get through the door. But before we can squeeze through the bodies to get to one of the rear entrances we run into my three least favorite people in the entire world: Diesel, Bullshit, and Road Warrior, who have a really loud band called Smut and live in Van Nuys. Dandelion and H.C. knew them before I came along, so the guys are always trying to pretend like I'm on the friend by association list. The other thing they're always trying to do is get us to go to their house, which they call Smut Central. Just hearing about it sounds awful enough even without going there. I think that my friends are ready to go but I don't want to join them. I'll admit that Smut sound good when they're practicing in

Mother Sandy's backyard, but they smell so bad that one cancels out the other.

Diesel, whom I've only known for a few weeks, already has this annoying habit of sticking his finger under my chin and stroking me like I'm a cat and tonight he does it again.

"Hello, pretty blond kitty. I'll give you something delicious to drink if you meow nice for Diesel," he croons.

I wish I had a very long string of strong beads to choke him with. Maybe the fishnet choker will work if I pull hard enough?

Oh, I have to banish these terrible thoughts! I'm not being very nice! Ma and Pa are right about me being an evil girl headed for the pits of hell!

"Oh, I'm not very thirsty right now, but if I am I'll tell you!" I'm so nervous as I try to get the wicked thoughts out of my head that I say something ridiculous. I want to wring my hands too, but I have my bag of jewels getting in the way.

Diesel lifts his dark brows. "I'll be waiting for that!" he assures me, and for the rest of the night, I can't get away from him.

"You have to go through the front. No guests backstage until later. Sorry." A man bigger than the doorway is blocking our entrance through the back door of Gazzarri's.

Highway Child gives my ankle a light tap with her shoe and whispers, "Shark Gant."

So, this is the notorious giant Mother Sandy was talking about one day. Dandelion and H.C. had nodded knowingly when Sandy had explained how tough he was when it came to being a manager. Though he looks like an overgrown kitten to me, even the members of Smut don't give him any lip so he must carry some kind of clout. Still, as they change directions to return to the front of the building, I want my chance to explain about my jewelry. I make eye contact with him as I hold up my Carolina's Creations bag and shake it. His unsmiling face makes my voice, if not the rest of me, quiver.

"H-hello, Mr. Shark. I make jewelry for rock stars and-"

The sheep in wolf's clothing waves a stinky stogy at me in dismissal. "Listen honey, my name ain't Mr. Shark. It's Gant. And you can push your jewelry later, okay? I'll even give it to them if you want. But I can't let ya through the door because they ain't got time to meet and greet right now." His voice is pleasant, even pleading. As for my heart, it's fluttering like a drunk butterfly trying to break free from the confines of my rib cage, even though I don't know who "they" are other than a group called the New York Gems who are starting to make a mark on the Strip. I hope they're worth a bag of my best work, because now Mr. Shark is going to tell them some blonde has free jewelry for them. Maybe he'll even tell them that I'm a groupie and I have more than jewelry for free.

"Oh thank you, Mr. Shark. I mean, Mr. Gant. I'll be sure to find you later and you can give them the bag." My feet won't move from in front of him so Diesel takes me by the elbow and steers me away.

"C'mon, sweetheart. Let's make sure we get in through the front."

I look back at Shark Gant but he's closed the door.

Diesel and I catch up with the rest of our group.

"Hmph! What do you think of that? Can't get in the

back door. Do they think they're too good for us or something?" H.C. gripes.

"Mr. Gant said they don't have time for us," I explain.

Dandelion rolls her eyes. "Yeah, that means they're too good for us."

Silenced again.

We don't have any problems getting into Gazzarri's through the classic entrance. We're regulars and know how to work our way to the front of any crowd. Soon we're at the lip of the stage and waiting for the New York Gems.

"They probably suck but they have this big attitude." H.C. is still miffed by the snub at the back door.

"Well baby, we could always go back to Smut Central and you can be with the coolest band in L.A.," Bullshit slurs.

"Yeah, how about it, sweet thing?" Diesel moans in my ear, and I get a whiff of the "three Bs," as Dandelion and Highway Child call them, that he oozes: beer, body odor, and ball sweat. I don't even want to think about the last one and how Dandelion had to explain to me what "balls" are while Highway Child giggled in the background.

"No thank you. I have jewelry to hand out," I decline sweetly, and wait patiently for the band to take the stage. Eight o'clock comes and goes and then quarter after.

"Yeah, they think that they're better than their fans." Dandelion nods knowingly.

"Well, I'll give them a few more minutes then I'm heading to the Roxy. Some group called Why? is there," Highway Child snorts.

"Why," Dandelion echoes with an eye roll. She's also known to flip her hair a lot and does it now.

The Smut trio is just as restless but is waiting to see "the hot chick from the magazine covers." I don't even want to know who they're talking about.

Finally, the event takes place. I feel ready to faint when I see the mesmerizing lead singer of the New York Gems come out. Diesel takes the opportunity to slip his arms around me when I lean backward, nearly losing by balance in a sudden haze of love.

"Oh shit, there they are again! We saw them at the Troub, remember? And I told you I saw them at Cherry Red's party too!" Dandelion catches the gorgeous power of the quartet made up of three men and a woman, all magazine-worthy. They have to be the most glam of the glam groups I've seen yet, and I've been around L.A. for more than a year. I'd let any of the men put their shoes under my bed. But it's the female lead singer that has me ready to fall over in desire and panic.

In a matter of seconds I want to be her. And I want her to wear my jewelry. But stupid Carolina Clampett has a sack full of jewelry made with the usual male rockers in mind. The bold blonde is the first woman I've seen on the hair metal stage. And she's fronting a band! Now, I won't sleep until I see her again and have a selection of fine baubles for her.

I'm not the only one in love. H.C. can't tear her eyes away from the guitarist who has a Gibson that's embezzled with blue gems. Dandelion is teasing her and H.C. is complaining about how she has the right to check out at a good-looking man. Dandelion settles for that answer, but I think it's more than looking. I think H.C. is in as instant love with him as I am with the singer.

Don't get the wrong idea about me! I don't like girls! But this girl is something different. She gives me hope that I'll be able to become something besides a rock star toy. This girl has power. This girl has every gaze, male and female, following her from one end of the stage to the other the minute she appears in her tiny copper metallic dress and matching knee boots.

But I don't want to meet her. I'm too nervous. No, when the show is over and my friends want to get backstage I just want a ride back to Elsa's House so I can get some sleep after plotting how I'll get money from Elsa for beads and clasps and everything else I need for the visions I have in my head. Nevertheless, we end up behind the scenes. I wait on the sidelines hiding my bag of creations behind my back while my sidekicks meet the band. It's a pretty short transaction anyway; within a few minutes they're pulling me out the door.

"Well, you were the smart one, Carolina. They just acted like they were too good for us. You didn't miss anything and they probably would've turned their noses up at your jewelry," Dandelion gripes.

I couldn't possibly give them my jewelry without anything in the bag for the lead singer. That would be sinful!

"That chick is hotter than hot," mumbles Road Warrior, who hasn't said another word all night. We three girls all stare at him because when he actually does say something it's like the dead speaking.

"I doubt she's going to Smut Central anytime soon," Highway Child snorts. "But at least I found out the name of that guitarist. I have a new goal in life now." Enter wicked grin. "To get Nikk Saffire between the sheets. Mm, mm, mm."

"I'm always available for between the sheets work also," Diesel reminds us.

He gets roundly ignored.

We exit through the same door Mr. Gant was blocking earlier and follow a crowd of metal heads around to the front of the building and toward the Roxy. As I listen to the giddy banter about the New York Gems I hear the name of my new heroine several times: *Emerald*. What a magical name.

As if he could read my mind, Diesel confirms that her name is spelled with an apostrophe in it: Em'rald.

"I've been reading up on that rad bitch," he says proudly.

"Gee Diesel, I had no idea that you knew how to read," H.C. teases.

I don't hear anything after that because I'm off in my own emerald-studded fantasy in which the beautiful girl is wearing a fabulous necklace I made as she rules the stages of Sunset Boulevard. I'm safe in that world as we peruse that very thoroughfare until Marty picks us up early the next morning.

I go home and dream Sunday away.

"I wouldn't make that snob anything."

This is the kind of comment I have to listen to from Dandelion and Highway Child at school as I work feverishly on my art. It takes a week for "check day," but Elsa has government money to give me and I spend it all on Hollywood Boulevard buying items that I can string together to create the sugar-plums in my head for the girl I want to follow around town. Suddenly, the New York Gems are popping up on all the most important marquees. But my friends are mad about what they keep referring to as the "treatment" they received at Gazzarri's and refuse to see them again.

"They treated us so badly that we almost went home with Smut!" Highway Child reminds me, wide-eyed.

I have to hold my tongue again because I had no intention of going to Smut Central. It was me that said I wanted to go home to Elsa's when Diesel was laying on the sales pitch after our night that started with the Gems.

Holding my tongue is easier with my mind on my work. No matter where I am, my fingers are busy. Home or school, my kit and supplies come with me. Breakfast, study hall, lunch, gym, is all jewelry time.

"That sure is pretty stuff, baby," Cherry Red says when she stops by the breakfast table that morning. Meanwhile, my partners turn their backs on her and start talking loudly about our exploits whenever she's around.

"It's for Em'rald of the New York Gems," I tell her. A pleasant warmth travels from my heart outward to my extremities.

"Oh yeah, my momma and daddy know them. They come to our parties sometimes. You should come over, honey. Maybe you can meet them."

Just the thought of being face to face with Em'rald makes my hands start to shake so badly that I can't even hold my tools. A small pair of pliers falls out of my hand and under the table.

My voice is shaking just as much. "Oh, thank you. Maybe someday," is my reply as I feel around on the floor for the missing tool.

"She's just trying to reel you in," Dandelion warns me when Cherry Red bounces off looking gorgeous but lonely.

This time I think that maybe she's right. Cherry Red doesn't know that her offer scares me more than anything else. I decide I should avoid her. My friends are delighted. But things are about to get much worse at school.

I don't want to leave the house after classes and on weekends, nor do I want to be disturbed. I just want to be alone with my goal. But if it isn't Dandelion and H.C. dragging me backstage somewhere, it's Bunny Baby knocking on my door. Bunny Baby, though, learns how to entice me into opening the door.

"Carolina, I have some magazines full of Em'rald and the New York Gems," she'll say from the hallway.

Even though I'm dying to see what she has, I pause a minute before I open up. No way I want the likes of Bunny Baby to know she's got me where she wants me. I didn't run away from Ma and Pa to let people get me where they want me.

While I'm spending my government allotment on my wares, Bunny Baby is spending hers on glossy rock magazines and now that she knows how I love Em'rald, the occasional fashion tome to show me the model side of my girl crush. But seeing Em'rald in *Vogue* and *Harper's Bazaar* lowers my spirits instead of raising them. My eyes study the expensive clothes she's wearing on the pages then I scan the stuff I'm making for her and it sure does look like junk to me.

"Oh, I don't even know why I'm wasting my time. She's rich and famous already and doesn't need my jewelry," I moan.

Bunny Baby at not-quite-fourteen is a lot more supportive than my two adopted sisters.

"I'll go to the Gems shows with you so you can get your stuff to her."

I shrug. "I can't see that it really matters. Anyway, it'll take me another two weeks to finish what I want to. They'll probably be gone from L.A. by then and back in New York." This feeling of time running out is hanging over me and with everyone disturbing me, my agony is prolonged.

Bunny Baby shrugs too. "Well, let me know if you change your mind."

I certainly have every opportunity to see Em'rald again, even to meet her. But one of those rugs is about to be viciously yanked out from underneath me.

I walk to school instead of taking the bus because Elsa's is so close to Hollywood High. Lately, I've been going in early because the cafeteria is really quiet until the busses arrive and I have lots of room and a flat clean surface to lay all my stuff out on. The only place I can do that at Elsa's is to put it on my bed in my tiny room, but everything gets messed up every time I move and I like my supplies to be neat and orderly.

Morning time at Elsa's is loud. Girls are fighting over the bathroom and sharing clothes and blow dryers and make-up, making it hard for me to get anything done because sometimes they want things from me. Here at school, an occasional teacher may come in to get some breakfast but they don't usually bother me, being that I've been at the same table for weeks now without causing any problems. But I figure it's a curious teacher coming to check up on me when I hear a voice say, "Hey, Carolina. I can't believe you're here this early every day!"

"Well, I-" I'm in defense mode until I look up and see not a teacher looking back at me, but a boy named Mikey Morris who's very pleasing to the eyes.

"I-I'm just making jewelry!" I blurt, and I feel like I'm going to start dropping things again because "the enemy" is so close.

Dandelion hates Mikey, but Dandelion hates most people anyway. I guess I should be glad that I'm not one of them, but I wish both of my friends weren't so high-strung. One false move and they don't like someone. Like Em'rald. I can't fathom someone not liking her, even though I've never met her and have only really seen her once in my whole life.

"Mikey Morris is the enemy because he's Cherry Red's ex and is in the same crap band as my ex. Oh, and he seems to think like the rest of his lame band that they're getting a contract with Double Take Records." I remember Dandelion's words about Mikey when the school year began and I had to be "initiated." That basically meant that I had to be told whom I couldn't talk to at Hollywood High because my friends don't like the person.

To my chagrin, Mikey sits down at the table across from me and looks with appreciation at my works-in-progress. He's even respectable enough not to touch anything.

"Everything looks great. You have a special talent," he comments, nodding his head.

Mikey has a scratchy voice like you might expect from a guy who screams heavy metal several nights a week. I've never seen his band Hall Pass, being that every member is the enemy, but everyone except for Dandelion and Highway Child say they're great. Well, they certainly have the lead singer to die for. Mikey is one of the most popular boys in the school with his long blond rocker hair, shoulder tattoo, and jeans-and-leather slouch. I have to tear my eyes away, because he's gazing right into mine, blue eyes into blue eyes, and my breath is quickening.

"Th-thank you. That's very nice of you to say that." I zip my lip after thanking him, hoping he'll go away. Instead, he shines an adorable and bashful smile on me.

"Your accent is so cute. Are you really from South Carolina?"

I know I shouldn't tell him anything other than I have an older brother who is really mean and will shoot his head off if he keeps talking to me. But I'm not a good liar.

"Yes, I'm from South Carolina."

"Well, I'm glad you came to L.A."

If I could get back on the right track I'd be happy to be in L.A. too, but I seem to be getting further off the mark every day.

I let silence fall between us, hoping he'll take the hint and be on his way. Instead, Mikey sighs and admits, "Listen, I'm not here this early by mistake. I've been watching you and I'd like to invite you to see my band play this weekend."

Oh no. Oh no. This is very, very bad.

"Oh, I'm sorry, but I have a steady boyfriend." I guess I'm a better liar than I thought. This one falls out so easily that I don't even recognize my voice.

"Well, if he lets you run up and down Sunset with your two friends, he won't mind you coming to a Hall Pass show either."

Things aren't getting any better. I get the sneaking suspicion that Mikey Morris knows more about me than he's letting on.

I'm so flustered that I'm alarmed when the first bell sounds to usher in the new school day, like I've never heard it before. A steady flow of students just off their busses start to fill the cafeteria. Neatly but abruptly, I start picking up my beads and tools. Mikey Morris helps me without being asked and I'm well aware that we must look like we're together. I know Dandelion and Highway Child are going to appear any minute and demand to know what I'm doing with Mikey. Before this can take place, however, Cherry Red struts into the cafeteria from the door closest to the table we're at and stops cold a few feet away to glare at us, her eyes seeming ready to pop right out of her head. Then, like a madwoman, she charges at me and grabs my hair. A sickening sound comes from her throat; it's like an animal dying.

"How could you, you bitch? I thought you were the nice one of the three! You're so sweet to my face and behind my back you're making time with my man!"

I've never been in a fight with anyone before, but Pa used to pull my hair so I know how much it hurts.

"I'm not your man, Sherri. Let her go!" Mikey has Cherry Red by the wrists and tries to break her hold on my hair.

"You let me go!" she wails, while several students gather around us not to try and stop the fight but to cheer on the conflict.

The pain of having my mane pulled is almost unbearable but the memories it brings back are even worse.

How did my daughter turn out to be such a little slut? Pa's words echo in my aching skull. I duck and clutch my head.

Mikey successfully pulls Cherry Red off of me and I'm granted a few seconds of relief before a loud crash and the sound of hundreds of tiny objects falling on the floor makes me lift my head. My beads are rolling all over the cafeteria like tiny centipedes of all colors let loose from a jar. The plastic carrying case that separated everything is smashed and my tools and clasps are in a heap at Cherry Red's feet.

"No!" I moan, as Principal Paulson enters the cafeteria with his assistant principal Mr. Grey, both of them at a run, not realizing what Cherry Red has just done. Soon they're on the floor after stepping on some bigger wooden beads and are the new stars of the ugly mess I've created. Students are pointing and laughing at them because of me and my stupidity.

I fall to my knees in a fruitless effort to rescue a few beads that have rolled in my direction. This decision can't make me look any smarter.

"You bitch! I'm telling Em'rald not to wear any of your stupid jewelry, so you might as well just give up!" Cherry Red continues to lash out at me while Paulson and Grey recover from their falls.

Several teachers are now in the cafeteria trying to get control of the situation. Sirens howl outside. They get closer and closer. Mikey is trying to help me up off the floor, Cherry Red is screaming obscenities at me while Paulson and Grey drag her away, and more of the student body arrive for the school day. Dandelion and Highway Child materialize. Mikey has his arm around me and is looking into my face and apologizing for the scene he says he caused.

"I'll replace everything that Sherri wrecked," he promises.

He doesn't understand that she ruined things that can't be so easily replaced.

"Carolina, what is going on?" Highway Child demands, putting emphasis on every word the way Ma used to do when I was in trouble.

Dandelion eyes Mikey and I coldly and sneers, "I know exactly what's going on. Well, it's not like you weren't warned about who to stay away from." She flips her hair as she turns her back on me.

"Dandelion, I-" I know how badly things must look, but my friends have to know what's really going on. And what's really going on is nothing.

"Oh, don't even bother to try and explain. We tried to help you to stay out of trouble around here and you didn't listen." Highway Child shakes her head and follows Dandelion.

Now I don't have any friends! And maybe worse, I don't have any jewelry for Em'rald! Well, I may as well just go back to Ma and Pa at the rate I'm screwing things up!

A kindly teacher tries to comfort me but all I want to do is run. And run is what I do: avoiding the beads I take off for the other side of the cafeteria and go straight out the door as an LAPD cruiser pulls up outside of another cafeteria door.

My espadrilles are definitely not made for running down Highland toward Hollywood, but I do the best I can because the only other option is to go barefoot and the sidewalks are disgusting. I run over several stars with the names of celebrities on them, the same stars that were so exciting for me to see when I arrived in L.A. Now, they don't disappear under my feet fast enough. I don't want to be anywhere but back in my room, don't want anyone to see me, and don't want to talk to anyone except for maybe Elsa, who is a wonderful and understanding woman.

The front door is locked as usual when I get home and I have to ring the bell. Just my luck Bunny Baby, who's in junior high and hasn't left for the day yet, answers.

"Carolina, what are you doing home again?" she demands.

I push by her and run up the stairs. At this time of the morning I know Elsa is busy in the kitchen cooking breakfast like she always does for us. Things will calm down once the younger girls are off to school and I'll be able to talk to her. But as I slam my door, I hear Bunny Baby yell to her in the kitchen that "Carolina is home and something is wrong." Then Bunny Baby is pounding up the stairs behind me in bare feet and almost beats me to my door before I have a chance to lock myself in.

"C'mon, Carolina, what happened at school?" she pleads through the cracked wood.

"I just want to be alone right now. I'll tell you after school, okay?" I croak.

"Okay. I'll knock the minute I get home."

I know she's not kidding. Bunny Baby may be young and wear bunny ears, but she's persistent.

Once I hear the floorboards outside my door creak in a certain pattern that I've grown used to, I know she's gone to finish getting ready for school. It's finally safe to cry. To drown out my whimpering, I put a Kiss cassette in the cheap player Elsa gave me and envision myself in Paul Stanley's strong arms. I sob until I can't sob anymore.

Having spent a lot of my life in South Carolina bawling, I know I have a limit to how many tears are actually inside of me and once I'm done, I'm really done because there are only so many to go around. By the time I finish Elsa is tapping on the door and talking in a calm caring voice to me.

"Can we talk, honey?"

Elsa never had any children of her own. She's told us girls several times that she never found the right man. Her failure is our gain; she's the nicest adult I've ever met. I'm not at all reluctant to open the door to her. Having an elder to really talk to is new to me and even after a year the newness hasn't worn off.

I pour my whole story out to her. Well, at least the parts I can tell her. Elsa doesn't know the full extent of what Bunny Baby and I, and a few other girls living in the house, do when we leave the premises at night. I guess that proves I'm a liar, but I prefer to think of it as withholding information to protect the innocent. And to keep Elsa from giving us a curfew and ruining all of our fun.

"I don't want to go back to school, Elsa. Not ever. I don't want to see Cherry Red or Dandelion or Highway Child ever again." I'm sobbing again, finding another river of tears inside of me.

"Carolina, I was a little unsure of those girls when they showed up here anyway. And if Cherry Red is anything like them, you're probably better off without them."

I nod and listen intently to the options she lays down: I could change schools or maybe it would be better to just take a day or two off to get my bearings and go back and start again.

"With your head held high. You didn't do anything wrong and none of these girls have the right to tell you who you can talk to and who you can't."

Her words sink in. And I like them. I may be only fifteen, but like Bunny Baby, I'm not one to give up easily. If I did I would've never stolen enough money from Ma and Pa to catch the Greyhound to L.A. from Columbia, South Carolina. I would've never known to take a little at a time over the course of a year so they didn't notice. Elsa's pep talk makes me understand that not only must I stop those girls from bossing me around, I can't let them make me give up on my jewelry or give up on Em'rald either, no matter how bleak things looked after seeing my beads tripping up school personnel. One thing I do need right now, however, is time.

"Elsa, I don't want to change schools. But I think I need longer than a couple of days to recover."

"I'll tell you what then. How about I call the school and have your teachers collect the work you miss? Then one of the other girls can bring it home for you."

Elsa makes the best deals, whereas most other adults I've met just want to talk you out of what you want and into what they want.

I nod and sigh. "That sounds good, Elsa." I want so badly to call her "mom," but I'm terrified of being rejected.

Elsa kisses my forehead and tells me, "I have to get to the laundry. How about lunch at noon in the kitchen? I'll get a pizza for us."

Pizza is a luxury around Elsa's House. It costs a lot more to feed ten hungry girls with a party sized pizza than it does to create something interesting from government food, which Elsa is an expert at.

"Okay, and thank you," I agree.

Then I remember that I have to somehow get more beads.

Elsa furrows her brow. "I'm sorry, but I think it's going to have to wait until next month."

I nod solemnly. "I understand." My voice is weak.

And I do understand.

But as it turns out, I don't need to wait until November to start Carolina's Creations again.

"Some cute guy named Mikey Morris is here to see you!" Bunny Baby announces through my door the next day. Her voice is muffled because she's so close to the wood.

I toss my covers over my head and pretend that I don't hear. Mikey Morris has already caused me too much grief. I can't see go him, though his image is flitting around in my imagination.

"Carolina, did you hear me? Mikey Morris-"

"Go away, I'm trying to sleep!" I cry.

The hall goes silent. I fling the sheets and blankets off my head now and strain to hear what might be going on one floor below, but all I can make out is the slamming of the door. I jump out of bed, half tripping myself on a sheet tangled around my foot and catch Mikey, in snug ripped jeans and leather biker jacket, get in a loud car with an eagle on the hood and leave some rubber on the street in front of the house. When I open my door later to go to dinner, a plastic case full of several different beads has been left at my threshold.

I'm sorry, Carolina. I hope these beads help a little bit. Love, Mikey, reads a little note that has obviously been opened and refolded several times since he arrived.

The beads help. But it's the *Love, Mikey* that I can't quite stop thinking about even as I start stringing my magic again.

Mikey comes back and leaves something every few days. But he isn't the only person who comes looking for me.

"Those girls are here again and they're demanding that you come back to school if you aren't going to come to the door," Bunny Baby reports.

I've started to face her again when she comes with news. It only makes sense, since the whole world seems to be concerned about Carolina Clampett all the sudden and Bunny Baby has to run up and down the stairs an awful lot to keep me up to date.

"Oh, they'll see me again soon enough," I say casually, but inside I'm distraught just like the first time "those girls" were trying to get my attention.

"Well, I told them they owe you a really big apology because this is all Mikey Morris's fault!" Bunny Baby has a look of sheer determination on her face and her hands on her narrow hips. In spite of the fact that she's nothing more than a child with ears that light up, I'm comforted by her support. None of the other girls in the house are standing up for me, even the ones who go to Hollywood High and see my detractors every day.

"Thank you, Bunny Baby."

"So, you want me to tell them to go away?"

My feet want to hit the steps and tell them myself. But I nod and tell her that yes, she can tell them to go away.

Five minutes later, I hear some little objects causing the lone window in my room to tinkle.

"Carolina, we miss you and we're sorry. Come talk to us!" Dandelion calls. I see them down on the ground but the window is closed and is probably too dirty for them to see me. I see H.C. pick a small rock up from the sidewalk and toss it at the window. She has great aim, as if she has done this many other times. Something tells me she has.

I further contemplate going to talk to them, but the time is coming when I won't have any other choice. I decide to wait and have a little bit more peace until then.

Mikey continues to come and so do they. Dandelion and Highway Child pick up on the bead trick and start leaving me care packages with supplies and notes. Usually the notes echo their apologies but one comes through that reads, *The New York Gems are coming back to town to play the Stardust Ballroom. We have to get ready to conquer yet another club!* My cohorts have no idea that the Stardust regulars already know me as the "jewelry babe."

After two weeks of sleeping and thinking and beading, I have more earrings, necklaces, and bracelets to give to

Em'rald than I had before the Mikey Morris scene at Hollywood High. Maybe I even like the ones I have now better, because that has been my objective: to make something better come out of tragedy. Elsa told me to think like that.

It's almost time to go back out into the world with my chin up. I'm terrified that Mikey is going to keep pursuing me, that Cherry Red is going to beat me up, that hundreds of other students are going to be left with the vision of Principal Paulson and his assistant rolling to the cafeteria floor on the wings of my beads. But I make the decision to return on the Monday before the New York Gems hit the Stardust stage the following weekend. I can't let this opportunity get away. If worse comes to worse and I don't make amends with my friends, I'll bring Bunny Baby to the Stardust with me.

"You sure do get a lot of company. Now some fat guy in a cab is here."

It's the Sunday evening before I walk out the door of Elsa's to take on Hollywood High again. Bunny Baby, of course, is the bearer of this latest news.

I feel my eyebrows shoot up. "Marty is here?"

"Yeah, I think that's his name."

Whatever would Marty be doing here? I pad down the stairs and Bunny Baby opens the front door for me, showing me out with a sweep of her hand like I'm some form of royalty.

Marty is there on the sidewalk, his large, sagging body wearing clothes that are even larger and saggier than his bulk. Dandelion and Highway Child make a game out of being rude and mean to Marty, but he's always so nice to me. I like to see the good in people; that's one positive thing my parents taught me even if they could never see the good in me. Out there on the short, broken sidewalk in front of Elsa's house I notice that Marty has a handsome face. Some people might say, *he would be so good-looking if…* but I don't do that. I choose to just pick out that one quality that stands out and enjoy it for what it is. Then I find another one when Marty turns toward me, his hands shoved deep in his pockets: his eyes. He has very caring eyes, even if he gives me the once-and-twice over whenever I see him.

"H-hi, Miss Carolina." These few words sound so painful for him.

I extend my hands out to him to make him feel welcome and thank him for coming.

"What brings you here? This is a very nice surprise, honey," I assure him.

"Yeah, uh, I guess I shouldn't be here but I was real worried about yous. The other two girls were talkin' about some Cherry girl wanting to beat yous up for stealing her guy and I just thought, that doesn't sound like the Miss Carolina I know!"

I'm inclined to give Marty a friendly hug. He sighs deeply and pats my back with one clumsy hand. He has more body heat coming off of him than most of the rock stars I've met when they've just finished a two hour concert and are ready to chase around an underage Southern girl. I feel a bit soggy when I let him go.

"There's nothing wrong with you coming here and you're right; that doesn't sound like the Carolina you know because it isn't. I didn't steal anyone's guy."

He takes off his Dodger's cap, which he wears constantly, and fans his face. "So I was right."

"Marty, is that what Dandelion and Highway Child are saying about me?" I shouldn't ask because I'm probably better off not knowing, but I have to know. I can't stop myself from finding out the truth.

"Aww Miss Carolina, it doesn't matter what them girls are saying about yous. Yous is the nicest one and yous make them better people because of it. I love them two girls but they got a lot of problems and even more now that Miss Tulip is out and about again." Marty shakes his head and kicks a small chunk of loose pavement around the sidewalk.

Dandelion and Highway Child have told me about their little competition with Dandelion's mother. Fortunately, since I came along, Tulip hasn't spent much time on the scene because her husband is so depressed with his lagging career. But I met her several times at Holly Woods when I was pushing my jewelry at Derek Dagger's concerts and she was always cordial to me. Frankly, I'm not interested in any more enemies.

"You're saying some awfully nice things about me, Marty," I say with a blush.

"That's 'cos yous is an awfully nice girl. I'm glad yous is okay." Marty shuffles around and makes like he's ready to leave.

"I'm going back to school tomorrow, Marty, so I'll see Dandelion and Highway Child. I'll decide if they're worth being friends with anymore. It's my decision, not theirs." My voice quickens at the end because I want to be sure he knows that I'm the boss in this matter.

"Well, I sure hope that I'll see yous again going out on the town. But if I don't…" Marty takes a messy piece of paper out of his pocket and hands it to me, his fingers shaking. "Call me if yous need anything at all, okay? I still want to be friends with yous even if yous decide yous don't like those girls anymore, okay?" Marty is pushing for understanding a lot like I was a minute ago.

I take the paper and close it firmly in my palm. "I will, Marty."

It's then that I remember how he always looked pained when H.C. picked on him but took it a lot easier when Dandelion did. If I'm ever going to get an answer to that mystery the time is now. But I see how he's had his say and is moving about as fast as he can toward the cab. I let him go. We all have our own problems to worry about without nosing into the issues of others. And do I ever have a nerve-wracking entrance to make tomorrow!

No more going into school early for Carolina Clampett; the creation of Carolina's specialties now takes place strictly behind closed doors. That's another decision I make: never will what I love be taken advantage of by anyone again. I dress how I want to dress in my short, flouncy dresses and sandals and will not be talked back into hair metal garb by anyone, even if the stuff I have is kind of my style. Within moments of my arrival in the cafeteria at Hollywood High students start coming up to me and introducing themselves. At first I'm nervous, thinking I've made a whole school full of enemies. But when a girl from my English class gushes,

"That's so cool what you did to Paulson and Grey! You're my hero!" I know that just the opposite is true: Carolina Clampett is a legend for something she didn't even do! And she's panicking that the administrators think she did it on purpose! Oh, I must get to the office and talk to Principal Paulson!

"Hey sweetheart! Welcome back!" Mikey Morris appears out of thin air and pulls me into a warm embrace, smiling at me with even teeth that contrast so nicely with his tanned skin. No matter how hard I try, I can't stop myself from being just a little bit excited about being so close to him. Okay, I admit it, I'm more than a little excited. His older boy body is firm and lean and his scent is a pleasing mix of brand new leather and some cologne that he has applied just right, not too strong like the jock boys trying to hide their body odor.

I may allow myself the pleasure of letting the closeness of this boy who has caused me so many problems to fill my senses, but I don't allow him to know what I'm feeling. "Hello Mikey, and thank you for the beads." With determination, I keep my feet moving so he knows that I'm not so easily pulled in. Two weeks ago my disinterest didn't work, so why would I think it would work now?

"Hey, no problem, beautiful. Where ya headed? Want some company?"

"Oh no, not right now. I have to talk to the principal."

Mikey's smile disappears. "Well, I'm definitely not going there with you."

"Okay, then. Good-bye!" My footsteps are so small I must look like a bumbling mess.

"See you at lunch?" he asks, unsure of himself.

"Maybe!"

I peer down the hall in front of me, wondering if Cherry Red is lurking in a corner, ready to shove me into a locker. The coast looks pretty clear so I continue to the office.

"Oh my god, Carolina! Do we have news for you!" I'm almost to the office when Dandelion and Highway Child come clomping down a side hall acting like we just saw each other an hour ago and like nothing ever went wrong between us. No "welcome back" or anything like that.

Dandelion continues breathlessly, "Cherry Red's mother left her rich father and Cherry Red moved to Las Vegas with her just this past weekend! Can you believe it?"

"So now we don't have to worry about that bitch causing any more problems for us! The Hall Pass Honeys are no more. Now all we have to do is get rid of the band guys and we'll be happier than ever," Highway Child concludes.

My feet won't move now. I'm stuck to the ground as they keep chattering about other Hollywood High gossip but mostly about Hall Pass and Cherry Red. Gosh, I guess a little part of me was hoping that if Cherry Red is really gone, maybe it would be okay for me to be nice to Mikey. I mean, what's the problem if she's not around? But I can see that this is only wishful thinking. They still hate the Hall Pass boys.

"Oh, that's great!" Here I go trying to sound excited to please them again. What's wrong with me? "I have to talk to the principal."

I notice how quickly four hands end up on four hips and a whole lot of attitude gets thrown around. Two noses go in the air too and Dandelion flips her hair.

"Hmph, that's all you have to say to your best friends in the whole world on your first day back at school? And after we send you beads because we love you even though you won't come out to talk to us?" Dandelion snorts.

"And you send that little weirdo with the bunny ears out to collect the beads instead?" Highway Child adds.

I can't stop the onrush of guilt that seizes me and gives me an uncomfortable feeling in my chest, nor can I stop the apologies from gushing out of my mouth. My plan to see Principal Paulson is handily abandoned by these sisters of mine who need my attention more than he does.

"Thank you for sending the beads. I have lots of things to give to Em'rald now when we go to the Stardust this weekend." The spurt of words come out shaky and accompanied by hand-wringing.

My head isn't so high anymore. Having sisters sure is harder than I thought it was going to be. Maybe I don't even want to meet Elly May now. No telling what kind of demands she'll make on me!

"Well, we were worried about you," is all Dandelion will admit to before she says, "We're going to the cafeteria."

And Carolina Clampett dutifully follows them, three steps behind.

Ma and Pa are right. I'm stupid and worthless. But someday things will be different. Silently I make this vow to myself as I rush headlong back into sisterhood: *things will be different.*

Things at school are so calm that I feel like I've never left. I slide right back into classes, slink right back into my groupie trio, and am tossed back into social situations I wanted to stay out of. Just to be back in English class and learning new vocabulary and reading new books and writing new papers is worth all of it though, because I can feel myself getting smart. Then I go home and hover over my creations until one of the girls in the house tells me that Dandelion and Highway Child are on the phone wanting to go shopping or to Mother Sandy's.

The end of the week comes quickly and I'm feeling good about going to the Stardust on Saturday night to see Em'rald and her band. The only glitch in the plan is that Mikey Morris keeps coming around and doesn't care one bit that he gets the double stink-eye from Dandelion and Highway Child. I'm more caught than ever between wanting to please them and liking Mikey's company. He's sweet, generous, and concerned about my welfare. Something tells me that I'm his only friend too. He has stopped hanging around with the other Hall Pass boys.

"Something is going on and I want to know what it is," Highway Child sniffs as soon as he walks away from me Friday morning at breakfast.

I pretend to be looking at the box of assorted black and neon beads he's just presented me with, but I'm really peeking up through my bangs to watch him depart. Mikey doesn't seem to be as confident as he usually is; his steps seem to be tentative and his swagger is not so swaggering in spite of the denim and leather.

"He hasn't told you anything about Hall Pass?" Dandelion inquires, kind of like she thinks I know something that I really don't, like I'm keeping something from them.

"No, nothing. He just asks about me," I say, miffed.

"Well, don't be too flattered by that. He's got pretty girls everywhere who want him," Dandelion warns, shaking her index finger at me.

I *have* seen Mikey in the halls with other girls but they look like friends. And when he sees me he moves away from them and turns his attention to me.

No use telling them that I don't feel threatened, since I couldn't possibly be his girlfriend anyway. I let the conversation drop and it ends, at least until lunchtime.

"More big news! Hall Pass is done with Mikey! They threw him out and are looking for a new lead singer!" Dandelion announces in a way that bothers me because it sure does sound like she's happy about someone else's bad luck. In a more private tone she murmurs, "No one seems to know what happened between them but it must've been a doozie because they were all best friends when I was hanging around with them."

"Maybe Carolina can find out," Highway Child chimes in, with a lift of her eyebrows.

"Oh, no. That's none of my business." Decisively, I shake my head.

"Come on, you can do it!" H.C, urges.

"He'll probably tell her anyway," Dandelion says.

I feel invisible, like they're talking about me and I'm not there. Four days of calm and now this. Elsa may have had a good suggestion when she asked if I wanted to change schools. But at the very least I have to get to that concert at the Stardust tomorrow.

I don't see Mikey for the rest of the day and it's better off that way, even though not laying eyes on him for the whole weekend doesn't sound so great.

Stupid me, I think I'm falling in love with Mikey Morris. Things can't get much worse for me than that.

Like all the clubs we go to, the Stardust Ballroom is really a dive but it's so famous that it doesn't matter. A line of big-haired fans twists around the hulking disaster on the corner of Sunset and Western, because the word is officially out on the New York Gems: they are not only the prettiest but also the hottest hair metal act on the scene, and they're going places.

Inside, three quarters of the audience is half-naked girls, but Em'rald has a growing legion of male groupies vying for her attention. Mr. Shark is lording over the whole scene and I keep my eye on him because he will be getting a bag of jewelry for Em'rald at the first convenient opportunity.

"I don't get it why you have to give it to him and not just hand it off to her majesty herself," Highway Child says, her voice tinged with jealousy.

"And don't call him Mr. Shark. It sounds so stupid," Dandelion instructs.

Before I can defend myself, they start acting catty because they see Tulip Dagger chatting up Shark Gant. *Shark Gant.* I'm practicing it. No Mr. Shark. But can I call him Mr. Gant or is that stupid too?

"I see your daddy let her out of her holding pen tonight," Highway Child jokes.

"Huh. Daddy knows what's going on with us, but he's so depressed that he doesn't even care anymore. He's at Joshua

Tree this week with his band so she has time to play."

Last thing I knew Derek Dagger was still in the dark about Dandelion's groupie stardom. Though truthfully, I don't understand how he couldn't know. Because I'm supposed to be stupid but I know lots of things I'm not supposed to know. It's not like rumors don't fly around here. We already have a "reputation" for showing rock stars a good time.

Oh, how did I let myself become a part of this?

"What a weekend for him to be gone," Highway Child moans.

That's because my two sister want very badly to conquer the three beautiful boys of the Gems even if I'm thinking about conquering the beautiful girl in a much more civilized way.

"Hey, there's our three favorite girls. Big party at Smut Central after the show. We're gonna ask the Gems if they might want to drop by for the fun." Diesel, Bullshit, and Geronimo surround us, and as is so often the case, Diesel is the spokesperson. And yes, the drummer of Smut has changed his name again. He says he wants to be known as the drummer who always has a new name, but it sounds kind of silly to me and confusing too.

H.C. rolls her eyes. Dandelion flips her hair.

"Well, you let me know when they agree to show up at Smut Central and I'll be there too," Highway Child dares.

"Ya know what? Me, too," Dandelion decides.

"How about you, precious?" Geronimo does the token Smut move of tickling me under the chin.

"No thank you," I turn away quickly in refusal, though I know my friends have only agreed because they know the

New York Gems aren't going to Smut Central unless they have a really good reason, like getting paid lots of money to make an appearance.

No sooner do I feel like I'm on safer ground away from the unwanted pressure when someone smiles seductively and waves to me from across the crowded room. A few people milling about step in the way, but when they move again the gaunt, long-haired guy is still there. I lock eyes with Ricky Rude, the drummer of Hall Pass and one of the boys who reportedly kicked Mikey out of the band. Worse, he's Dandelion's ex-boyfriend. Now I'm forced to turn back to the Smut situation because acknowledging Ricky Rude is worse than bantering with Smut!

"We got a great band on the agenda," Bullshit mumbles with a drop of drool coming from one side of his mouth.

"Who would that be?" Highway Child is all ears now and Dandelion leans in for the info too.

"Us!" Diesel answers.

Dandelion and Highway Child think that we can't continue to ignore them completely just because they sound okay in Mother Sandy's back yard.

"We may have to pay them some groupie attention eventually because they're gonna be big," were Dandelion's words when they told me about Smut's alleged talent.

No amount of fame would make me sleep with these boys!

"Nothing like tooting your own horn," H.C. says sourly.

"Maybe you'll let me toot your horns instead?" Diesel is about to put his hands on her chest but H.C. pushes them away.

"Oh god, did you see who's here?" Dandelion cries suddenly, her face going blank.

"Who? Anyone good?" H.C. demands.

"Ricky Rude and the other two Hall Pass losers. And what do you know, they're looking right over here." Dandelion puts on a pose full of attitude as she glares over at Ricky and friends.

Maybe Ricky Rude is here to try and get Dandelion back. It's the best I can hope for.

"Ricky isn't looking at you. Carolina, are you messing with all these guys behind our backs?" H.C. accuses when Ricky clearly ignores Dandelion's eye contact.

"No! Absolutely not!" I feel tears flooding my eyes. Sisters sure can be mean and jealous. Maybe I don't want sisters after all! "I've never even talked to those other three boys!" I hate myself for my attempt to explain away Ricky's attention. The more I talk the guiltier I sound. I need to shut up.

My gaze wanders to the exit, but my hand wanders to my purse, bigger than the one I normally carry because my bag of jewels for Em'rald is in it. The bulge gives me the comfort I need to stop me from running out the door. If any other band was rocking the Stardust I'd go back to Elsa's and talk to her about changing schools immediately.

Our conflict is interrupted by the house lights going down and the stage lights coming up. The New York Gems, "back in L.A. after a tour of the east coast," are introduced. Pink and blue lights start flashing before Em'rald appears in the tiniest of gold dresses and highest of platform heels that pick up the colors. Highway Child can't close her mouth because she's so spellbound by the lead guitarist whose name

I know from rock magazines is Nikk Saffire. He plays a sapphire blue Gibson. Ricky and company are forgotten that easily. By me, too.

"You're drooling like Bullshit over Nikk Safffire!" Dandelion guffaws, pointing and laughing at H.C.

"Stick it, Daddy's little girl!" Highway Child is really upset even though I can tell Dandelion is only trying to rib her. "I'm not drooling. I'm just looking at him trying to get his attention. I mean, we aren't here to watch goldilocks strut around, are we? Bitch!"

They start pushing each other so Diesel and Bullshit have to pull them apart. A lot of joking ensues about how they love girl fights. And Highway Child still hasn't closed her mouth over Nikk Saffire.

The concert lasts for two hours. Then, the Gems, who are, according to Dandelion and Highway Child, "stuck up" and "too good for their fans," actually put down their instruments and walk right down into the crowd to take pictures with anyone that wants one and to shake hands. My girlfriends are in the middle of the action with smiles plastered on their faces. They try to drag me along but I have my own agenda and a troublesome one at that.

Shark Gant is sticking close to Em'rald as she is bombarded with photo requests. I need to get my bag to him, but by getting near him, I'm getting near her and the thought cripples me. I'm not nearly ready to come face to face with such greatness. Lucky for me Shark gets distracted by the Gems bassist, a bleach blond name Danny Diamond who looks like he belongs on a surf board. I quickly pull my sack out of my purse and rush over to them.

"Mr. Gant-"

"Hey, darling, you got love in that bag for me?" As Danny Diamond slurs the words, a prevailing smell of alcohol washes over me.

"Your name Mr. Gant?" The giant manager guy narrows his eyes at the bassist before he turns back to me and in a much nicer tone says, "What can I do for you, love? You want a picture with one of the band members?"

Oh, he seems so kind!

"Um, no, Mr. Gant. I was just wondering if you could give this jewelry to Em'rald." I offer the bag to him, ready to make my escape.

"I knew I remembered you from somewhere. You're the girl who was supposed to give me something for Em'rald last time we were in town, weren't you?"

He remembers me! Oh, I was hoping he wouldn't.

"I'm sorry! I had to go and couldn't find you!" I'm talking fast and stumbling over my words.

"I'll tell you what, honey, why don't you give Em'rald the stuff yourself? I'll bring you over." He puts his bear paw on my narrow wrist. His touch is surprisingly gentle.

"Oh, no, I can't do that! Please just give it to her!" I shove the bag into his chest and turn to run away. But I smack right into Diesel.

"Hello, gorgeous! Nice to see you up close and personal!"

"I have to go, sorry!"

Diesel won't let go of one of my arms, so I pull him with me. When I look back over my shoulder at Mr. Gant, he has the bag and is looking at me strangely and shaking his head.

Then he hands it off to some other guy. Pretty soon my stuff is all over the side of the stage and he's going through it like he's looking for illegal drugs or a mini bomb. Oh gosh, maybe he is! Maybe that's what Mr. Gant thinks because I acted so strangely! I need to go back and explain myself!

I start to pull Diesel back toward Mr. Gant, but he says, "Oh no you don't! We boys have to talk to you girls about something!" He leads me along until we find Dandelion and Highway Child, who are with Bullshit and Geronimo.

"So, did you tell them the good news?" Diesel asks with a snicker.

"No man, we were waiting for you," Geronimo gurgles.

"All right, spit it out, because we want some rock star sex and we definitely aren't getting it here," Highway Child huffs, tapping her foot on the floor, another move that both of my friends have perfected.

From the attitudes they display I can tell they didn't have much luck with Nikk Saffire, Danny Diamond, and the drummer Jack Ruby who are still chatting with fans.

"Well, maybe you have another chance because guess who's coming to Smut Central?" Diesel is giggling like the girls at Elsa's now. I don't know how he does it but he reminds me of Bunny Baby.

Dandelion rolls her head. "Sure," she sniffs.

"No, really. Just talked to the fashion model herself and told her she had to see our band, so she's rounding up the boys. And by the way, my instincts tell me that her and Nikk Saffire are swapping spit and other bodily fluids on a regular basis."

Highway Child explodes so hard that I'm ready to see lava flowing out of her head.

"That's a lie. They aren't even anywhere near each other! And what kind of instincts do you have anyway, Diesel, other than finding friends that drool?"

"Funny!" Bullshit can't get enough of this comment.

"And you know what else, your mama is hot to trot and can't wait to get to Smut Central and see the boys tear it down. The woman has taste." Geronimo pokes Dandelion in the shoulder even as his eyes roll around in his head from being so high on whatever his bad habit of choice is tonight.

Dandelion pulls back. "Mama is going to your party?"

Highway Child is so stunned that her lava flow halts. They eye each other and a decision is made within seconds.

"I guess it wouldn't hurt," H.C. says casually, like she hasn't been turning them down for months.

"I'd like to go home," I speak up.

"Why, so you can meet up with Ricky Rude?" Dandelion accuses.

"No, because-"

"Because you're gonna meet up with Mikey Morris," Highway Child finishes for me.

Again, I cower.

"When are we leaving?"

Diesel rubs his hands together gleefully. "I'll go get the truck."

I just know this is going to be the worst night of my life.

"What the hell are we doing?" Highway Child wails, holding her arms over her head as we fly up the 101 Freeway in the back of the Smut Mobile, which is a pick-up of several different colors with the band insignia spray-painted on the side.

"Something tells me that Em'rald isn't getting here in the back of a pick-up truck," Dandelion gripes, glowering at H.C.

Marty's cab is following the truck a few cars behind. Tulip Dagger is in the back with Diesel doing I don't want to know what.

"Oh please, you don't really think they're gonna show up, do you? And didn't you get us into this because you want to stay one step ahead of your mama?" H.C. nags.

I'm hugging my legs and trying to keep my dress from flying up as they have yet another tiff.

"Well, I didn't exactly hear you protesting." Dandelion puts on her best buttery voice as she mocks H.C.'s earlier "It wouldn't hurt" line.

Their conflict makes the time go by faster and takes my mind off the fact that L.A. is cold at night in October. Geronimo is driving too fast and is changing lanes frequently. What a terrible end this would be. Ma and Pa shaking their heads as they identify my bloody corpse, and saying, *You should have gone to church more often, you terrible girl!*

The truck roars up the 405 Freeway and exits in Van Nuys. We barrel down a well-lit street filled with girlie clubs under flashy signs and ugly, boxy concrete buildings. A few quick turns and we're pulling into the short driveway of a squat house with a rusted fence around the yard. The grass is dried out and looks like it hasn't been trimmed all year. Cars are everywhere and every light seems to be lit, including several flood lights in the small square of a backyard that's crammed with people who either look just like the members of Smut or are girls who are way too pretty for them. A young blonde is yelling at an older couple in the next yard as Geronimo and Bullshit lead us back. The couple is pleading for someone to turn down the metal music screaming from a stereo with four large speakers blaring at can't-think-straight volume.

"Evening, Mr. and Mrs. Katz. Wanna join the festivities?" Bullshit hollers, giving them a mock-friendly wave.

The couple is soon slamming the door

"Beer over here, girls," Geronimo calls as he grabs three cans of warm Budweiser and tosses them to us. Mine falls at my feet and I pick it up out of courtesy, not because I plan to drink it. Beer disgusts me and makes me throw up. Kind of like Smut.

We're all uncomfortable with the rough party crowd and sit down on a tipsy bench that the boys must drag out for big events.

"How do we get back to Hollywood?" H.C. wonders aloud.

"Well, I guess we're just gonna have to ride with Mama in the cab," Dandelion answers.

"Is now too early to get out of here?"

"Maybe Nikk Saffire will show up and then you'll be happy."

"You just had to say that, didn't you?" H.C. stands up and straightens her short cut-out dress. The bench almost throws Dandelion and me off because the ground is uneven. It's almost like being on a see-saw in a children's park.

"We'd better keep our eye on her." Dandelion moves closer to me as H.C. struts over to a food table that doesn't have anything on it worth eating. In fact, just looking at it turns my stomach.

Junk food and half-rancid sandwich meat and cheese are on paper plates. Someone is obviously a real party planner around here. I see a few of Smut's friends pick things up, inspect them, and put them back down. One big guy dressed head to toe in leather even takes a chunk out of a piece of roast beef then puts the other half back on the plate. That gets H.C. back to the bench.

"Did you see that?" She's curling her lip and holding her belly.

"Oh, sit down, will you? We need you to balance this thing out before we flip over," Dandelion screeches. I can feel her shivering because her leg is pressed up against mine.

"We'd better go," I suggest, and the three of us conspire about how to make our getaway. I look forward to moments like these, when we act like real comrades and I'm included in the decision-making process. If we had more pow-wows like this I would feel so much better about our trio and maybe even being a groupie wouldn't be all that bad.

But our escape plan gets grounded when Tulip shows up on the arm of Diesel. They both look drunk and disheveled. Dandelion and Highway Child are stopped in their tracks as Tulip and Diesel are treated like King and Queen Smut. I'm not so impressed but my friends feel differently.

"Your mama is taking over our show." I think that Highway Child says this only to get Dandelion going.

"She can't take over our show. We can't allow that." Dandelion's voice is flat, emotionless.

The music on the stereo stops abruptly and three horrible

men push people aside to pull a tarp off of a drum riser and guitar amps set up on a small patio made of pock-marked concrete. Diesel brings Tulip over to the stage while a microphone is dragged out of the house and plugged in.

"Welcome to Smut Central, all you Smutheads out there. It's time to rock and roll!"

And that's all it takes for the three losers to turn into hard-driving musicians. Of the one hundred or so people already in the yard, every head seems to be catching the beat of the barn-burner Smut is crunching into. In spite of my desire to refrain from being one of them, the head of Carolina Clampett is moving too, even as I swear out loud that I'm not a Smuthead.

Tulip Dagger, in a zippered black leather dress and knee boots, is up on a storage crate lettered with the words "Smut Stuff" and is gyrating to the music, enraging Dandelion and H.C. I think she's beautiful and I admire her ability to be the only one up there with Smut even if it is only Smut. I know all about her notoriety and hating her is just another thing I can't do for my friends. In spite of my earlier feelings about coming here, I'm getting happily dizzy from the cool night air carrying Smut's energy into L.A. metal history on the hips of Tulip Dagger.

I try to stop myself from enjoying Smut, but I can't. The more Smut plays, the more I admire their transformation. They're harder and dirtier than our hair metal guys but they're beautiful animals just the same when the power of their music takes over. More people are filling the yard and now the party is practically the size of a concert at one of the clubs on Sunset.

"They're ten times better than they were last time we heard them," Dandelion admits.

"Well then, it's time to put them on the conquest list," Highway Child decides, even though we really don't have a formal list.

Their friends crush in and bombard the patio but Smut keeps hammering away.

I'm shivering now. Not because I'm cold, but because I'm getting won over, though maybe not the same way I was instantly pulled in by the New York Gems. It's a gradual, building interest coupled with an uneasy feeling. I'm full of doubt that I'm doing the right thing. I just know I'm not but it sure is hard not to catch Smut fever in the thick of it all.

"Hey gorgeous, looks like you haven't opened that beer yet. How about some wine?" A very handsome young man is beside me with a narrow bottle of sweet smelling liquid. I don't even realize I'm still clutching the can of Budweiser until he points it out.

"Well, I don't really drink," I protest as he tosses the can aside and closes my fingers around the cool bottle that smells so nice. "I'm much too young."

"Aww, a little vino won't hurt a bit. Looks like you need to loosen up some to really enjoy this experience." He sits down on the bench between Dandelion and me and greets her and Highway Child too. He certainly doesn't seem like a friend of Smut's; he's so well-spoken and nicely dressed.

I tip the bottle just a little and the wine warms up my mouth. Mmm. Delicious.

Two more helpings appear for my friends. We start giggling a lot.

Smut looks better and better with every sip.

In my grape-induced fog my eyes settle on a blonde near the patio, head and shoulders above mostly everyone else. It's Em'rald! And she's clearly appreciating Smut's performance as she stands with Shark Gant and the rest of her band. Oh, she's here! And she approves of Smut!

That's all the convincing I need.

"Yes, let's put them on the conquest list!" I exclaim.

"Carolina?" H.C. says suspiciously, but breaks into giggles.

I turn the wine bottle upside down and chugalug it until it's gone, meanwhile almost tipping our bench. We just barely stay upright.

I lose track of Carolina Clampett's affairs after that, but some pleasant thoughts are whirling through my head, the favorite one being that Em'rald has to be my sister too. Elly May, Em'rald. Ma and Pa had to like them better than me to name them with the same letter of the alphabet, but that's okay. Just knowing I have two beautiful blond sisters instead of one makes it okay.

The handsome wine guy's smiling face appears to be floating around without the rest of his body. He has a steady supply of drinks for all three of us. But that isn't all he has.

"Smut wants you three girls to play a game. Only twelve of their favorite girls get to play. Are you ready?"

"Oh, a game!" I gurgle, and then I'm upside down and staring at the ground while someone with dirty boots carries me across the dead grass, across the patio where Smut has ceased to play their instruments though I don't remember when they stopped, and into the rear door of the house. I'm lowered to the floor then helped up into a standing position, though holding myself upright is becoming more and more of a challenge with the ticking of the cheap clock on the wall.

The clock is the only thing on the wall and the floors are void of furniture.

"It's time for one o'clock, two o'clock!" Geronimo suddenly appears with his pants unzipped. "And you're gonna be six o'clock!"

This must be some kind of great honor so I sing, "Oh, thank you!"

A clock game! What could be better than that!

More girls are being brought into the room and they're stumbling and giggling too. The same three guys who pulled the cover off of Smut's instruments are putting us in a circle. So cute! Are we going to play something like Ring Around the Rosie? Or wait, Mother May I?

"Oh, can I please be the Rosie and everyone can make the ring around me?" I throw my arms around the neck of one of the big bruisers.

"Huh?" He looks at me in confusion, but then he must remember the rules of the game. "But don't you want to be six o'clock?" he asks.

Six o'clock! Of course, I want to be six o'clock!

My stomach isn't feeling so good now as Mr. Big tells me to bend all the way over and put my hands on the floor in front of me. What a terrible position to be in with wine in my belly! And then that awful man makes it worse by throwing my dress over my head so I can't see anything! But I peek up from underneath it and see that Dandelion, Highway Child, and the rest of the girls all have their hands on the floor in front of them too, and then the shouting starts: "Four o'clock!" "Eight o'clock!" "Eleven o'clock!" and the three members of Smut have their pants around their ankles and are running around behind our girl circle like silly little boys playing with their hot dogs.

Why don't they call six o'clock, why not six-

Em'rald is in the doorway. My sister is in the doorway. I meet her eyes. Smile, wave. She turns and disappears.

My stomach can't take any more of this bending over stuff. I hurl all over the floor in front of me just as I hear someone yell, "Six o'clock!"

But I'm disqualified! No fair!

My memory cuts off.

"Oh good, you're finally awake. Where the heck were you last night?"

My eyes flutter open and somehow I'm in my little bed in my little room at Elsa's house. The sun is filtering through the dirt on the window and Bunny Baby is bouncing on the edge of my mattress like a nosey, pesky younger sister.

"I-I-" I stutter, because I don't know what to say, don't remember a thing, don't even know how I got where I am right now. But a sudden recollection of twelve pretty girls standing with their butts up in the air in a room with a soiled beige rug rolls through my mind and the memory that I was one of them stops my vocal cords from functioning.

Bunny Baby moves in closer. "It's okay. You can tell me. I was the one that answered the door when Marty brought you home at four this morning so no one knows anything but me. I was waiting up for you. Did you party with the Gems? I'm so jealous!"

Her screechy speech makes me aware that I have an enormous pounding in my head that is sensitive to any kind of sound that normally wouldn't annoy me.

"Yes, the Gems," I lie.

Diesel, Bullshit, and Geronimo are laughing and running around in back of us, calling out times on a clock, just the top of the hour. And depending on the time, depending on what time the girl is on the "clock," that's who gets…oh, I don't even want to think of it!

I threw up and saved myself the embarrassment of being a part of this terrible game!

"Is Em'rald really beautiful close up?" Bunny Baby persists.

Em'rald. Em'rald saw me playing the sex game! My sister saw me! Oh, what could be worse!

"Yes, beautiful," I murmur.

"And the guys are sexy, right?"

That man with the muddy boots pulled my dress down to cover my butt and hauled me through the back door and out into the rabid crowd again. *You broke the rules of One o'clock, two o'clock, dumb bitch!*

"Oh, yes!" I shake my head, trying to clear it of the awful thoughts coming back to me.

"You'll have to tell me all about it once you feel better." Bunny Baby skips to my bedroom door, but before she leaves she turns and assures me, "Your secret is safe with me!"

One more thing. Only one more thing has to happen and I'm done with Dandelion and Highway Child and Holly-wood High, too. I'll run my own show and make new friends at a different school. I'll only do what I have to do in order to get the rock guys to wear my jewelry and maybe tell their friends about my work. But I'm not following those girls anymore. I love them in an odd way, but they make bad decisions. Their bad decisions become mine.

They don't even try to contact me that weekend. I hope they're all right. And I want to thank Marty for bringing me home safely. But it will have to wait.

Monday morning and Dandelion and Highway Child are as casual as can be, like nothing happened on Friday night of any significance. They're unemotional until Mikey Morris makes his usual attempts to talk to me at lunch time. They don't know that I've started to come in early again to talk to him. Just to talk to him. No jewelry-making in school.

"Doesn't he get it that we're on the wish list of every rocker on the Strip?" Highway Child brags.

Dandelion just yawns.

I haven't told them that Mikey is on my wish list.

Two more days go by quietly and I start to relax and for-get about Smut and their game.

Mikey is so sweet. I've started to let him hold my hand and he strokes my skin with his thumb as he smiles into my eyes. I allow this as long as no one is around, of course. He knows to either disappear or move away when any nosey people invade our space.

The teachers at Hollywood High are very kind to me too, and they understand my desire to learn and be smart. I forget about my decision to change things if anything else goes wrong. Because it's going to be all right. Really, everything is going to be fine.

And then it's Thursday.

The clock in the cafeteria tells me it's almost 7:00 a.m., which I call "Mikey time," because that's when he's been showing up. My stomach is in knots of desire, thinking about seeing him. My hand wants to be warm inside of his and feel that little stroke of his thumb. Maybe I'll ask him to take a walk with me so we can find some place to kiss. He's been so patient; I've been so reluctant. He's playing to win and I'm playing to let him. As much as Dandelion insists that he's not going anywhere, especially now that he's on the outs with the rest of Hall Pass, Mikey is convincing me that he is going somewhere and he wants me to go with him.

"Carolina, I'm auditioning with other bands and I just know I'm gonna find the right one and we're gonna go right to the top," he dreamed aloud yesterday when we had our half hour together.

"I know you'll find the right band," I'd said, my throat tight with jealousy. But my envy is my own fault. I've let things go for weeks and weeks already, letting my friends make decisions for me. I should've trusted my own gut feelings about Mikey from the first day I talked to him.

I'm running all this over in my mind for the hundredth time when I feel a presence behind me. Someone's hands slip over my eyes.

It's not Mikey. I know it's not Mikey. It's not anyone I know, though the stranger does smell like leather and something stale.

A mischievous chortle comes from the throat of the person in question and my fear factor rises. Oh, it couldn't be a member of Smut in my school! They've come to get me to play their disgusting game!

"Who are you?" I demand, tugging at bony wrists to get the person's hands off my eyes.

"Relax, cutie. It's only me!" Ricky Rude tosses himself down at the table next to me and flops his elbows behind him. "How you doing? I saw you at the Stardust the other night and I've been dying to talk to you. One of my buddies said you came in early. So, here I am!" He reaches out and pulls at the long, loose braid I've swept to one side of my face. I thought Mikey might like my hair like this.

Mikey. Where is Mikey?

Instinctively, I inch my rear end away from Ricky. But for every inch he takes a mile.

"Come on you cute little thing, I ain't gonna hurt ya! You want a ride home later? I got my own car now!" Ricky is sticking his face close to mine, running his finger down my nose, leering into my eyes. And his breath is not very nice.

"Oh, no, no ride home!" I say quickly.

Hurry Mikey, please!

"Aww, come on!" Ricky flings a gangly arm around me and rubs his clammy cheek against mine.

"Please..." Oh no, it sounds like I'm begging. Now he knows I'm scared. I'm still so stupid.

As Ricky crushes his face against mine, Mikey turns the corner into the cafeteria. Oh, déjà vu time! Mikey could be that awful girl Cherry Red catching Ricky with me! His reaction to seeing Ricky trying to kiss me is the same as hers was seeing her ex-boyfriend with me: rage!

"What the hell is going on here?" he demands, fists out and ready to pound into Ricky.

"Carolina and me were just getting to know each other a little bit. You got a problem with that?' Ricky is cocky, doing this shadow-boxing move as Mikey bulls forward, full force, both fists flying. Seconds later Ricky is flat out on his back on the cafeteria floor and has blood pouring out of his nostrils. Mikey is holding his right fist with his left hand and wincing.

"No, no, no, not again," I curse, as I stand up and head for the same hallway Mikey just came from. This time I'm not going out the front door and into the scattering of students that are starting to show up for the day. This time I'm disappearing from sight without anyone noticing and never stepping foot in this place again.

"Hey." Mikey catches my arm as I flutter by, but I pull away.

"No, I have to go. I have to get out of here," I try to explain.

I can't even hear my voice due to the cymbals crashing in my head. *Get out, get out, get out.*

The only person I want to talk to now is Elsa. I turn back only once to see Mikey, shoulders sagging in dejection, watching me run away.

I'm only out of school for another week before Elsa can have my records transferred to Fairfax High on Melrose Avenue. For a few days I feel like every student in my new school knows about Smut's degrading game and how I lost my six o'clock position before I could even play. They've heard all about me and how I've had sex with rock stars to try and make a name for myself as a rock and roll jeweler at the age of fifteen. And worst of all, they know how I followed Dandelion and Highway Child into a groupie lifestyle I didn't really want to be a part of. Carolina Clampett: weak, stupid, gullible. A doormat that reads: *Welcome. Please wipe your feet on me.*

Instead, I get a fresh start at Fairfax High. No one knows me other than a few faces I may have seen out on the Strip dressed in black and neon or in some club that we're all too young to be in. The girls are friendly, the boys are cute, and the teachers love my burning desire to learn.

"It's your time to thrive now, Carolina," Elsa tells me with a motherly smile when I express my gratitude to her for all she's done for me, all she's helped me to do.

"I hope so," I say doubtfully.

Because something is missing whether I want to admit it or not.

Bunny Baby stays out of the clubs with me for a while and we look at local magazines and papers with all of the up and coming rockers in them. When she turns fourteen at the beginning of 1984 and starts to get boobs, she's ripe for the rock star picking.

"I'm ready to go out chasing boys again whenever you are," she whispers to me after blowing out her candles on the cake Elsa bakes and decorates for her.

"I'm ready now," I whisper back, without hesitation.

She ditches her blinking ears and looks at least sixteen but keeps her rabbit moniker.

Bunny Baby and I go to the clubs and to Holly Woods and, keeping a good look out for Dandelion and Highway Child, we avoid them for months.

"Remember the signal if you see them," we remind each other before entering any door on Sunset.

I always bring my jewelry but the guys don't care about me unless I'm offering something besides what's in my little bags, and I'm not offering. These new boys coming up on the Strip now are so shallow, they won't even talk to me unless they get what they want. Mikey wasn't like that. I miss Mikey. But he doesn't come around and I can't risk being in the vicinity of Hollywood High to seek him out.

Bunny Baby and I see the Gems two more times before they're gone from L.A. to cut an album and tour the country. And even though I expect that my "sisters" will be throwing rocks at the window of my room at Elsa's, no one comes for me. I don't like the peace and quiet as much as I thought I would.

I miss Dandelion and Highway Child and crave the excitement they brought to my life, even if I used to think they led me in the wrong direction sometimes. And now that I have some real control over my affairs, I decide that I won't hide if I see them again. Stand right up to them is what Carolina Clampett will do, and will declare her equality and individuality!

I'm as ready for them as I'm ever going to be.

It's April 1984, and the nonstop action out on the streets of Los Angeles is stirring me up inside so much that I'm looking at every pair of teenagers with long dark hair hoping that it's *them*. Sometimes the people aren't even girls, but boys jumping on the glam metal bandwagon. As for whom I'm really looking for, they don't seem to be any-where that I am even though I suddenly want them to be.

Fate intervenes before we can come face to face in the Rainbow or the Roxy or Gazarri's.

I finally get a little bit of company.

"Someone is here to see you," Bunny Baby announces, just like she did when I was taking a break from Hollywood High and the whole world seemed to care about where I was and if I was all right. Now, seemingly, after all of these months I only matter to one person. But I can relate to that better. It's what I'm used to.

Bunny Baby shuts the door of Elsa's behind me as I step out onto the sidewalk. I know she's watching me through one of the side windows like she always does and maybe she's even gathered some of the other girls to watch and to try and listen to what I say.

"H-Hi, Miss Carolina. Sure is nice to see yous again. Me and the girls really miss yous."

Marty is as sweet and sincere as ever, his hands stuffed deep in his front pockets, Dodgers cap on, heavy feet shuffling on the pavement.

I never did thank him for bringing me home safely from the Smut party.

"I miss all of you too, Marty," I admit, my eyes misting over.

"They didn't send me, Miss Carolina. Honest, they didn't. I came here 'cuz Dandelion and Highway Child are havin' a hard time of it and they need yous to hold 'em together."

The concern in Marty's eyes is real.

"Marty, are they okay?" I panic.

"Dandelion's gonna leave us, Carolina. She's goin' to Europe on tour with her daddy and she might never come back! And nothin' Highway Child says to her will change her mind!" Marty shakes his head and scuffs the ground with his sneaker.

Oh no! My sister is leaving and could be lost forever!

I swallow hard and glance back at Elsa's door before I face Marty again.

"When is she leaving?" I ask coolly, evenly

"The day after tomorrow. We ain't got any time to waste!" Marty, sweating worse than usual, swipes at his forehead with his big arm.

The day after tomorrow!

My hands join together in front of me, but I catch myself before I can start wringing them. With all of my concentration, I will them to fall to my sides. I smooth my dress down calmly as two roads open up before me. The one to the right is the one I'm currently on: a straight road with fresh pavement and few road blocks. Bunny Baby waves from up ahead, beckoning me to stick with her. The one to the left is a bumpy, curving joy ride that promises roller coaster thrills and just happens to lead right to Marty's cab. Highway Child and Dandelion are on the edge of it with their thumbs out, looking wild and free.

"Oh Marty, we can't let her go!" I exclaim.

I grab his hand and drag him toward the cab.

That crazy road leads me right back to where I came from.

TULIP

I kept the secret of my disappointment, my shame, my shock locked inside of me for weeks. Derek didn't notice until he hit us with the news of his European tour. He saved the announcement and used it as a Christmas present for Dandelion and me.

"Guess what? Daddy has the best surprise ever for his two favorite girls," he sang after we had opened all of our presents that Christmas morning in 1983.

Dandelion and I shared a warm smile, something that didn't happen very often anymore, thinking that maybe Daddy was planning to cook for us, which always turned out badly but was likewise always a great memory to laugh about later.

"I'm ready for my pancakes, Daddy!" she'd teased him.

"Oh no, honey, it's better than pancakes!" Derek had a sneaky, crooked grin on his ripe lips, the same smirk that had won me over when I could've had any rock star on the planet, and did. When I'd had all of them, sometimes several in one night.

"Tell us!" I demanded happily, my heart leaping with joy, because it had to be great news. Hopefully it had something to do with money, because we were running up credit card bills at the speed of light. Yet we kept throwing parties for our friends so it would appear that everything was perfectly fine in our world.

"I've been offered a long tour of Europe and I've decided that we should move out of this hellhole and get a nice place in England or France. Chas Greenwood is giving us his house in the British countryside to live in while we're looking for something to buy and it's a damn mansion. We're actually doing him a favor moving in because-"

I lost him, remember nothing about why we were doing Chas Greenwood a favor.

Move out of L.A., my hometown. My beloved hometown. The only hometown I've ever known, in spite of the jet-setting lifestyle I've led since my teens. Move to the European countryside. Long tour of Europe. Not what I was hoping to hear. A jaunt through America and keeping our home in L.A. would've been much more to my taste. But there was that issue with Dandelion to deal with too. I couldn't just think of myself, had to be concerned for her too, after what I'd seen.

Dandelion looked like she'd just seen a ghost. And Derek is not a stupid man; he picked up on the hush that fell over both of us.

"Come on, don't you think it's time to start fresh as a family? Aren't you happy that I have a new gig that's gonna put me back on the blues map? I get to cut a new album while we're there, too," he said, futility entering his tone.

Dandelion sucked a hearty gust of air through her pretty nose, and bravely said, "Daddy, that's so great. I'm very happy for you." And she stood and ran to him and threw her arms around him, even as I sat stiff as a mannequin and collected the daggers shot at me from over her shoulder by Derek Dagger.

"What the hell, Tulip? What the hell?" he raged that night in our bedroom, after a silent Christmas day between us.

"I have to tell you something," I moaned.

"Well, get talking. Because I haven't been able to figure you out for weeks, and now this. What is going on with you, woman? Are you leaving me for one of those young creeps messing up my career?"

Derek hated the hair metal scene from the beginning and now that he knew Dandelion was firmly ensconced in it, now that so many of his friends told him the stories of what she and her two partners pulled all up and down Sunset week after week, his loathing had increased. So did his finger-pointing in my direction. But he let her go. He let her do it, pretended that she was still pulling the wool over our eyes with her lies about where she was going, what she was doing, and with whom she was doing it. I'll admit, she had us believing those three friends of hers from Hollywood High really were church girls, at least for a while. But that crumbled away pretty quickly and left us the parents of a world-class liar.

"It's the only way to bring her back. Let her get it out of her system and she'll see it's not what she wants," was her father's theory.

But not mine. Back in my heyday, the more I got, the more I wanted. And with the scene constantly changing in the 60s and 70s, there was always something and someone new to want. The 80s glam scene initially intrigued me and I had some beginner's luck with the hair bands when I was sneaking my updated fashions past the prying eyes of my hubby and daughter, but the extreme narcissism the musicians started to display when the look and the sound started to take off hardly impressed me. Even the punks, whom I found vile, were more down to earth than these lipsticked screamers.

I moved toward Derek, wanting his affection while I told him my worrisome story, but he raised his hands in front of him to ward me off, shaking his head.

"Just tell me what's been eating at you so badly that you can't even be happy about starting a new chapter in our lives that's going to put me back on the radar screen."

And so, I sank down on the edge of our bed and, as tiny guitars were thrown all over the room from cut-outs in the shade on the lamp on the bedside table, I told him what I had seen at the Smut party. The scene that wouldn't leave my mind, even as a career groupie. That *game* I had seen my daughter and her friends play with the guys in the band.

"One o'clock, two o'clock? Do I want to know the details of this game?" Derek was balling and unballing his fists by now.

I told him the details as he shook his head and stared at me in disbelief.

"I'll kill 'em, Tulip. Just tell me where I can find 'em." He was calm, collected. Because Derek rarely lost control over anything.

"But Derek...she liked it. That's the worst part. The whole thing hardly phased her," I admitted dramatically.

That's when the finger-pointing started.

"How many times did we talk about this? And now it's happening. Our kid has turned out like you instead of me."

He may as well have socked me in the mouth, because that's what those words felt like.

"Derek-"

"And what exactly were you doing at that party? And where was I?"

"You were at Joshua Tree, so I figured I'd go and check up on her and-"

Of course I could never tell him what happened in the back seat of Marty's cab with Diesel, the lead singer. But at least what we did was private and was what most red-blooded rock stars and groupies do in the back seats of cabs and limos and other vehicles. Not like that game. That game with so many people watching and cheering on those dirty boys.

"And I guess you just happened to get invited to the same party she did?"

When I started trying to explain again Derek cupped his hands over his ears and talked over me.

"Don't even say anything else, Tulip. I warned you."

Derek stayed there with his hands over his ears until he was ready to move on to the next page of our discussion, which was more like the end of the book.

"I'm tired now. We'll talk about this again after I think more about it."

I agreed in a whisper.

Though I hoped that dropping my secret would afford me some relief, that was hardly the case.

We didn't talk about it for weeks.

The beginning of Derek's tour of Europe was April 15, 1984 and the days and hours were flying by without an answer. I didn't know if we were coming or going. But every time I tried to discuss it with him, his hand would go up, that shapely hand that could play a woman every bit as amazingly as it could play a guitar.

"I'll let you know when I have a solution. You don't have to ask me again," he said, after my third feeble attempt to broach the subject.

Meanwhile, the Strip got wilder every day with new hair band boys and the girls that loved them heating up the streets to boiling and I didn't understand or want to be a part of any of it. I wanted to have my circle of friends who idolized Derek, who had lived the rock and roll glory we had and hoped we'd live again when this unexplainable trend ended. Instead, I had to watch as my husband and daughter came together again and left me out of it. Dandelion was always a daddy's girl. Derek was winning her over again. She started to stay home more and was even picking up a guitar and taking lessons with him. Her grades at Hollywood High went up that semester. The phone rang constantly in her room and those terrible friends of hers, particularly the highway waif, must have been pulling their long hair out. I was on the outside of it all looking in, jealous on the one hand but on the other happy that I didn't have to watch my own daughter moving to the head of the groupie class of her generation.

Only after wooing her back to his hip bone did Derek come up with his "solution" to the problem.

His face was vibrant and full of color for his only daughter as he spoke to me and raved about the renewal of his faith in fatherhood.

"I'm so proud of our girl, Tulip. She's really turning it around. And she and I have come to an agreement that will probably please everyone involved."

We were in the bedroom again and Derek was undressing for the day. He was still favoring the embroidered jacket made for him by Dandelion's dumb little Southern friend Carolina Clampett who, rumor had it, thought that Elly May Clampett was her sister. A fictional character! Well, she did have some talent even if she was brainless. He handled the jacket with kid gloves, laying it carefully on the back of a chair in the room where he could grab it just out of the shower the next morning.

"You made a decision without including me in it?" I demanded.

"Easy does it. I'm pretty sure you're going to like it." This time his palms were facing the floor, urging me to calm down.

My chest, perhaps my most famous asset, heaved up then settled again and I stared at him coldly, awaiting my fate.

"Tulip, let's be honest here. Dandelion will go right back to being a groupie if she's around you." Derek sat down on the bed with me and massaged my shoulders to take some of the sting out of his words. "And you two have built up a conflict between you over the past year that has turned into some crazy competition for her."

"Derek, the conflict started longer ago than that! It started before she was even a groupie," I spit, shaking my head in sorrow.

"So, even longer than a year. Even worse. And that makes our decision even better."

"Don't keep me in agony any longer!" I cried.

Derek nodded with more understanding than he'd given me in a long time.

Then, he dropped the bomb.

"Dandelion wants to come on tour with me and wants to be away from you for a while. So, how do you feel about staying here and holding down the fort?"

Holding down the fort. *Holding down the fort.* HOLDING DOWN THE-!

I tried to stay calm but my hands were shaking. And when the bomb exploded and tossed out vibrant shades of every color in the L.A. kaleidoscope, my eyes widened to take in the brightness as if I was watching fireworks. But my voice…my voice was even.

"Well, I suppose I could try it," I mumbled, attempting to sound unimpressed.

I could try it for sure. I could try penetrating the Sunset Boulevard scene once more without anyone in my way. One more shot at becoming the undisputed queen of hair metal. Showing my daughter who is boss. Three decades running and no one better than Tulip Dagger. What a pleasant thought.

And, it wouldn't hurt a thing to find out what our daughter

had really been up to – or had stooped down to might be more accurate. Whatever I discovered could be dutifully reported to her father and his conviction to keep her under control would be hardened.

"I thought you might say that," Derek said.

We didn't speak any more about it that cool February night. But I rewarded him in other ways for the pleasant fate he and my daughter had resigned me to.

They left yesterday, Derek and Dandelion, on a Boeing 747 bound for London, England. Marty drove and I, the mother in mourning, rode in the front seat with him while the slightly tarnished king of the blues and his stunning daughter rode in the back like they were in a limo. Which of course, we should have been.

Mother in mourning, my ass!

But I went through the motions, letting Derek entertain himself with the idea that I was really in grief, like I was a bad girl being punished somehow, and if I was really good then maybe he would "have me flown out" to Europe to join them. Poor Derek, the last several months have been very hard on his psyche, so hard it seems that he has forgotten that Tulip Dagger has seen the world on the arms of the most famous rockers of all and that at this point being "flown out" anywhere is rather passé.

I wake up to a lovely empty bed in a lovely empty house and my first thought is: time to work on that damn wardrobe. Eyeing my closet from the leather bed, I'm rather appalled that I have to shop before I can correctly hit the town. Any up-to-the-minute fashions that I'd smuggled into the house, including those neon pink shoes that I know damn well Dandelion stole, had to be stashed away and anything hanging on my side of the long closet had to look like I was going to one of Derek's concerts. But that worry is irrelevant now and I relish a day of pouring through the racks of Another Man's Treasure. Even better, I don't have to worry about his precious daughter looking back at me from over a rack.

"Marty, pick me up at eleven o'clock?" I call dispatch at Marty's cab company to set up my ride for the day.

"Sure, Miss Tulip. See yous then," he agrees happily.

God, I wish he'd stop putting that damn stupid "s" on the end of "you." And I'm getting tired of having to deal with the cranky dispatch woman at the company who's been answering phones her whole life, poor hag. I've been asking Marty for months to be my exclusive driver but he insists on staying with the company to get other jobs.

"And now you have to drive Baby Dagger and her friends around too." I've made several such comments, to which he always clams up. But I've seen the stray sequins or lost bead in the back of the cab and they coincidentally match the outfits that I've seen in her closet. Marty clearly has other allegiances besides me. Another thing I don't have to worry about now that my family has left me.

I hum happily as I wonder what surprises are in store for me over the next year of freedom.

For a full week, I case Hollywood Boulevard for the finest in latest fashions. On the credit card they go. Derek will never know, because by the time the bills come in he'll be sending me money from the tour to pay the mortgage and to keep our friends coming to our parties. I sift through Every Man's Treasure once per day, as they get new offerings daily and I can't bear the thought that some other groupie will get the ultimate must-have fashion before me. It's on the last day of the week of shopping that I get a surprise; in this very store, the Dandelion-less Highway Child and Carolina are going through the same racks I am. For the first time in the history of the world, Highway Child has some emotion besides disdain on her face for me. But it's not her that approaches me, it's the blonde that Derek talks about frequently, always wondering if we could somehow invite her over for a visit via Dandelion.

"She's such a breath of fresh air, Tulip. A nice little Southern girl. If we had her over maybe they would party here where we could watch them instead of all over those bars." That's always his excuse. But I know what he really wants. He's partial to blondes, the younger the better, and that innocent act gets the strongest of them every time. I know those types. Dirty little sluts underneath it all. I wasn't born yesterday!

This one has a chest that rivals mine and is loaded with the dilly, thick-accented charm that drives even the smartest of men crazy with lust. The steps she takes toward me are small and annoying, and before she even speaks she's doing this maddening hand-wringing ritual that I saw her do backstage a couple of times, though I really tried not to pay any attention to her at all. The whole time, Highway Child is standing ten feet behind her with her mouth hanging open in a half smile. She looks like she just got out of the dentist chair and her mouth is numb.

"H-hi, Mrs. Dagger. How are you?" Carolina says tentatively.

We're actually the same height, but I lift my head and look down my nose at her.

"What can I help you with, honey? Do we know each other?"

The way she swallows looks very painful and she glances back at her sidekick who still has that ridiculous look on her face.

"Um, kind of. I used to come to Holly Woods when your husband was-"

I cut her off. "Sweetheart, so did half the world."

What I want is to throw her off balance so both of them know I'm not someone they can come to if they want information about my daughter. But she's a persistent little flea and doesn't back down.

"We're friends of Dandelion and we were just wondering if she's gone to Europe with her daddy."

She's penetrating me with those big blue innocent eyes of hers and patiently waiting for an answer. The other one looks terribly uncomfortable from over her shoulder.

"Well, if you were really good friends of hers wouldn't you know?" I ask in return.

At this point it would be best to turn and leave but I'm not done looking at the new arrivals, so I bow my head and hope they go away. However, this Carolina girl must not be able to read social cues, because she leans across the top of the rack and says, "Thank you for talking to me, Mrs. Dagger," before she stalks away, shoulders slumped.

Her posture bothers me; she looks hurt. I'm not without

a heart, but I do my best to ignore it. They don't leave and what's more, they keep glancing over at me. Damn illegitimate brats. But I have plans for the next year of complete freedom and I have enough clothes to get me by now. I make a necessary exit and don't look back.

Derek kicks off his European tour in Brussels, Belgium and the word from across the pond is that he's better than ever. I can feel his enthusiasm seeping through the phone receiver. He doesn't need to know that he's disturbed one of my dress-up sessions.

"A sell-out, Tulip! Those people in L.A. don't know what the hell good music is anymore. Europeans know the best when they hear it!" he raves.

"Congratulations, baby! I'm so proud of you!" I pull my black skirt an inch higher to show more leg as I cradle the phone between my shoulder and chin.

"And baby, our girl is doing so well! She's being my best little companion and Daddy's little spring flower again."

"Good news all around," I comment, distracted by my own business.

"She didn't want to talk to you," he intones cautiously. "But we'll work on that."

"I understand, Derek. Things will improve. Absence will make the heart grown fonder."

What a line!

"Tulip, I miss you already. Gonna have to start checking out the groupies if you don't come over and see us every once in a while." Derek's voice is thick, like the man that can't go without sex for more than a couple of days at a time without chewing his hand off. Derek is that man and he enjoys making me think that he's such a loyal husband even while he makes me out to be the naughty girl, the cheating wife.

Here's the real truth: Derek and I have an agreement. He's my number one, I'm his number one. We share a child and a home and we don't bring things like sexually transmitted diseases into our relationship. We're careful, protected. Other than that, we both have our indiscretions. Do I get jealous? Sure. Does he get jealous? Absolutely. But we're also discreet. Everyone ends up happy in the end.

"But baby, you left me behind for a reason," I remind him.

"Yeah, yeah, I know. And I think we did the right thing. She'll get it out of her system before we come back to L.A. and will be ready for college when we return," Derek agrees through the crackling connection.

"And you know I'll come when you have the breaks between legs," I offer with a bored sigh.

That was part of the deal between us, but the first break won't be for another two months. There's an extra perk in it for me too, as I'll be able to catch up with some of my old flames tucked away in their palatial mansions outside of London.

"I'm gonna miss you until then, baby."

"Remember our agreement, honey. It'll be okay. Just save the best for me and I'll save the best for you." I'm grasping for things to say to comfort him. Damn him for dragging out this conversation. Doesn't he understand that I have better things to do than talk about subjects we've been over and over a thousand times?

He doesn't speak for a moment and I wonder if we've lost our connection. But then his concerned voice comes through again, sounding like he wants to have a heart-to-heart even with a continent and an ocean between us:

"Tulip, maybe we should talk about our agreement again. I mean, we're getting older, we have a kid who knows everything we're doing now, and we have to be good examples."

I turn my back to the mirror and throw a look over my left shoulder. The backs of my thighs…worrisome. If the sun hits my skin a certain way it looks dappled, loose, even *fat*. The skirt gets pulled down an inch again. And it certainly doesn't help my ego to have my husband tell me I'm old. Thirty-five is a beautiful age to be for the rest of your life!

"Well, maybe we should talk about that when I come to see you," I suggest, trying to keep the annoyance out of my voice.

"Tulip, you're gonna run around with those stupid kids with make-up on while I'm gone, aren't you?" Derek demands, sounding choked up.

"Derek, you know I can't just sit at home for a year and wait for my family to come back. I'll go out and see what kind of fun I can have. And whatever happens…happens," I say casually, allowing my eyes to drop from the mirror to focus on the conversation so I can get rid of him faster.

"Tulip, I know you better than that. You have big plans, don't you? And you're gonna keep this competition going with our kid even from six thousand miles away?"

Derek knows me better than anyone, probably because he was one of the only people I've known who cared to explore the real me over the years. But damn if I'm telling him anything more than I already have.

"Derek, every minute of this conversation is costing us a lot of money. We'll think about all of this and discuss it again when we're face to face, okay? Until then, stop worrying. It's you and Dandelion I love."

More dead air before I hear a young female voice in back of him and it isn't Dandelion. Then, "You're right. I'll call you again soon." And he's gone.

I shake my head as I hang up the receiver.

Saved by the underage Belgian groupie.

I step out of the skirt and toss it aside; a bad purchase. The black spandex scoop-neck long-sleeved dress is much more to my liking. I cinch it with a wide black belt…magic. Not only does it highlight my hourglass figure, it's a perfect backdrop for my shimmering blond hair that falls to the middle of my back and is petal-soft from enjoying two hundred brush strokes a day. I choose the black number as my opening-night outfit. For make-up I add signature red lips, and brown pencil to my gently arched brows.

The years I wear on my face are noticeable, but I have to wear them proudly. My life experience trumps even my physical beauty. Rather than trying to be twenty years younger, I have to remember to be Tulip Dagger. Because being Tulip Dagger is what got me where I am today and it'll get me where I want to go tomorrow.

I'm ready to be every rocker's fantasy. Again.

I know the big names of hair metal almost as well as I knew the names of the past two decades.

The burning hot New York Gems aren't in town. Flame Game is in Europe. But I have my choice of Here Kitty, Kitty, Scarlett Rouge, and another band heating up the Strip called Hijinks fronted by an electrifying blond named Mikey Morris who is making a name for himself with every show that he does. Or, I could see "Hollywood High's Very Own Hall Pass" at a dump in Van Nuys, not far from that terrible Smut Central where I saw my daughter play that shocking game. I heard Dandelion talk about Hall Pass once when I was eavesdropping on a phone conversation she was having with Hippy Chick and I got the impression that she knows them personally. Nevertheless, I decide to start my new adventure with Scarlett Rouge, even though I'm not completely impressed with them. They aren't particularly sexy and are older than the typical band, but what they do have is that manager who also happens to work with the New York Gems, Shark Gant. The Gems have three delectable men that I would love to add to the notches on my belt. Since Gant isn't any spring chicken, he may like the attention of an influential groupie over some fourteen year old brat with massive hair. Buttering him up will warrant me better access to the band boys. You have to investigate all the channels in this game of chance.

Gazzarri's looks like it's been raided by Hollywood High students that in turn raided Frederick's of Hollywood. I wade through the jailbait, hoping to spot Shark Gant. Instead, on my way backstage, I run into a roadie that it would take six of to equal one Gant.

"Sorry, the boys don't want any grandmas backstage." That's the line I get from the scrawny creep who is wearing a t-shirt that reads "Freak" on the front and back. Clearly, he hasn't recognized me yet. Or, maybe he can't see at all.

As much as his spiel bothers me, I have to laugh in his face because he's twenty years older than me!

I give Freak a friendly little shove and protest, "Oh please, don't you even know who I am?"

He looks me up and down, drawing unkempt salt-and-pepper brows together.

"No, and I ain't got time to find out!" he scoffs, and out he goes into the crowd to round up a pair of stick-legged blonde girls. They appear to be twins and look like they're still in middle school.

"Hey girls, you wanna meet the band?" Freak's tone has totally changed, but I don't have time to be insulted. Competition in this game is fierce at best and the most successful groupies have skin six inches thick.

I still can't lay eyes on Shark Gant, who is pretty hard to miss.

While Freak is busy with his affairs, I skate right through the backstage door. That easily, I'm face to face with two members of Scarlett Rouge who, unfortunately, look even worse in person than they do in publicity photos.

"Whoa, are you someone's mother?" a bleach blond with meaty arms and caked on make-up asks, elbowing a squat guy with long, dark hair who's tossing drumsticks around like a juggler until he sees me. One of the sticks falls on the floor and as he bends to pick it up he peeks up my dress. A typical rock star move. Maybe I'm getting somewhere.

"Now come on, boys, is that any way to treat one of your biggest fans?" I tease, even though I don't know a damn thing about Scarlett Rouge's music and frankly, don't care either. That's one of the major differences between the 60s and 70s and today; I used to care about both the men and the music coming out of their amplifiers. Derek is at least right about the dreadful sound if not the look of glam rock.

"Wait, she is someone's mother! Remember the chicks with the peanut butter?" the drummer howls, then they both start high-fiving one another.

Peanut butter? My daughter is known as a "chick with the peanut butter?" Oh, Derek is going to tear his hair out!

"Boys, look who I found for ya!" Freak comes bursting through the door with the twin stick figures. He throws his hands up in the air and whines, "Didn't I tell ya that the boys don't want any grannies back here?"

"Bye, bye, granny!" the awful men chant, waving at me while Freak escorts me out the same door I came in.

"And stay out. Don't you have a family to raise or somethin'?" Freak waves his hand at me dismissively and sulks away.

"They're so mean unless you're sixteen and blond."

As I'm trying to regain my composure a soothing female voice comes from behind my back. When I turn I wish I hadn't, for I'm faced with a teenage girl who is dressed decadently, but is from a population of backstage sluts that I've always steered clear of: the dreaded fat girls.

"Oh honey, it's all part of the lifestyle," I say flippantly, dismissing her comment.

"It doesn't matter what they think, anyway. I think you're still beautiful," she tells me very matter-of-factly.

Oh dear, is she trying to pick me up? I've had girls attempt it, but I'm strictly interested in men. Not that I've never put on a girl-on-girl show to get a rock guy's attention. But he would have to be pretty special to do that.

"Thank you. Have a pleasant evening." I can't stop the hint of sarcasm that enters my tone as I move away from her.

"I'm not a groupie because I want to sleep with these guys. I want to be a manager someday and I'm trying to make connections," she explains quickly, like she's desperate for me to continue giving her attention.

This generation doesn't seem to get it when you're trying to get out of a conversation with them. I remember that dingy Southern girl named Carolina in Another Man's Treasure and shudder.

"Good luck," I say with a nod as I take a few more steps away from her.

Every step I take is shadowed by her steps.

This overweight teenager is following me!

"Shark Gant doesn't manage this band anymore. He's concentrating all his efforts on the New York Gems. So, I'm free to take Scarlett Rouge over and I'm trying to. But Freak won't let me backstage because I'm not skinny and gorgeous," she complains.

I appreciate the information about Shark Gant but find her whining ironically funny, so I snort, "Well, welcome to rock and roll."

Does she think we work in a bank?

"That was pretty cool the way you just walked right through the door when Freak was with those other girls. Did you see the band? Did they say anything about looking for a manager?" the hefty girl persists

I roll my eyes at her. "Honey, musicians don't worry about managers when they can think about sex and beer and getting high on pot that they get for free from fans." I'm completely frank.

"Pot? Mrs. Dagger, obviously you don't know this scene very well. These guys are all high on cocaine."

For her information, I'm well aware that coke is prevalent in L.A. now. Lord, I hope that Dandelion and her friends are smart enough not to get involved in that!

"And by the way, my name isn't honey. It's Katie, but my groupie name is Kitty Kat."

The young lady is starting to show her true colors. I can tell that she's not the usual feather brain acting stupid to earn the honor of spreading her legs for a one-night stand with her favorite band member. I never was that girl, either. I could always hold my own in conversation. But I was and am beautiful, of course, unlike this ghastly heavy girl in front of me.

I'm saved from telling her that her name is too typical when the lights flash a couple of times and the owner of Gazzarri's appears to introduce Scarlett Rouge. Momentarily, the band members run out on stage and start beating on instruments to create some terrible racket that they call "original songs." They look silly in their spandex pants and vests with nothing on underneath; the get-ups are better saved for younger and prettier boys. Kitty Kat sticks close and tries to engage me in conversation a couple more times but I'm not fair game. In fact, I feel compelled to move on. After a quick lipstick touch-up in the ladies room mirror I proceed to the pay phone to call Marty to come and rescue me from a Scarlett Rouge concert that rapidly takes on the feeling of a fate worse than death.

"Where to next, Miss Tulip?" Marty asks as he pulls away from the curb just down the street from Gazzarri's.

I'm feeling very low as I peer out at Sunset Boulevard overflowing with young girls in tight dresses with teased and dyed hair. They laugh while they throw looks over their shoulders at some bad boy they're wiggling their tight rears ends just a little more than usual for. Just barely staying upright on heels that elongate their firm legs, while they somehow hold each other up. The boys love it.

My mood has little to do with the nonsense that happened in Gazzarri's, but more the prevailing thought that I haven't been an outsider looking in at the world of rock since I was Dandelion's age and learning the ropes of meeting the men of my dreams. Something about this new era of music makes me not want to be a part of it, makes me want to party with my own established kind and hope that it goes away soon.

"Miss Tulip?" Marty repeats.

I come to my senses. "I'm rather tired already, Marty, and I think I'd like to go home." I yawn for effect even though I'm really not very sleepy.

"Yous okay? That's not like yous at all." Marty peers at me suspiciously in the rear view mirror.

It's an odd comfort that Marty is concerned about me. Now that Derek and Dandelion have left me behind, Marty is probably the person in L.A. that I'll count on the most. And, he sees me at my worst and keeps his mouth shut, so I know that he can be trusted. In fact, you might say that he's a little too trustworthy.

Two words pop into my mind: *peanut butter*.

I wonder what Marty really knows about Dandelion and her friends.

"I don't know a darn thing, Miss Tulip," he spouts quickly, no doubt trying to absolve himself of guilt but at the same time proving how guilty he is of knowing a lot of facts he could be telling me. "All I do is drive, just like with yous."

"Marty, we've know each other a lot longer than you've known my daughter and her little sidekicks. Derek and I are trying to get her back on the right track and…"

"All I do is drive, Miss Tulip," Marty hits his point home, and I know that my effort is fruitless.

Maybe what I really need to do is abandon my infiltration plan instead and find out exactly what my offspring has been doing to give her such a stellar reputation after so short a time.

But do I really want to know?

Well, yes, I do. As a matter of fact, as her mother, I have to know.

I stare at the door to Dandelion's bedroom and recall what Derek warned me about before they left:

"She's all worried that you're gonna be in her room looking at her stuff. I told her to lock the door and I'd hide the key, so she doesn't lose it while we're gone. Stay out of there, okay?"

To which I'd retorted: "How am I supposed to go in there if the door is locked and you have the key hidden?"

Derek had laughed and wagged his finger at me. "I couldn't ever keep you from knowing what you want to know and I still can't."

I smile at the memory because of course, Derek was and is right. When I want to know something there isn't any stopping me! Which is why I feigned sleep the night of this verbal intercourse and through the darkness saw Derek inter the key to Dandelion's room into the same leather jacket that she'd found the key to his money box in. I can enter her room anytime without either one of them every knowing it. After all, why would Dandelion be worried about it if she wasn't hiding the secret to her backstage success behind the locked door? I could find out the answer to the peanut butter joke and the one o'clock, two o'clock fiasco with the turn of a little gold key.

But not this time. I shake my head and turn away. My curiosity has not reached epic proportions. Yet.

I couldn't ever leave the City of Angels for very long. It's the only place that really feels like home because it's always been my home, even when I was off touring with this band or that or being flown into some exotic locale for down time with a household name lead singer or world-renowned guitarist who couldn't be without me. My own mother brought me into the world here after my real father disappeared, and raised me with any number of men who came in and out of our lives, some of whom became my "stepfather" but most that didn't because they didn't stay around for long enough. Los Angeles is the long lifeline on the palm of my hand; I know it equally as well. It's the beating of my heart, if that's not too cliché. But as Marty drives me around at any time of the day or night to run errands and take care of business, my stomach turns to knots because I feel like I'm losing my comfort zone to a burgeoning population of limitless denizens that I don't want to fraternize with.

I may have to find out the full extent of my daughter's shenanigans, but rather than set foot into another of the West Hollywood establishments where I'm suddenly twenty years too old to be noticed, I pull out my summer 1984 calendar and start planning parties for the faithful gang of hangers-on Derek and I have accumulated over the years. All the while I'm trying to convince myself that I have not lost the glam rock battle, I'm simply uninterested in being a part of it. It's my choice, not theirs. If I really wanted to be on top I could be. I could grovel like these teenagers are doing, like my daughter and her friends have done.

Back in the day, the guys I knew and loved were more accommodating, more accepting. They haven't changed so why should I? That visit to Europe after the opening leg of Derek's tour that I was dreading now sounds like a wonderful reprieve back into the world that I'm accustomed to.

I don't hear from him for weeks and when I do, it's in the middle of the afternoon on a party day. The eight hour difference between Western Europe and L.A. makes for some oddly placed phone calls.

"Tulip baby, how are you?" Derek is distraught, a total about-face from the optimistic star back on the rise and father of the year recipient he sounded like the last time we talked.

"I'm good, darling. Getting ready for a fun night. Thanks for the money, sweetheart. All the bills are paid and I'm having our friends over tonight." Derek had sent me a very generous amount of money that, as expected, covered my credit cards bills too. Not that those purchases got me anywhere. But one never knows when one is going to need hair metal fashions again.

"Tulip, it's all starting to fall apart on this end," he wails, on the verge of tears.

My face must go white as a shiver works through me. The tour is falling apart. The money is going to stop. Back to funding life through credit cards.

Or...

"Derek, are you drinking too much?" I ask carefully, as my husband is notorious for being in control when the chips are up and for drowning his sorrows in booze when they're down. He's not a violent drunk nor a public one, but I fear that his problem is ruining his health on some level. He never wants to talk about it, but dismisses the issue with a flourish of his hand.

"It's not that. The tour is going great and we're writing for the new album. It's our kid I'm worried about. Some band of wild-haired monkeys with lipstick and eyeliner showed up at the Amsterdam show to see her and she took off with all four of them! And they're married and have children! Can you believe it, Tulip? Our girl, loose in Amsterdam with four married men! Some Flame Game assholes!" Derek pauses and I swear I can hear the gurgling of a bottle of liquid he's pouring down his throat. He continues, "We have to talk about our agreement! We've taught her to disregard the institution of marriage!"

When Derek starts throwing around laughable terms like "the institution of marriage," I know he's under the influence of Jack Daniels.

But wait…did he say "our girl" is running wild in Amsterdam with the splendid members of Flame Game? My face flushes from the envy coursing through my veins.

I consider telling Derek about the peanut butter joke but decide it'll only make matters worse.

"We'll talk about it when we see each other. I wish you were here with me to party."

I do miss my husband. But I've invited a couple of upstart guitarists who idolize Derek to the party tonight, so I'll be fine until I see him.

"That's still a month away, Tulip! There's no telling what might happen between then and now!"

"Derek, what good do you expect a change in our agreement to do for her? To stop her from being a groupie overnight?" I demand.

Silence. But I know he's still there because I hear the liquid coming out of the bottle again.

"You're right, Tulip. It isn't going to do any good. So what do we do?"

We? I'm powerless to do anything from Los Angeles.

"I don't know," I admit.

"Can you come sooner? We have to put our heads together on this! I'll fly you in whenever you want, wherever you want."

I glance at my calendar up to the end of June, when I'm supposed to go to London. The parties sound much better than watching my daughter run around Europe with metal guys who would rather be with her than their families.

The apple doesn't fall far from the tree.

"Well, let's see what happens," I decide.

It's a decision that will come back to haunt me.

I have a two-night-a-week agenda of parties that is supplemented by invitations to other bashes. The result is that I'm on the go five nights a week and basking in my own element. Sex with the two youthful blues hopefuls is divine. Though they do get a bit competitive for my attentions at times, I let them know that there is plenty of Tulip Dagger to go around.

Getting from place to place in Marty's cab still warrants me a look at the streets of West Hollywood and the follies taking place there at any and every time of the day or night. I get jabbed by little knives whenever I see the world I've let pass me by. But the big jabs come when I try to set foot into that world again, a sure sign to stay out of it. Nevertheless, when an invitation comes from my friend Melinda for a party that will likely have lasting repercussions on my relationship with my husband and daughter and really, with myself, I'm not able to say no.

"Honey, mark your calendar! Clarence and I are throwing the world's greatest graduation party for our baby and you must be there!" Melinda Aikman's nasally voice drones through the receiver after she wakes me well before my desired time, and on a Sunday morning after a party! Which she was invited to but turned me down for another affair. Which makes me want to give her a curt "no thank you" before she goes any further into the details.

Melinda, who was a groupie coming up in L.A. the same time I was. Melinda, who married into a lot more money than I did by choosing a businessman instead of a rock star. Melinda, who most often can't stand up straight or keep her eyes from crossing at any party because she gets so shit-faced.

"I'll see if I'm free, love. What's the date? I'll let you know later on."

She quotes the last weekend in June, which is after the date I'm scheduled to fly to London to see my family. So I have a valid excuse not to go to her damn party at the gilded mansion in Bel Air that should be what we live in and would be if Derek didn't spend his money on useless things or drink it away with his band mates.

"Oh Mel, I'm so sorry, but-"

"The whole gang is coming. I've invited hundreds and Clarence is paying big dollars for Cloud's favorite bands so you can't possibly miss the fun. It wouldn't be like you, Tulip Dagger!" Melinda giggles.

I roll my head toward the clock in my bedroom. Nine-thirty in the morning and Melinda is already on her way to being drunk. Or maybe she's just carrying over from the evening before, wherever she was. The tone she uses when she talks of her and Clarence's only daughter "Cloud" grates on my nerves. Spoiled little bitch. Dandelion can't stand the sight of her and avoids her at Hollywood High like she has bubonic plague.

"Mama, she has no style whatsoever for having all that moola," Dandelion complained to me. "Such a wannabe."

Bubonic plague would be better than having no style! At least my daughter and I agree on something once in a while.

"No really, Mel, that's the weekend after I-" I should hang up on her. Should really...

"Hall Pass is up first. Cloud knows them from Hollywood High. Then Hijinks comes on next and the big draw is gonna be the New York Gems. We had to pay a pretty nice sum to them to do a house party. Of course this isn't just any house party." Melinda cackles, sounding terribly uppity.

My eyes are wide open now. Maybe this is an event that I need to attend after all. Derek hasn't bought my ticket to London yet and I can always tell him that I need a few extra days to take care of business here in L.A.

"That sounds like quite a party, Melinda. I'll let you know as soon as I can." I stick with my plan to not sound overly anxious about anything traitor Melinda offers.

"Do make every effort to attend," she babbles.

Oh, I will. I certainly will. In fact, even before I manage to shake her off the phone I pull out Derek's touring and recording schedule and call him in Oslo, Norway where he's doing two shows which I presume are sold out. He's in his room and not alone.

"We're writing, Tulip. What's up?" Derek doesn't like to be disturbed during the creative process, but it's important that he knows that I need a slight delay in my visiting schedule. Better to tell him now than to buy a ticket that needs to be changed.

"You're interrupting a writing session for that? We can't

talk about this another time?" he scolds, as if I'm supposed to have a crystal ball and know that he's "writing." Anyway, he sounds drunk.

I decide to level with him.

"Listen, Derek, I've been hearing a lot of things about Baby Dagger around town and I want to get to the bottom of some of these rumors. Melinda is having a party at the end of June that could put me in contact with some of her friends, some people who might know what she's been up to. I'll skip it if that's what you want. But I'm pretty sure that our main concern is getting our daughter back on track and we can't do that unless we really know what she's been up to."

In the same way that Melinda got my attention, I have his now.

"Well, if that's the case, I'm glad you called."

So I thought. We discuss a date shortly after the weekend of the party for me to meet him and Dandelion in London.

Too bad I won't be in town to celebrate the 4th of July. But I need my independence from the glam crowd and by then, maybe from my own crowd too.

I'm pleased with the plans we've laid out.

I see Melinda Aikman several times before her over-the-top graduation party for the spoiled Cloud, who is going on to study law at Harvard. Personally, I still think it's better to have a daughter who has style than one that has none, even if she is going to Harvard and my raunchy girl is running around Europe with raunchy boys.

On a lunch date at the Rainbow, Melinda leans over the table at me and murmurs, "Cloud says all the boys talk about Dandelion at Hollywood High. And all the girls do too. I'm sorry Tulip, but she said that your daughter is a slut." It takes three drinks before she has the nerve to tell me this and the three drinks are straight shots of Tequila.

"Is that so, Melinda? Well, Dandelion tells me that your Cloud is a wannabe, she just doesn't know how to be," I say, leaning even closer to her. I'll admit, it's a total revenge line. Even though Melinda and I have known each other since we were teenagers, there are still some lines that you don't cross and she's just done it.

"My Cloud a wannabe? Hardly, Tulip! She's not going to Harvard because she's spending her time chasing future rock stars!"

Melinda is such a hypocrite. How easily people forget where they came from when money comes into the picture.

I want to have my say but don't want to push Melinda so far that I get uninvited to her party. So I try to settle it by patting her hand and thanking her for her interest in Dandelion.

"Derek and I have her on the right track. She's doing well in Europe."

"Cloud says the boys from Hall Pass used to be friendly with her and one in particular tells some very dirty stories about her." Melinda sounds now like she's revealing a scandal. Her eyes are wide and her voice is hushed.

If there's one thing I hate it's a parent who repeats what her child tells her as if it's gospel. I never tried to be Dandelion's friend. I haven't even tried terribly hard to be a parent either, when you get right down to it. But Melinda Aikman is one of those terrible adults who tries to be "older sister" to her daughter so she doesn't feel like the pushing forty adult that she is.

"Have you heard them for yourself?" I ask with a tip of my head.

Melinda downs a fourth Tequila, practically taking it out of the waitress's hand.

"Of course not, honey. Cloud doesn't really get involved with that kind, she's just heard rumors."

"Well, let's just leave them as rumors then," I suggest.

But I really am quite interested to meet those Hall Pass boys at the graduation bash the very next weekend.

Silly little wannabe Cloud is running around her graduation party in a namesake frock of tulle and lace that Melinda must have rushed out and bought in a fit of inspiration after our conversation about our children. Admittedly, it's a sexy and obviously very expensive piece of clothing, but it would look better on my own daughter and she would add the rock and roll attitude to match. The words that came out of the throat of Melinda's child about my Dandelion are still irking me, even if we do have our differences.

"Mrs. Dagger, thank you for coming!" Cloud gushes, and, proving she's a girl after her mother's heart, her eyes fall to the baby pink envelope in my hand that she presumes has money in it. Only it doesn't. Just to be a thorn in her mother's side, I've gotten Cloud a gift certificate to Another Man's Treasure, which she will probably never use. I figure that it's her only hope to get her style on track.

"Cloud, I wouldn't be anywhere else in the world! I have to report everything that happens here to my little slut daughter so she knows what she's missing while she's touring Europe with her father."

That gets rid of the annoying little gnat. I stuff the pink envelope back in my purse. Maybe I'll spend it on myself instead.

Chateau Aikman looks like the goddamn White House, only the White House isn't pretentious and the chateau is; it screams, *Look at me, my owners have money coming out of their crazy asses!* Built from the finest marble, the balustrade that was fashioned after the President's home boasts a dazzling million-dollar chandelier that's lit for the evening and tosses a golden light over the fabulous patio that stretches out from in front of it for what seems like miles. The forty-two rooms of the mansion, twenty-one on each side, hug the marble patio. Melinda and Clarence always entertain in the front of the house because that's where you get the full immensity of the property and anyway, Melinda doesn't like anyone in her pool, being that she's a germaphobe in addition to being an alcoholic.

Surely the gardeners and landscapers will be busy as soon as the party is over, being that a stage has been set up on the perfectly manicured grass and the precious blades are getting overrun by post-pubescent teenagers who certainly don't look like the friends of a proper young lady on her way to Harvard. Quite the contrary; I see Cloud downing a goblet of red wine, half of which ends up all over the front of her virginal whore dress.

"My darling, you look wonderful tonight." Melinda drapes herself around my neck, stinking of Tequila.

Of course I look wonderful tonight. I put on my make-up, brushed my long blond hair, and slithered into a red column of leather cinched with a wide matching snakeskin belt. This is such a head-turning style for me. And heads are turning.

Melinda, on the other hand, looks like an overused dishrag in that way of women who work too hard to stay young-looking. Her body is a wrinkled mess in a black dress with a plunging neckline that shows off the fact that she spends a lot of time in a tanning bed. Personally, I think over-tanning makes a woman look older. I prefer my creamy, lightly sun-kissed complexion. Melinda is only two years my senior but looks a decade older!

"You too, honey. Looks like it's going to be a great party."

Cheek kiss.

"Too bad Derek can't be here with us! And Dandelion too!"

Dandelion would've refused to come. When Cloud used to attend an occasional party at our house with her parents Dandelion would have nothing to do with her. Melinda knows this full well so I'm not quite sure why she keeps bringing up her name.

Before long, however, it becomes apparent that if I have it in for Melinda and Cloud because of what Cloud has been saying about Dandelion, they have it in for me even more.

The group called Hall Pass from Hollywood High take the stage and play for almost an hour. While they sound good enough, I can only take them so seriously; they're a boy band, barely out of diapers! They're even too young for me and I don't exactly go through life with one arm tied behind my back! Cloud and her friends are tearing their hair out over them. Once their set is over and the equipment of the next band, Hijinks, is being set up by the same young roadies who set up Hall Pass, Cloud tosses herself at the lanky drummer. I watch as she takes him by the arm and seems quite intent on finding someone in the crowd of revelers. If I'm not mistaken, I see her make eye contact with her mother whom in turn nods her head in my direction. Why, it's me they're looking for and within moments, they're standing in front of me.

"Mrs. Dagger, I just wanted to introduce you to Ricky Rude. He used to be a good friend of Dandelion's and knows a lot about her," Cloud sings as she clings to the young man's arm to keep from falling over.

Ricky hits me with a pie-eyed grin before he slurs, "Oh yeah, Mrs. Dagger. I know Dandelion from the top of her head to the bottom of her feet and everything in between. You might say I've seen every inch of her and she's seen all twelve inches of me! You might even say that I've taught her everything she knows, though I think she got the groupie instinct from you."

I'm momentarily taken aback by the nerve of this little nobody. My mouth moves but nothing comes out of my throat at first.

Tulip Dagger never loses her voice for very long.

I bite back, "You should have your filthy little mouth washed out with soap. My daughter wouldn't have anything to do with the likes of you!"

Cloud looks mortified that she's caught in the middle of an unexpected mess she's managed to orchestrate. She stays quiet and peers around me with doe eyes, no doubt looking for her troublemaking mother to save her. But the boy still hasn't had his say.

Wagging his finger at me he brags, "Don't be so sure of that, Mrs. D. Your little spring flower taught me a thing or two, actually."

"Well, I guess I'll have to teach her a thing or two about her tastes in men. Obviously they have to be worked on." It's a desperate line and I say it with a pounding heart. As I stomp away from the giggling boy-man I'm thankful to run into Anne Hayes, another lifelong friend and clearly a better one than Melinda Aikman.

My conversation with Anne works to lower my heart rate. But I'm not completely in the moment because I suddenly spot Dandelion's two friends, Carolina and Hippy Chick, kanoodling with members of the band that is up next, Hijinks. The dumb blonde is pressed up against and has her head on the shoulder of the lead singer, Mikey Morris, whom I've just read is being courted by several record labels whether he brings the rest of the band with him or not. The despicable Hippy Chick looks like a penniless hitchhiker in short-shorts, cowboy boots, and a tube top. She's comfortably attached to one of the other band guys.

"Tulip, you look like you've just seen a ghost!" Anne says laughingly.

I flick my eyes back to Anne, feeling like I've been set up by Melinda. The bad vibes just keep getting piled on. I wonder if I can trust Anne enough to discuss it with her.

"I'm sorry, Anne. I was supposed to be flying out to see Derek and Dandelion but stayed in town a few extra days because Melinda wanted me here. I'm a bit overwhelmed by my change in schedule and all of this in general." I pass a hand over my forehead to emphasize my unease. A bit dramatic, but in times of distress you have to do what you can to find out who your friends really are.

Cheek kiss.

"Sorry to hear, Tulip. But I can understand why you wouldn't want to miss an affair like this! Cloud is such a lovely girl and Melinda has done so well for herself. I mean, look at this!" Anne shakes her head as she gazes around at the three hundred and sixty degree splendor.

As I thought. Anne is not the one to talk to. Derek has to be the only one. Soon I'll be with him.

We're interrupted by a pushing and yelling match that erupts between Ricky Rude and Mikey Morris. Shark Gant, escorting his prized Gems around, is just the man to break them up. While he's busy with the young rockers, Melinda insists that I'm formally introduced to the New York Gems.

I'm more than pleased to come into contact with the delightful blondes Danny Diamond and Jack Ruby, bassist and guitarist of the Gems and poster children for glam rock. Meanwhile, lead guitarist Nikk Saffire is nothing less than a towering god of sneering beauty. But the ultra-perfect model-turned-rock star Em'rald is simply too much to bear. In my opinion, women of the rock and roll world shouldn't be competing with the boys, they should be loving them.

"If there's anything cool about all this glam shit, it's her. It's the girl leading that group." That's what Derek had said during one of his rants about the music that was putting him out of business.

"I'm a big fan of Derek's," Nikk assures me.

"Well, I'll let him know. Maybe I could set up a meeting," I say with a lift of my eyebrows.

A meeting, my ass. I'll set it up, but Derek won't be there.

The model ruins the moment.

"I met Derek a long time ago," she tells me.

Which I already knew.

Derek admitted to a run in or two with her many years ago in New York City, of which he never told me the outcome. But I can guess what it was: up and coming teenage model wanting to glom onto a famous blues guitarist so his name could take her to the top. Then Tulip Dagger came along and landed him instead.

"When he was still single," I point out. "He's told me all about his potential love interests."

"Oh, but Derek was never-" she starts, and I desperately want to hear her deny that Derek rejected her advances. But once again, Melinda isn't on my side.

"Oh, come and meet my good friends Jay and Sara!" she suddenly exclaims, tugging on Em'rald's long arm.

Em'rald offers me a snooty scowl before turning away to be introduced to friends of Melinda's I don't know. Nikk Saffire slips an arm around her as if to comfort her.

Later in the evening, I'll see her looking much happier. Because before the night ends she will be the undisputed star of the whole show. After the performance the New York Gems put on for the rich residents of Bel Air and a few stray rock kids from Hollywood High, there is no doubt in anyone's mind, not even mine, who the kings and queen of glam rock are.

But this is not my world. I need to go to London.

It's the wee hours of the morning. The only way I ever see this time of the day is when I'm watching the sun rise in the arms of an emotional lover looking for inspiration from the brightest star. That isn't the case this morning. Tulip Dagger, who has never had a sleepless night, is up at the crack of dawn two hours after arriving home from the party. Staring at her daughter's bedroom door. That room holds secrets, I know that now. Secrets of Ricky Rude, Smut, Scarlett Rouge and peanut butter, Flame Game, and who knows how many other glamorous boys roaming the streets of West Hollywood and the world. But I think of Derek, the only one I can trust. The one I'll see soon. He has to be able to trust me too. I have to keep my promise. No, the key stays in its "secret" place. I turn away from the door. Again.

I'm packing to leave for London when the doorbell rings. Looking outside, I see a postal truck in front of the house and our postman Ken in his ridiculous blue shorts at the gate. I'm not in the mood to see him today. His wife will have to do the trick until I get back.

He has a manila envelope in one hand. I wonder who it is from.

"Package for you, Mrs. Dagger! It says not to bend it so I can't push it through the slot," he calls when I open the door.

I wasn't expecting to be seen by anyone today, so I rush down the sidewalk in a faded dress with my hair pulled back and no make-up on. I see how Ken's smile fades when he sees my natural self. They all want the illusion. Derek is the only one who loves the real me as well as the dreamy me. Ken doesn't ask to come in. I take the envelope and move swiftly back to the house.

Contains photographs. Do not bend.

No return address is on the envelope. I just know I'm not going to like this.

I steel myself to see my daughter naked and in embarrassing and compromising positions as I tear it open with shaking hands, but it's worse than that.

I'm holding a small stack of garishly colorful photos of Dandelion with rock stars. But they aren't just any rock stars. They're some of my favorite European lovers from days past. Legendary guitar master Mark May. Then-and-now aging heartthrob Keith Wolf, lead singer of the Wolf Gang. Early metal guitar god Jeff Jacobs. All in their forties, all looking quite pleased to be with my teenage daughter.

My face burns with the heat of betrayal. She just couldn't stick to her own kind – could she? I'm supposed to end the competition but she doesn't have to. We'll see about that.

I rush to my bedroom closet and pull the key to her room out of Derek's jacket pocket.

As I toss open the door my heart feels the same as it did when I was at the party the other night after Rude Ricky's spiel. From every inch of every wall the eyes of Dandelion's hair metal heroes mock me in their flashy outfits that belong on girls, just like Derek said. Her closet is full of things that I don't know where she got the money for. Shoes, including my missing neon pink pumps, are neatly line up on the floor of the closet. Her drawers are much the same. Where did she get all of this? She must be giving the boys exactly what they ask for to accumulate these fashion treasures.

Dropping down on my knees I toss up the bedspread with musical notes all over it and look underneath the queen-sized bed. Because of the poor lighting nothing seems to be under there, no secrets. But then I just make out a box pushed into the very corner. Like a snake in the grass, I shimmy under and grab the top to drag it closer. I'm sweating by the time I have the box on the bed.

Taking the top off, a notebook with a red cover comes into a view. Underneath, more pictures plus a vast array of folded notes attack my senses. I intend to make short shrift of the notebook, but when I open it I see that she has written something on the inside cover in fancy lettering:

How I Became a Hair Metal Groupie:
The Step-by-Step Guide to Backstage Action
by Dandelion Dagger, age 16
Copyright 1983
Hollywood, California, nine double oh rock and roll

Oh, she has to be joking. Writing a book on being a groupie when her mother was the pioneer? Furious, I toss it aside. Otherwise I'll destroy it.

I start in on the pictures. None of them are necessarily dirty, but they are suggestive. Backstage, tour bus, hotel rooms. The notes, on the other hand, are different. *This is what I want to do to you when we see each other again.* It would take two days for me to look at them all, but I take out a handful and can't believe what I'm seeing and reading. Some of the notes are from my lovers in Europe. They've made secret trips to Los Angeles just to see her and never once mentioned it to me, even the ones I keep in touch with regularly.

More friends that I thought I had that aren't really friends when the going gets ugly.

And the going is getting very, very ugly.

My daughter will not carry on like this. This means war.

I don't bother to shove the box back under her bed before I rise to my feet and pluck a small clump of dust out of my hair.

There's no time to linger or to cry over spilled rock stars. I have a plane to catch to London.

But first, I have a gift certificate to spend at Another Man's Treasure.

DANDELION

Mama and Daddy are total hypocrites. It's just fine that they had their fun for two decades and are still having it, but oh no, not me! They cornered me with their dopey scheme in London and tried to make some hairbrained deal with me, meanwhile claiming to be a shining example of monogamy that I had to follow. Poof! Just like that! No more fun for Dandelion Dagger who is just getting going!

I had to get them off my case, so I said, "Okay, it's a deal," and I even shook on it. But behind their backs, I had several of Mama's old boyfriends as well as my own conquests climbing the walls for me and taking big chances to pick me up in limos behind the venues Daddy plays at, while he was on stage and Mama was off somewhere not keeping the deal she helped Daddy dream up. I had to get ample rock star action for the rest of Daddy's European tour somehow, even if I got caught. But I didn't. Before they even noticed I was gone, I'd be back. Not my preferred way to be with my lovers, but it worked while it had to.

Well, that's all over now. Because I turned eighteen in January of 1985 and the minute I got back from Daddy's tour I packed my stuff and high-tailed it out of the Hollywood house and into Mother Sandy's with H.C., into the room across from her. Now we can walk down Hilldale to Sunset and be in the thick of it all in five minutes and I can write my how-to groupie book without Mama nosing into it the way she did while I was in Europe. The arrangement is working out perfectly, other than Daddy calling once a day.

"I miss my little spring flower. Come home to us, will you, honey? You can do whatever you want to do but come home to us so we won't worry about you," he pleads with me.

But I've decided to live my own life, because when he gets really drunk his pleas turn to things I don't want to hear: "I wish you would find a nice guy and just be with him. I wouldn't even care if he wore lipstick, as long as he was good to my little spring flower!"

"I'm sorry, Daddy, I'm not ready for that yet. But I do love you. You know that, right?"

I do. I really do. But something is going on with Daddy and I don't really want to be around him right now. He had a good tour but the album he put out flopped. He doesn't know why no one bought it, why the critics hated it. One thing Mama and me agree on is that Daddy drinks too much, and that might have something to do with the terrible music he put out. But he always bounces back, so I'm not going to worry too much. Once this low phase passes, maybe I'll even go home.

"Oh no you won't!" H.C. yells as soon as I hang up the phone.

We giggle together. She's probably right.

No, she's exactly right.

Daddy can wait. Right now, it's all about me.

HIGHWAY CHILD

Dandelion go home? Over my dead body! She owes it to me to stay right where she is now and she knows it! Especially after leaving me with Carolina Clampett, who just wants to fall in love with Mikey Morris even though I know damn well he's screwing ten other girls behind her back. And with Carolina warbling night and day about how beautiful Em'rald is and how her goal in life is to be her personal jewelry maker...I've had enough!

Dandelion and me, we're soul mates. Nothing can stand in our way. Not even that Daddy of hers crying to her on the phone because his career is over and he's a damn alcoholic.

I just barely made it through the year without her. The only reason I hung around with Carolina is because she has an "in" with Shark Gant, the monster-sized manager of the New York Gems. He must pity how dumb she is or something, because when he sees her coming he makes sure he takes the bag of jewelry she's made for her heroine and the other three guys in the Gems before she starts stalking him. It's one of those guys, one tall, dark, and sexy Nikk Saffire, who keeps me at Carolina's heels. I'm not looking to fall in love like she is, but I could potentially change my mind when it comes to him. He's got so many girls bowing down at his feet he doesn't even pay much attention to me, but that will change. Now that Dandelion is back, I know he'll come around because her and me, we always get our men. But I don't want her to know I'm soft on him, even though she kind of figured it out from the beginning. All she needs to know is that I want to put him on my list of "haves" and take him off my list of "haven't had yets."

That slime ball Diesel keeps trying to make a bet with me that Nikk Saffire is in Em'rald's pants, but I didn't believe it from the start and I still don't believe it. Whether or not it's true doesn't make an inkling of difference to me anyway. What does make a difference is that the Gems are on the rise and are becoming big stars, so suddenly they aren't in L.A. as much as they used to be. Nikk Saffire has left me behind.

For the first fourteen years of my life, everyone left H.C., even her own parents. But I'm slowly turning those tables. Dandelion loves me and swears she'll never leave me again, not even for her daddy, and I believe her this time. Just like she came back to me, I know Nikk Saffire will too. I'll wait. Because I've been through a hell of a lot worse.

CAROLINA

Finding Mikey Morris in the ladies room at the Roxy with Highway Child is the worst thing that could have happened in my life. I really thought Mikey loved me and we were exclusive. That one of my two biggest dreams was going to come true and I was going to marry a guy who was about to be a rock star. Likewise, I thought H.C. was my friend. She sure didn't stop hanging around with me when Dandelion went to Europe with her daddy. H.C. kept right on showing up at Elsa's and even tried to talk me into moving into Mother Sandy's with her. I love Mother Sandy almost as much as I love Elsa, it's like having two mothers, but I couldn't see being that close to Highway Child, especially when Dandelion wasn't around. I only teamed up with her again because I thought we could stop Dandelion from leaving with her daddy. We were too late. And there I was, back in the thick of things with H.C. with her saying nasty things about my two sisters Elly May and Em'rald. By that time, I couldn't shake her and I still can't and she thinks that I don't know why.

It's because of Nikk Saffire. She thinks everyone, especially me, is too stupid to know she's in love with him. Even Diesel knows it. Oh, but I don't want to talk about that terrible person and his band and that awful Smut Central H.C. has tried to drag me back to! I just want to lick my wounded heart and hope that someday I'll have another chance to find true love with a rock and roll boy.

For a while there, Mikey almost replaced my jewelry in importance, but this feeling inside of me told me I was making a mistake. I won't make it again. Until I meet a real man, my jewelry dream is priority.

I have the same feeling about Dandelion when I hear her lying to her daddy. That feeling that she's making a big mistake. Her daddy may have chased me around his dressing room, but I still think that when it comes to Dandelion, he's sincere. I admire the fact that he loves her. I wish my Pa loved me like that and wanted me to come home so much that he would accept me the way I am even though I'm a sinner in his eyes. Sometimes I'm about to tell Dandelion what I think, but I stop myself, knowing she'll just laugh at me and then H.C. will pile on and make fun of me too and start saying mean things about my sisters. I'm better off with my mouth shut.

After all, what does a dummy like Carolina Clampett know!

TULIP

Sometimes, it pays to have friends in high places.

Derek made one album with his new label during the tour of Europe, it hardly sold, and he was promptly dropped. No one would pick him up.

"I'm washed up, Tulip. Washed up at forty," he moaned over and over again.

Then the marathon drinking started, accompanied by the desperate phone calls to his daughter living the high life one street above the peaking action on Sunset. I listened to their conversations and even though I heard only his side, it never failed to sound like she was leading him on to think that she would come back home.

"Really, honey? You're thinking about it? I can't wait for the day when you come back," he'd sing softly to her, his handsome face glowing for a few special minutes.

But it didn't happen.

Now, about those friends in high places.

It was 1986 and hair metal ruled the world with seemingly no room for Derek to break back into the industry he'd spent his life in. Melinda and Clarence and several of our other moneyed business friends pooled together a stack of endorsement funds to put Derek's name back on the marquee at Holly Woods to see if a weekend of shows might jumpstart his career in our beloved hometown. The proud bluesman tried to make it sound like he wouldn't accept their "charity," but I knew how happy he was. And L.A. was happy to have him; the shows sold out in a few weeks and we eagerly anticipated his "comeback."

"Me and the boys are gonna head to Bangkok and have some fun after the shows," Derek told me the morning of the Friday show, the first of two.

"That's great, honey," I answered, because all of his problems had really taken a toll on my wild times. I had been "good" for months and it was high time for me to be "bad," if even just for the week or two that he would be away with the boys.

"I can't wait to see our girl tonight. I'm hoping that she'll want to come to Bangkok," he said hopefully.

We had not seen Dandelion in over a month at that point. She had promised to be at both shows. Unfortunately, the little brat didn't keep her word for the Friday show. Derek was shattered.

"She doesn't care, Tulip. She doesn't love me anymore," he wept that night after his two-encore performance, even though it was a total triumph otherwise.

I didn't settle for a phone call to Mother Sandy's. I showed up on the doorstep. Inside the door, I heard Sandy talking Dandelion into coming to the door and she finally did, but I had to speak to her through the screen.

"Your father is heartbroken that you weren't at the show last night. As far as I'm concerned, if you don't make it tonight, you aren't a part of my family anymore," I spit.

Yes, it was harsh. But so was her rejection of her father's success, even if it was only temporary.

She showed up. But she did it on her own terms, with her two friends in tow and with every rocker who was there following them around like they were the only three groupies in L.A. Derek was thrilled, but his happiness didn't last long when she acted like she hardly had time for him. Oh, he tried, but those hair metal boys hanging around backstage thought they owned the goddamn place and that they owned her, too. Well, I guess they practically did. Their names were on the Holly Woods marquee every other day of the month and she was on their marquees with the antics she and her friends got up to.

That evening, the opening act came off the stage and Derek's roadies set up for his show. I sat with him in his dressing room as he made final preparations for his second and final performance. He slipped on his favorite embroidered jacket and turned to me with a sigh.

"Tulip, I mean it this time. Dandelion has to come back home and we all need to change our lives once and for all and be a real family," he said gruffly, Jack Daniels in one hand and a Fender Strat in the other.

I nodded my head, knowing I was just as much to blame for all of this as anyone. And he was right. If we couldn't change we couldn't ask her to.

"When you get back from Bangkok we'll do it," I promised, my resolve firm.

He kissed my forehead. "We'll both have one last good time and then get serious."

"It's a deal," I agreed, and we sealed it with a firm handshake and a firmer embrace.

I followed him out the door as he was being introduced onstage. It just so happened that Dandelion was waiting on the side of the stage right where he would pass by. She wore a sweet smile on her face, like Daddy's little spring flower. But Derek wasn't a forgiving daddy at the point, he was a fed-up one. And I heard what he said to her on his way by.

"Dandelion, find yourself a real man and fall in love. Never mind all this carousing."

They were the last words he would ever say to her.

She turned her back on him and ran out of Holly Woods crying.

Derek turned his back on the world and never came back from Bangkok.

DEDICATION

This book is dedicated to my guardian angels: my beloved mother and father, Albert and Jennie, and my sister Margo. This book is also dedicated to my sisters Marie and Jeanne, and my niece Amanda.

ACKNOWLEDGEMENTS

Thank you to my sister Marie for reading my books, even though the *New York Times* is much more your thing.

Thank you also to my friend and fellow author Judy Kentrus, for all the guidance you've given me, even when you had your own work to do and your own problems to overcome.

CONTACT INFORMATION

If you enjoyed *Girls Gone Groupie*, please help other readers find this book:

1. Write a review: www.amazon.com
2. Write a review: www.goodreads.com
3. Follow me on Facebook:
   www.facebook.com/bkstoneauthor
4. Follow me on Twitter:
   twitter.com/bkstoneauthor
5. Follow me on Instagram:
   nstagram.com//bkstoneauthor
6. Visit my website at: www.brendakstone.com and sign up for my newsletter.

Brenda K. Stone is the pen name for Barbara Lebida, a native of Western Massachusetts who loves to write, travel the world, hike the world, and go to rock concerts. When not engaging in these particular adventures or the several other activities she enjoys that leave her no time for rest, you can find her "doing research" with her nose in a rock and roll biography and her black bunny Gert not far away, probably sleeping.

COMING SOON!

Girls of Glam Rock Series, Book 2
Gunning for Groupie Gold

A spotlight that starts as a pinpoint of brightness before growing larger is pointed toward the top of the stage. My mouth joins many in the "agape" position as Sammy is lowered from the ceiling, spinning slowly so we can get every drool-worthy angle, his wrists bound in leather over his head. Every ripple of his arms, chest, and narrow waist pops. His black leather snakeskin pants are low on his hips and they hug his delightfully bulging thighs like electrical tape wound too tight. His legs are open just enough to get a load of the Gunn family jewels…and what a load they are, indeed. The poor boy must be happily strangling and I'm cheerfully prepared to set him free.

"Oh, he's perfect!" Carolina screams, covering her eyes.

"Indiana should be proud," is H.C.'s comment.

Smoke billows around Sammy as his feet hit the floor. The illusion is easily understood: the Gunn Man is so hot that he's making the stage steam. He pulls his hands free of the bindings and throws the long length of leather to, of all people, Mama! She opens her cover up and drapes the souvenir around her neck, pouting at Sammy like she already has him bagged.

Sammy laughs and lets out a "Whew!" as Mama bounces up and down yelling, "I'm Tulip, baby! You know me! I'm the most famous groupie ever!" I can just barely hear her, so it's highly doubtful that he can. For that I am unquestioningly thankful. What's more worrisome is the fact that her bikini top is just about ready to take a turn for the worst.

H.C. gives me *the look*, the stink eye that says she's in great distress. "Your mother!" she scoffs.

My mother turns to us and flings the leather around with unbridled confidence.

While the band is playing an extended intro to "Bang, You're Dead," Sammy runs his hands through his tousled tresses that fall to the middle of his back, and sidles up to the microphone to flash a sneaky smile. Adding a cute wink, he says, "What a greeting. I think we should have come to L.A. a long time ago." He expertly pulls the microphone out of the stand and starts belting out the lyrics in a stunning voice that some say should be singing opera instead of being wasted on heavy metal:

> *Yeah it's true I'm as tough as nails*
> *Gonna light your soul on fire*
> *Wicked woman rockin' leather and lace*

Got me burnin' with raw desire
I'll bring ya to the edge
But I won't let ya slip
Careful not to hedge
As the guitar starts to rip
Bang, you're dead, seein' red
All these crazy visions reelin' through my head
Bang, you're dead, seein' red
Got my hard lovin' baby in my heavy metal bed

That moment when his vocals carry out over the crowd is like a collective orgasm for seventeen thousand frenzied people, a second in time that makes everything suddenly right in the world. We feel the power shot of the Gunn Runners, poised to become the biggest band on the music scene.

Sammy Gunn shows his appreciation for all of us that waited so long for him to come to the hard rock capital of the world. He points to the Porn Sluts in between verses and says, "Thanks, girls," as they shake their furry sign emblazoned with lipstick. Running to one end of the stage, he strikes the ultimate rock star pose with his feet apart and his arms making a "V" as a teenage boy takes his picture. Then, he reaches out to slap hands with the boy. Next, he looks down at we three girls rocking out and sings, "I love L.A. more and more by the minute." We all blow him kisses, reaching up to him, and he stretches forward to touch our hands. His fingers are strong and burning and that tanned face is unlined, unmarred. I wink when he squeezes my digits. He lifts his eyebrows at me and says, "Hey, Wonder

Woman." Mama glares at me and stops flapping her leather around. The beat of my rock and roll heart matches the thump of the drums played by the extraordinary Mark Winn. Sammy and I have made a special connection. My heart's prayers have been answered.

Oh Daddy, he's The One!

Tonight is the defining night of my life. I whiz right past lust and land in front of love's door. Hard.